Also by
KATHRYN ORMSBEE

Candidly Cline

Growing Pangs
(illustrated by Molly Brooks)

VIVIAN LANTZ'S SECOND CHANCES

VIVIAN LANTZ'S
Second Chances

KATHRYN ORMSBEE

HARPER

An Imprint of HarperCollinsPublishers

Library of Congress Cataloging-in-Publication Data
Names: Ormsbee, Kathryn, author.
Title: Vivian Lantz's second chances / Kathryn Ormsbee.
Description: First edition. | New York, NY : Harper, [2023] | Audience: Ages 8-12.
| Audience: Grades 4-6. | Summary: After trying and failing to break her years-
long curse of bad first days of school, eighth grader Vivian Lantz wishes for a
do-over—and gets stuck reliving this year's horrible first day over and over again.
Identifiers: LCCN 2022037387 | ISBN 978-0-06-306004-3 (hardcover)
Subjects: CYAC: First day of school—Fiction. | Time—Fiction. | Middle schools—
Fiction. | Schools—Fiction. | Gay fathers—Fiction.
Classification: LCC PZ7.O637 Vi 2023 | DDC [Fic]—dc23
LC record available at https://lccn.loc.gov/2022037387

Typography by Corina Lupp
23 24 25 26 27 LBC 5 4 3 2 1
First Edition

To Lorelei.
Meeting you for the first time was the coolest thing ever.
I can't wait to keep meeting you as you grow.

ALLOW ME TO introduce myself. My name is Vivian Lantz, I am four feet, ten inches tall, and I am under a lifelong curse.

I mean it. I've been cursed since practically birth, and here's how: I've never had a good first day of school. Not one.

It all began on my first day of pre-K, when I accidentally knocked over an industrial-size tub of rainbow glitter during nap time. The way my dads tell the story, when they picked me up at Green Sprouts Preschool, I was a sparkly forty-pound chunk of toddler, and that was the day that my older brother, Arlo, started calling me Unicorn Barf, or Barficorn for short.

My first days didn't get better from there. Name a grade, and I'll fill you in on the deets.

Fourth grade? Stepped on a hornets' nest at recess.

Second? Hawk Ryman broke my nose by throwing a stapler at my face.

Fifth? My appendix burst in world history.

In kindergarten, Jill Peever cut my bangs with craft scissors, and let me put it this way: she was not a licensed cosmetologist.

Then there was third grade. That was the year my family moved from Chicago to Austin. The whole Texas thing was new to me, but Ms. Fischer, the school's music director, didn't get that memo, because who did she pick during opening announcements to come onstage and help the auditorium sing "Deep in the Heart of Texas"?

You guessed it.

I didn't know a single word of the song, and when we got to the part where everyone claps as loud as they can, four times in row, I jumped off the stage and didn't stop running till I was locked in a bathroom stall, bawling my eyes out.

If I had a dollar for every time some fifth grade boy charged me in the hallway after that, yelling, "'The stars at night! Are big and bright!'" I'd be a multimillionaire.

I'm not gonna lie. The rest of my elementary school career was tough. (See *Exhibit A*, appendix bursting, and *Exhibit B*, hornets' nest.) But sixth grade was the start of middle school. It was a chance to make a new name for myself—*literally*. I decided that I would start going by my middle name, Mare, instead of Vivian. Mare sounded more sophisticated. Intriguing. Fun!

In homeroom, when Mr. Osment read my name off the

roll, I told him that I actually went by "Mare." He gave me a funny look.

"Mayor?" he said, double-checking his clipboard.

"Mare," I corrected, pronouncing it the right way, so it rhymed with "hair."

"Mayor," Mr. Osment repeated wrongly.

The kids around me started to snicker.

Amanda Cravens leaned in and said, "Uh, okay, *Vivian*. I guess I'll go by Governor now."

Then Justin Schmidt shouted, "My name is President!" and the whole class cracked up.

It took a while for Mr. Osment to calm everyone down. Once he had, he turned to me, looking tired and kind of annoyed, and said, "Mayor. Is that right?"

I mumbled, "Just call me Vivian."

By the time lunch rolled around, I was sitting alone at a table, chewing a fish stick and ruing the day my dads had given me a weirdo middle name that Da claims is an Irish version of Mary but *looks* like another name for a horse and apparently *sounds* like an elected city official.

That's when a girl in a pink sequined dress appeared before me.

"Whoa," she said. "I love Relevane, too."

I stared at her, my mouth crammed with food. I didn't understand. How could this stranger know about my all-consuming love for Relevane, the greatest book series of all time, written by the legendary Q. S. Murray?

Then I saw that she was pointing at my backpack. There was a patch on the zipper pouch, colored green and gold—the colors of the Elystrian Court. The embroidered letters spelled out the Elystrian motto: *Ascend in dignity*. You'd have to be real fan of the series to understand the reference, and no one at school ever had. Not until this fateful moment.

I blinked at the girl, fried fish going soggy in my mouth. I didn't recognize her from Travis Elementary. She had golden-brown skin and long brown braided hair. She wore an enamel pin on her dress collar, shaped like two interlocking hearts—the crest of the Elystrian Court.

I gulped down my food, awestruck.

"I'm so excited about the movie," the girl said, setting her tray on my table. "But how are they going to cast Torin? No mere mortal is good enough to play him."

"Torin's my favorite character," I said breathlessly.

"Right? He's so noble. Who gives up their birthright like that?"

"Have you been to BookPeople yet?" I asked. "They're throwing a party when book five comes out next month. I went to the book four party, and it was *so* fun. People even dressed up for it."

"Seriously?" The girl gaped at me. "I have the perfect Sage

Miriel costume from last Halloween."

"We should go together!" I blurted. Then I blushed. I was making plans for a Relevane party, and I hadn't even introduced myself.

"I'm Vivian," I told the girl. "Mare" was a thing of the past.

"Cami," she replied, plopping into the chair beside me. "I moved here last month from El Paso."

I couldn't believe my luck. It was my dreaded first day of middle school, and I was making a friend. A friend who loved Relevane! I felt like I'd stumbled into Wistwander Field—this place in the world of Relevane where wayward travelers drift into dreams so vivid they feel like reality.

Bad first days can majorly suck—believe me, I know—but once in a blue moon? They end up leading you to your best friend.

Cami Ruiz and I were inseparable from that day forward. It didn't matter that we weren't popular or that we didn't do the usual school stuff, like band or sports or student council. We had each other, and we had Relevane. We dressed up for the party at BookPeople, and we went to the midnight premiere of the first movie. I even wrote Relevane fan fiction that I shared with Cami—and *only* Cami.

Our friendship wasn't all about Relevane, though. Cami helped me name all the creepy porcelain dolls in my family's vintage shop. I helped her make a homemade hedgehog kite for the ABC Kite Fest. Cami swooned over Ervin Rahbar playing Prince Eric in *The Little Mermaid Jr.*, and I ranted about the injustice of Alex Fernandez—soccer star and goalie of my heart—going to the spring dance with Drea Bernal. We got our ears pierced on the same day, and we promised we'd get our first tattoos together one day, too.

Cami even helped me through my bad first day of seventh grade, when I got food poisoning from expired turkey bacon Da had cooked. Five hours after breakfast, I was projectile vomiting in the Bluebonnet gym during a game of dodgeball. Cami held my hair back as I barfed more bacon chunks in the bathroom, and afterward she gave me two sticks of cool mint gum.

I never thought the day would come when Cami wouldn't be around. But that was before Mrs. Ruiz got a new job in Orlando and Cami's family moved away this June.

Summer hasn't been the same without Cami. No visits to Schlitterbahn Waterpark. No lazy days spent eating mangonadas at the frutería on Braker Lane or laughing at Trixie, my family's rescue pug, while she does zoomies around the kitchen. Sure, Cami and I still text each other, but it's not the same as when she lived five minutes way.

The worst part about Cami leaving *now*? I have to face the first day of eighth grade without her.

Here's how I see it: eighth grade is the end of the road

for me. It's my last chance before high school to get a new reputation—one that doesn't involve me puking turkey bacon in the gym. I wasn't expecting a miracle. I know my first day of eighth grade is bound to be cursed in *some* way, but I was hoping—desperately hoping—that it would be more good than bad.

That seems impossible now. How am I supposed to have a good day without *Cami*? She's the only reason that my last two cursed days were livable.

It's been bad enough just making it through the summer. I don't have other friends to hang out with. Even my brother, Arlo, has been busy playing bass for his band, the Neon Spurs. So I've spent most of my days alone, taking Trixie on walks, rereading the Relevane books for the three-thousandth time, and helping out at my family's vintage shop, Be Kind, Rewind.

That's where I am today, on July twentieth—the eve of my thirteenth birthday and a scorcher of a Wednesday here in Austin, Texas. According the KXAN morning news meteorologist, it's going to get up to 115 degrees today. *Yowch.*

It's late morning, and I'm working in the back room. Most days, I'm down to earn a few bucks by helping out with inventory, but today I'm sweating bullets and thinking how I'd rather be in Q. S. Murray's Marladia, with its misty, mile-high waterfalls and snowcapped mountains.

"Yo, Barficorn."

I blink, coming back to reality.

Arlo is holding out a transistor radio—one of Pop's flea market finds. Judging from the look on Arlo's face, this isn't the first time he's tried to get my attention.

"I *said*, do you think you could find a spot for this?" Arlo motions toward the shop and adds, "Maybe on that peacock table up front."

I take the radio.

"Sorry," I tell Arlo. "Guess I was spacing out."

"Did you hear that?" Arlo asks our dads. "Barficorn is delirious from the heat. This wouldn't be happening if we had central AC."

"*Arlo*," Da says tiredly from where he sits at the back-room desk, tapping new entries into a spreadsheet on his laptop. "We've been over this. There's no way we could break even this year with a huge home improvement cost. The window units work fine when it's not summer."

"But summer is nine months out of the year," Arlo mutters.

"That is objectively not true," says Pop, waving a paisley-printed umbrella in Arlo's direction.

"It's a matter of cost-benefit analysis," says Da. "Maybe you're too young to understand, but—"

"Here we go." Arlo throws up his hands. "I'm turning eighteen in three months. I could be forty, and you'd still say I'm too young."

I leave my dads and Arlo fighting in the back room. This past year, Arlo has been arguing with Dads *a lot*—Da, especially.

Stepping into the shop, I spot the table that Arlo mentioned. It's a coffee table with brass feet shaped like peacock tails that Da found last month at an estate sale in Buda. I nudge aside a stack of old *Screen Life* magazines to make way for the radio, and as I do, something else on the table catches my eye. At first, it looks like a tiny, formless purple blob, but when I pick it up, I see that it's a spiral of purple construction paper.

I snap to attention, noticing more of the paper spirals on the shop floor. They're leading away from the peacock table in single file. My heartbeat kicks up. I know a bread crumb trail when I see one.

Straightaway, I put down the radio. I'm on the case.

The trail leads away from the table, winding around a tufted ottoman, and past a plastic penguin figurine. Then the trail of flowers leads *up*. The spirals are stuck—taped, maybe glued?—along the side of an A-frame bookcase. I follow them to the top shelf, across a row of book spines, and down the bookcase's opposite side. They circle a yellow umbrella stand twice, and then the trail stops—right at the front door.

Clearly, there's only one thing to do about that: I unlock the door and fling it open.

There, on the front porch of Be Kind, Rewind, are ten—no, *twenty*—vases, stuffed with flowers. I recognize the kind of flower right away: they're *hyacinths*, and every single one of them has been made from construction paper. Now I get what the purple spirals are: they're hyacinth *blooms,* and here there are dozens more of them, glued along green paper stalks, forming paper bouquets. The flowers are all kinds of colors. They're purple, sure, but also pink, white, red, and orange. And the hyacinths aren't even the main attraction. They surround a wicker table, and on that table is a wrapped present. I step closer, reading the tag attached to the gift. It says, *To Vivian.*

I'd know my best friend's handwriting anywhere.

I grab the present, tearing away the wrapping paper to reveal a book. The cover is a dazzling royal blue, adorned with a gold-foiled border of . . . *hyacinths.*

Here's the deal with hyacinths: they are the favorite flower of Sage Miriel, who discovered how to magically speak to their roots in book three of the Relevane series. That's how she passed secret messages to Torin during his garden walks, when he was under house arrest at the Autumn Palace.

Once, when we were in sixth grade, Cami and I tried to pass our own messages through a dandelion patch in Cami's backyard. It didn't work, but we made a pact that day. We vowed that if either of us ever encountered magic in the real world, we'd tell each other. We called our pact Code Unicorn. There haven't been any Code Unicorns yet, but it did turn into a joke. Like, "I wanna make out with Alex Fernandez, but that'd take a Code Unicorn." As for hyacinths? They're still special to me and Cami. We've drawn them on just about everything: class notes and bookmarks and each other's shoulders. They're our *thing*.

Cami made these paper hyacinths by hand. She found this hyacinth journal. And she must've done all of this *weeks* ago, before she left for Florida. She planned this whole thing in advance. Best. Friend. Ever.

As I rest my fingertips on the journal, a zap of energy tingles up my spine. I catch my breath, and I swear that for a split second, the gold hyacinths seem to *move*—petals blooming outward, stems budging upward. I blink, and the movement stops. I must've been seeing things. All the same, the tingling remains, prickling up the hairs on my arms.

Eagerly, I open the book and flip through its blank, lined pages. It's a place for jotting down all my thoughts and stories. This journal and the hyacinth trail that led me here—it's the perfect birthday gift.

So why do I suddenly feel like my intestines have turned to mush?

Tears prick my eyes as the truth hits me: it *is* the perfect gift, but Cami's not here to give it to me.

"Happy early birthday!"

I whirl around. Dads and Arlo have snuck up behind me and stand in the doorway. Arlo is wearing a goofy smirk. Dads exchange a knowing glance, and that's when it all comes together: Arlo was the one who suggested I put the radio on the peacock table. He was in on this. *Everyone* was. They even surprised me a day early, when I wouldn't be expecting a birthday present. So I can't cry *now*.

"This is the coolest," I say, mustering a smile.

"It's not over yet." Arlo holds out something: my phone.

I grab it from him as he says, "Looks like you got a text."

The message is from Cami: *Hope you love Part One of your present! I found it at the shop, of all places. Now on to Part Two.*

My head swims. *Part Two?*

Right then, a second text message comes through. It's a link. I click it, and an internet tab pops open. I recognize the logo at the top of the page: *MeetNGreet.* It's this app where you can pay for celebrities to record personalized videos. Last year at school, Amberleigh Allen got one from Thea Gardner, who's in the big Netflix show *Silver Bloods*, and kids were talking about it for days.

One thing I know about MeetNGreet is that it's pricey.

Amberleigh said her parents spent *three hundred dollars* on Thea's one-minute message. So I don't get why *I'm* on Meet-NGreet now. Not until Q. S. Murray's face appears on my screen.

"Wh-what?" I stammer.

It's a message from Q. S. Murray.

For *me*.

Q. S. Murray is notoriously hard to get a hold of. She doesn't have social media or a public email; she doesn't go on book tours, and she didn't even show up for the Relevane movie premiere. She is basically a hermit who comes out of her cave once every two years with a new Relevane book. So, seeing Q. S. Murray on my screen is *impossible*.

But then the impossible happens. The message starts to play.

"Hey there, Vivian! This is Quincy Murray, calling from my office in Boston to wish you a very happy thirteenth—"

For a second, I lose my hearing. My ears seal up, and I feel like I'm being transported through the hollowed tree portal Torin discovers in Willowlight Pass. But then I'm back in the real world, where Q. S. Murray is talking. *To me.* Panicked, I pause the video and look up at Dads and Arlo with wide eyes.

"It was Cami's idea," Pop offers. "We all pitched in to make it happen."

I nod vaguely and wheeze, "I—I think I need some space."

Arlo snorts, chucking me on the shoulder and saying, "Okay, weirdo."

He trots back into the shop.

Pop tells me, "We get it. She's your hero. You want to savor the moment."

I nod in a rapturous daze.

"Happy early birthday, kid," Da says.

He and Pop sling their arms around each other and head inside, closing the door.

Now it's just me and Q. S.

I sink down, sitting on the top step of the porch. Then I rewind the message and press play.

"Hey there, Vivian!" Q. S. Murray greets me again. She's sitting in a sunlit peach-colored room. Black hair frames her fair face and glasses are perched on her nose. She speaks in a strong, steady voice, and I hang on every single word.

"This is Quincy Murray, calling from my office in Boston to wish you a very happy thirteenth birthday. According to your friend Cami, you're about to start your last year of middle school. She wrote here"—Q. S. Murray squints at something off-screen—"that your first days of school have always been . . . difficult. Something about a curse?" Her eyebrows lift. "Well, that *is* serious. I'd like to help."

My breath collects in my throat. Q. S. Murray is going to

help me break my first-day curse? I feel like I'm in a dream.

"I remember eighth grade," Q. S. Murray goes on. "It was challenging. But it's also the year I started writing articles for my school paper. I kept on doing that in high school, and eventually I became the editor of my college newspaper. Writing the news is what inspired me to write *other* things . . . like a certain book series that I've heard you enjoy?" She smiles, revealing pearly white teeth. "Now, about this pesky curse of yours. I have some advice. Do you know why I joined my school paper? It's because one day I looked around and realized I wasn't doing much for myself. I went where my parents drove me and learned what my teachers taught. Life was simply *happening* to me.

"But here's what's up, Vivian: big breakthroughs don't come from sitting around, letting life happen to you. *You* have to happen to *life*. That's how you break curses—you take the power into your own hands. So, start happening! Try something new. Your friend tells me that you're also a writer, so you might consider joining your own school paper. Write for others, and write for *yourself*, too. Write down your goals! The more you see and repeat them, the more often you'll be reminded to go after what you want.

"Well, that's it from me, Vivian. I'll be sending you *all* the good magical vibes from here in Boston. Now, go out and happen to life this year!"

The message ends, Q. S. Murray's smiling face frozen on my screen.

I can't believe it.

Q. S. Murray knows who I am. She knows about my *curse*, and she has deigned to provide me with words of infinite wisdom.

Quick Relevane history lesson: in book one, Torin the Rogue begins his journey across the Six Commonwealths of Marladia after he gets a vision from the Relevanian Oracle. She's the one who convinces Torin that his aunt, the Grand Duchess of Relevane, is planning to murder him and that he must escape to the land of his enemies, the Elystrians.

Well, today? Q. S. Murray has been my oracle.

This MeetNGreet? It is my vision.

And it's going to change everything—including my life-long, good-for-nothing curse.

2

I WATCH THE video again and again. As days go by, I memorize every word. It's all I can think about, and soon Q. S. Murray even shows up in my *dreams*, tossing her long black hair and telling me, "Vivian, *you* happen to *life*."

I can't go back to normal after this.

Up until now, I saw my predicament this way: sure, my first-day curse sucks, but it's common knowledge that no hero *becomes* a hero without facing obstacles. Plus, Cami made it so that my first days weren't *all* bad. I decided that I could live with that.

When Cami moved, I freaked out about facing the curse all alone again. But *now* my path is totally clear. I don't just have to hope for a first day that's more good than bad. I can do better than that. I can alter the course of my future. No one in high school will think of me as Vivian Lantz, the girl with the exploding appendix who got stung by four dozen wasps and puked up her breakfast in gym. I can blot out my past with a bright, shiny present. I can reinvent myself. I can be Vivian Lantz, the coolest girl from eighth grade. I just have to follow Q. S. Murray's advice.

Q. S. Murray told me to write down my goals, so that's what I do first, before anything else. I get out my most prized possession—the hyacinth journal that Cami gave me—and open it to the first, crisp page. It takes me longer than expected—two whole hours, to be exact—but in the end I write down my three most important goals.

Behold:

VIVIAN LANTZ'S FOOLPROOF PLAN
FOR THE PERFECT FIRST DAY

1. Get a new style
   (Because I've never <u>had</u> a style before.)
2. Join the school paper
   (Because that's how Q. S. Murray got her start.)
3. Make Alex Fernandez my boyfriend
   (Because this one's obvious.)

This is my Master Plan. It is the key to breaking my curse. It is my guide to reinvention. And it is, as I have already noted, *foolproof.*

Most of the plan will have to wait for the first day of school. For now, I'm focusing on goal number one: getting a new style.

I hadn't given much thought to fashion before now. In sixth and seventh grade, I figured a good pair of jeans and a T-shirt was all I needed to get around. You could say that I let *style* happen to *me*. Well, that ends this school year. Q. S. Murray told me to try something fresh, and what's fresher than a legit makeover?

As of now, I'm happening to *clothes*. To *makeup*. To *hair*. *I'm happening to life*.

The life-happening starts with a drive out to a thrift shop called Loose Threads. I ask Arlo to drive me there, but I don't tell him that I'm modeling my style after Lissa, the keyboardist in his band. Of all the girls I've seen—at school and online—Lissa's style is the one I like best. It's all big T-shirts and ripped jeans and fun, fringed vests. Like, style, but *comfy* style. That's perfect for me.

Arlo waits outside the dressing room as I go through practically fifty outfits and finally buy three, using a big chunk of the money I've saved from working at the shop. I'm so ready to show off my new look that I put on one of the outfits right away, changing into a David Bowie T-shirt, silver-studded headband, and electric-red shorts.

"You look rocker chic," Arlo observes as we leave the store.

I beam, tugging the asymmetrical hem of my shirt. I *feel* rocker chic.

A few days later, I go with Da to Target, where I buy tubes of mascara and lip gloss that, according to YouTube makeup tutorials, will complement my fair complexion and brunette hair.

Then, on the day before eighth grade begins, Arlo drives me to Atomic Hair Salon. Dads always pay for me to get a back-to-school haircut; that's nothing new. But this time? I ask for something revolutionary.

"Bangs," I tell my stylist, D'Andra.

"They're work," she warns.

"I can take it," I reply.

Because I, Vivian Lantz, am happening to hair, and my rocker chic ensemble won't be complete without bangs. When D'Andra is done, she spins my chair so that I can see myself in the mirror. And it's *good*. I was made for bangs.

"Whoa," Arlo says when he sees me.

"Yeah," I reply.

That's how it is with me and Arlo. We don't have to say much to say a lot.

Arlo doesn't ask nosy questions about my makeover, which I appreciate. I haven't told anyone about the goals in my journal—not Arlo or Dads or even Cami. It's not that I don't trust them; it's more that I think of my Master Plan the way I do a birthday candle wish: I don't want to jinx it by saying it out loud.

That's why I haven't even told Cami about Q. S. Murray's curse-breaking advice. All she knows about the MeetNGreet is that Q. S. Murray wished me a happy birthday. It sucks, keeping a secret from Cami, but it's only temporary. I'll tell her everything once I've broken the first-day curse—just not before. I'd rather shock everyone with the magnificent Eighth Grade Vivian I've become, rather than show them the girl I *want* to be.

And that starts now.

Dads are in for a surprise when I waltz into Be Kind, Rewind.

"Bangs!" Pop shouts.

"Ack!" Da cries, clutching his chest.

I can tell they approve.

Da says he's got enchiladas waiting for us in the oven, and we chow down on dinner before watching a rerun of *I Love Lucy*, Pop's favorite old-timey show. Afterward, tucked in bed, I go over the plan in my hyacinth journal one last time. I'm snuggled next to Mistmorrow, a plushie horse made to look like *the* Mistmorrow—Sage Miriel's trusty steed—with midnight-black hair and violet eyes. Rain patters on the roof, and I nestle deeper into the sheets as I review my goals.

Number one? Check. New style acquired. I cross it out with a satisfying *scritch*.

Number two: *Join the school paper.*

I've loved writing since before I even learned to spell. I used to make construction paper books for Dads to read, and I wrote poems in fourth grade that I would be *super* embarrassed for anybody to get a hold of now. Then, in sixth grade, I started writing Relevane fan fiction.

I love writing those stories, but I do have a teensy problem with finishing them. As in, I *haven't* finished a single one. It's exhilarating to start a story with a fresh, big idea. But after I make it a few chapters in, it's like the words get away from me. I introduce too many characters and send them on too many quests, and then the story feels too epic to ever end.

Then there's the issue of sharing my writing. Some kids post their fanfic online, but I don't want total strangers reading about how I think Prince Lorace and the Mage of Fairwood should run off and get married. That's why I've only ever shared my Relevane writing with Cami. She doesn't make fun of me for how mushy I make the romance, and she doesn't complain when I stop one story midchapter to start a new one.

One day, though? I *do* want to finish a book, and I *do*

want to share it with the world. I want to be an author like Q. S. Murray. I've just been kind of stuck on how to get from here to there. For one thing, there aren't any creative writing clubs at Bluebonnet Middle School. The only thing close to that is the *Jaguar Gazette*, which always seemed boring to me. Nonfiction? No, thank you.

But Q. S. Murray joined her school paper, and look how life turned out for *her*. What if the *Jaguar Gazette* could take my writing to the next level, too? Here's the way I see it: articles are way easier to finish than fantasy novels. They're only, what—a few hundred words? I could do that. Plus, if I were a journalist, random kids would be reading my writing. I could get used to that feeling, one article at a time. This is my chance to *happen to writing*.

That's why I'm going to talk to Ms. Rose—my new language arts teacher—tomorrow after class. She's the adviser for the *Jaguar Gazette*, and so long as she thinks I can cut the mustard, I'll be a student journalist by this time tomorrow night.

When my eyes flit to goal number three, my heart starts pounding like a marching band drum.

Alex Freaking Fernandez. He's been my crush for twenty-three months straight. It all started in sixth grade. Practically every morning before school, I watched him and his friends hanging out by the bike rack. Alex would gut laugh over something his best friend, Neil, said, and I'd imagine what it would be like to be Drea, Alex's girlfriend at the time. What if that was *my* arm draped over his shoulder? What if *I* was sharing a 7UP with him?

I came close to finding out once, when Pop dropped me off at school early and I found Alex sitting alone on one of the turquoise benches outside. He was on his phone, playing a game with the volume on full blast, and he lost his grip right as I was walking past. The phone went flying, hurtling toward the concrete, and in that instant, I had the reflexes of a wild gazelle. I lunged and caught the phone as it was inches from total screen-smashing destruction.

Alex stared at me in shock. I was pretty shocked myself.

"Dude," he said, as I handed the phone to him. "You're my hero."

Then Neil ran up, shouting something to Alex about *American Ninja Warrior*. I backed away to give them space, but Alex's words clanged in my head, louder than the school bell: *You're my hero.*

His *hero*. Sure, I hadn't saved him from a perilous fall off the Cascading Cliffs, like Sage Miriel does for Torin the Rogue. But I'd been Alex's real-life hero, and in that moment, I knew that he was my Torin. My soulmate. My meant-to-be.

If Neil hadn't interrupted us, what else would Alex have said to me? Would he have asked if I wanted to hang out sometime after school? Sit next to him at lunch? I used to daydream about the day Fate would throw us together again. But my daydreams didn't come true in sixth grade, or seventh. So now I'm gonna happen to *romance*.

Here's the deal: to get to Alex, I've gotta get in good with Amberleigh Allen, who is only *the most popular girl at school*. She sings solos in all the choir and talent shows, and once she was even chosen to perform the national anthem at a Round Rock Express game. She lives in a giant house in Barton Hills, and her parents have vacation homes in Palm Springs and Vail. Amberleigh's pretty, too, with dark brown hair that she wears in a flawless high ponytail. But the most important factoid? Amberleigh is practically the president of Alex's group of friends.

Last year, I would've been too freaked out to even say hi to Amberleigh. But that was before I concocted the Master Plan. Now, I've worked it out. Sure, Amberleigh is popular, but it's not like she's Nestrende, the unapproachable goddess of the Elystrian Temple. She's mortal, and so are her friends, who seem pretty nice overall. Gemma Cohen signed my yearbook in May with a *Wish I knew you better!* So, there's that. All I have to do is get in good with Amberleigh, and I'll finally be close enough to Alex to win his heart.

For the past two weeks, I've been planning my move: I'll show up to school early and make a beeline for the bike rack. I'll walk right up to Amberleigh's group, with my new bangs

25

and rocker chic style and expertly applied makeup. They'll be speechless, since they won't recognize me at first, and that'll be my chance to say, "Cute shoes, Amberleigh."

No matter what shoes she's wearing, I will say they're cute. Then Amberleigh will say "thanks," which will break the ice with her friends, and we'll get to talking, and that'll be the start of Eighth Grade Vivian and her new life.

See? Foolproof.

I close the journal, resting my hand on the golden hyacinths, and feel the tingling zap of hope fill my heart.

A month ago, I felt as lost as Torin in Wistwander Field. I was lonely without Cami. I was nervous about eighth grade. But now, I shut my eyes and picture my bright future. Tomorrow, I will have style. I'll become a serious writer. I'll get a boyfriend. I will be *cool*. And if I can be cool this year— popular, even—maybe it won't hurt so bad that Cami isn't by my side.

"Tomorrow, I break the curse," I whisper to Mistmorrow.

Mistmorrow says nothing. He's a horse of few words.

Carefully, I set aside the journal containing my Master Plan. Then I switch off my bedside lamp and settle in for a good night's sleep. After all, I'll need top-notch shut-eye if I'm going to make tomorrow a good first day.

Scratch that.

The *perfect* first day of school.

3

"WHOA, WHOA, WHOA!"

I wake to the sound of rain on the roof and Arlo's voice shouting from downstairs. I sit up in bed, half awake, and paw my phone off the nightstand to check the time: *6:13 a.m.*

Whew. I didn't sleep through my alarm.

But it's six in the morning. Why the heck is Arlo up? That's not like him. We're lucky if he rolls out of bed two minutes before Pop drives us to school.

Then again, this year is different. Arlo bought his own car in June, which means he'll be the one taking me to school. Maybe car ownership has inspired Arlo to act like a responsible adult, and he's taken it upon himself to cook for the family. That's what this is: a surprise gourmet breakfast! I wonder if he's making pan—

"Dads. Get down here quick!"

That wakes me all the way up.

This is *not* about breakfast. Something is wrong.

I jump out of bed, throwing open my bedroom door and racing down the hall. Arlo is at the bottom of the stairs, and it's when I notice his sopping wet hair that I put two and two together: rain, plus wet hair, plus shouting, equals . . . *flooding.*

The shop has sprung another leak.

A short history of the Lantz family business:

Both of my dads grew up in Texas. Later, they moved to Chicago, where they got married, adopted me and Arlo, and ran a shop for thirteen years. Then Pop got a call from his sister, Aunt Ximena, who offered to sell him her place in Austin. Next thing you know, my dads were moving back south, and Aunt Ximena was hightailing it out of the city in an RV for what she called "early retirement on the open road." Now we get postcards from her sent from Reno, Marfa, Albuquerque—all over the Southwest.

Meantime, Dads run their shop out of Aunt Ximena's old place. They do better business in Austin than they ever did in Arlington Heights. Da says it's because of the shop's prime location off South First that Be Kind, Rewind has stayed in business for the last five years, through good times and bad.

"Location, location, location," he says when we have a busy day, folks bustling in to buy Victorian couches or lava lamps or—*ugh*—creepy porcelain dolls. Everything here is one of a kind, and once it's gone, it's gone forever. The shop is old, but it's fresh, because it's always changing. That makes it special. *Magical*, even. Aunt Ximena said as much when she gave Dads the keys to the place.

"There's something in the air here," she told us. "Or maybe it's in the floorboards or the eaves. It's magical, wherever it's at, so use that magic wisely."

That's a nice thought, but the shop feels slightly less than magical on mornings like this, when it springs a leak for the *thousandth* time.

"What's wrong?" I ask Arlo, at the same time he asks, "Where's Dads?"

Right then, like they've been summoned by the Great Relevanian Horn, Da and Pop come racing down the hallway with Trixie yapping at their heels.

"The damage?" Da asks breathlessly.

"My whole bed," Arlo gripes.

Pop tousles my hair as he and Da pass me on the stairs.

"Morning, Viv," he greets me, casting back a wink.

Pop's a pro at staying chipper in bad situations. Da? Not so much. He charges ahead of us like an angry bull into the shop's back room.

Our family's living situation is what you'd call . . . unconventional. The bottom floor is the shop, and the top floor is our home. I guess that sounds cool in theory, but it's actually just *cramped*.

Last year, Arlo moved from his upstairs bedroom to the

29

back room after announcing that he wanted more space. Dads warned Arlo that he'd have less privacy during the day and that the downstairs windows tend to leak. Arlo said he didn't mind.

I'd say he's reconsidering that now. He and I share a wince as Da's cusses float out of the back room.

We all know to give Da space, since he's the best at figuring out practical solutions. Sure enough, after a minute, he stops cussing and moves on to instructions: "Arlo, get rags from the laundry closet. Diego, the water drum from out back. Vivian, I'll need you here."

We've got our orders, so the three of us get moving. I head to the back room, where I find Da fighting a gush of rainwater. When I get closer, I see the source of the trouble: the wooden frame of a window has rotted and split, allowing water to pour onto Arlo's bed and a whole shelf of inventory boxes.

"Woof," I say.

"Here's the plan." Da grunts, hauling down one of the boxes. "Move all of these from point A"—he motions to the site of the flood—"to point B." He points to the far corner of the room.

I take the soggy box and get to work. Soon Pop and Arlo join us, and Da puts the rags and emptied water drum to use. The four of us move the boxes out of harm's way, and only after that's done do we stop to take stock of the damage. Pop lifts a velvet dress out of a box and shakes his head, saying he'll have to spend the morning washing and line drying the damaged clothes.

"I could stay home from school to help," Arlo suggests.

Da gives him a look. "Nice try."

"What?" Arlo protests. "It's for a good reason."

"Not good enough," says Pop, patting his back. "Plus, I don't think Vivian would appreciate her chauffeur bailing on her."

Arlo turns to me, a conspiratorial sparkle in his eyes. "You wouldn't mind, would you, Barficorn? Eighth grade's a joke, anyway."

Eighth grade.

School.

Oh *no.*

I whip around to read the clock over the back-room door. It's a whole *forty minutes* past when I was supposed to get up.

I had this morning planned down to the second. I *have* to get to school early to make my big impression on Amberleigh and her friends. If I'm not there at seven forty-five, my Master Plan falls apart.

I check the clock again. It's seven twenty, and school is a ten-minute drive away. I'll have to move at lightning speed, but I can still do this. I *can.*

"We gotta go!" I yelp at Arlo, pushing past him. "Be ready in ten!"

I careen out of the back room, up the stairs, and into my room. I grab the clothes that I hung on my closet door last night—acid-washed jean miniskirt, daisy-printed tights, yellow ringer tee—and put them on at breakneck speed before dragging a brush through my hair and swiping on mascara and lip gloss.

I grab my phone from the bed, then do a double take of the nightstand. My hyacinth journal sits there, gold blooms sparkling despite the gloomy light. On impulse, I grab it, stuffing it into my backpack. I want my Master Plan close. I'm gonna need all the help I can get.

Then it's back to business. I charge down the hallway, skidding into the kitchen so fast that the soles of my Vans screech on the tile. I don't have time to make the breakfast I'd planned: buttered toast with scrambled eggs. Instead, I open the cupboard and grab a sleeve of Pop-Tarts, shoving those into my backpack, too.

I nearly somersault down the stairs, and Trixie, who's already riled up, barks at me.

"Sorry, girl," I say, stooping to scratch her ears. "It's one of those days."

That's when I notice the smell. My gaze drifts to a spot behind Trixie, where an unmistakable mountain of poop sits atop a vintage rug.

"Trixie," I whisper, horrified. "*Nooo.*"

I step closer and notice a yellow puddle staining the rug's fibers, too. Trixie's done *all* her business here. Just great.

As I survey the damage, Trixie cowers, averting her eyes. Poor dog.

"It's okay," I tell her. "Storms are scary, I know."

Then, with a beleaguered sigh, I run back upstairs.

I grab a bottle of carpet cleaner, paper towels, and a trash bag, and I return to clean up the scene of the crime. When I'm through, I frown at the rug, which still doesn't look back to normal; there's a thin, beige outline of Trixie's pee. But my quick cleanup will have to do for now. I toss the soiled paper towels into the bag of poop, and I'm off again.

In the back room, Dads are picking through the salvaged boxes. Arlo eyes me skeptically as I grab my rain jacket from the coat closet and shove the poop bag into one of the pockets.

"You *really* want to go to school, huh?" he asks.

I tighten the toggles of my rain hood, nodding emphatically.

Arlo shrugs, like he's saying, *Your loss.*

"Are you going in that?" I ask, motioning to his boxer shorts and ripped Aerosmith tee. He doesn't even have shoes on.

Arlo trots over to the coat closet, fishing out a pair of flip-flops. "Got a spare outfit in the back seat. Band life."

I roll my eyes. Lately, it seems that all Arlo can talk about is "band life."

"Happy first day, kiddos!" Pop calls, as Arlo and I head out the back door into the pouring rain.

"Love you!" Da adds.

I blow a kiss to them both and slam the door after me.

Moments later, I'm sitting cross-legged in Arlo's Honda Civic, trying to ignore the major corn chip smell. Arlo's car has been messy since the day he bought it, crammed with band equipment and fast-food containers. Today, the mess is on a whole new level. There are big cardboard boxes of who knows what stacked in the back seat, topped with dirty, wrinkled laundry. *That* is what Arlo calls "band life."

As Arlo shifts into drive, I pull down the passenger visor, checking the mirror to be sure my mascara hasn't smudged.

"Got someone to impress?" Arlo asks, turning down the rock station he's been playing.

"Just trying to be presentable," I say, like today is no big deal even though it's the Biggest of Deals.

I tug out my phone and find a message from Cami:

Hope it's a good day!

My heart smacks against my ribs. Even though I haven't told Cami my curse-breaking plan, she knows how scary first days are for me. Her text is super thoughtful, but it feels wrong. Cami and I shouldn't be texting each other from hundreds of miles away. We should be heading to school *together*. I push away the icky feeling, though, and remember that this is a big day for Cami, too. It's her first day at a new school, in a completely new city.

That's why I write back, *GO, DOLPHINS!!!*

Dolphins are Cami's favorite animal. They're also the mascot of her school in Orlando, and we decided that this is a good sign.

I eye the hyacinth journal peeking out of my half-zipped backpack, wishing more than anything that Cami were here. But I can summon my courage, even with her gone. I can change my middle school destiny, like Torin changed the fate prophesied for him by the Relevanian Council.

"Seriously, dude?"

I look up from my phone and see that we've stopped. Through the swish of wiper blades, I make out a line of glaring red taillights.

"What's going on?" I ask, looking around.

"Must be a wreck," Arlo says, waving a hand at the station wagon in front of us. "This guy almost caused another one by cutting me off."

I look at the clock. It's seven forty. Normally, we'd be five minutes away from school. Now, there's no telling.

"Remain calm," I whisper to myself.

Arlo side-eyes me. "It's all good, Barficorn. Just a little traffic."

"Y-yeah," I say.

I'm trying to stay positive. Today will *not* be like every other first day of school. Today, I've got a plan, and no traffic jam is going to stand in my way.

"You got band practice today?" I ask Arlo, trying to take my mind off the delay.

Arlo's silent for so long that I think maybe he didn't hear me. When I look his way, he seems . . . *off*. He's quiet, eyes unfocused.

"Arlooo?"

That snaps him out of it.

"U-uh," he says, glancing at me. "Yeah, something like that."

I nod, looking out at the rain-slicked parking lot of a Starbucks. The car ahead of us creeps forward, but the traffic light turns red again, and we're stuck waiting, the Civic's engine rumbling like an upset stomach.

I've been debating mentioning something to Arlo. It's a conversation I overhead between Da and Pop a few days back. Now, with time on our hands, I figure I might as well let it out.

"Da says you're going to have to give up the band before you go to college."

I venture a glance at Arlo. His knuckles are pale as he clenches the steering wheel.

"Da doesn't know anything," he replies stiffly.

I shrug. "He knows *some* stuff."

"Yeah, well, I'm not going to college."

I blink at Arlo, shocked. Sure, he's been spending a lot of time with the band, but I still assumed he was planning on going to college. A couple of years back, UT was all he could talk about. He was going to study sound engineering. What changed?

I shake my head at him. "Why not?"

"You know, Barficorn," Arlo says, "life isn't like one of your fantasy books, with a beginning, middle, and end. It's not that clean-cut. If you do it right, life's improvising. Like music."

I squint at Arlo, but I don't understand what he's getting at. All I can think to say is, "I *like* my fantasy books."

I cross my arms, wondering if I should feel insulted, but the next moment, Arlo cracks a smile. He shakes his head and says, "I wonder sometimes how we're related."

I know the literal answer to that: through our birth mother, Anna Clarke, in Chicago. My dads adopted both me and Arlo from her, and the five of us meet up every few years for dinner. Anna's nice. I've got her brown hair, and Arlo's got her blue eyes. But I know that Anna isn't what Arlo is *actually* talking about. He just means we're different—even with the same mom. Arlo loves the band, and I love Relevane. I can't comprehend why he would ditch college, but then again, I'm not sure that he'd understand my Master Plan.

"We're moving," I point out, as the car in front of us inches up a few feet.

Traffic is letting up, but not fast enough. By the time Arlo swings the Civic under the school awning, it's two till eight, and there's no sign of Alex Fernandez or *anyone*. He and his friends must be inside already, finding seats for opening assembly.

I suck in a breath. Things aren't going according to plan so far, but I can still pull this off. I've got Q. S. Murray's words to guide me. I've got moxie. I've got *bangs*.

I jump out of the car, lugging my backpack onto my shoulder.

"See ya at dinner!" I shout at Arlo, slamming the passenger door.

When I glance back, he's giving me a funny look through the windshield. He's *off* again. Maybe the traffic got him more rattled than he let on, or he's nervous about his own first day of school—his *last* first day of school, if he's not headed to college. That's a big deal.

I wave at him, hoping that he catches the positive vibes, but his only reply is a weak nod. Next thing, he's zooming out of the parking lot. I watch him go, wishing I knew what was up with him.

Then I refocus. *The plan.* I missed my first chance, but I can still find Alex's group of friends inside. They always pick the same seats in the auditorium, toward the back. Maybe I can grab one nearby and make my stellar first impression there.

I set off for the school entrance. Yeah. I can do this. I can—

Wham! Something smacks into me. Pain drives into my right side, and I lose my balance, stumbling out from under the awning and into the pouring rain. Then I'm falling for real. My back hits the ground in a head-jostling thud. The air whooshes out of me, and I stare up, stunned, at the stormy sky.

As rain splatters onto my face, a voice above me says, "Oh my gosh."

That's when I get it: someone ran into me. We smacked into each other *hard*, and now I'm sprawled on the muddied grass, rain soaking every inch of my new clothes.

"*Ow*," I whimper, shutting my eyes.

"Oh my gosh," the voice repeats. "Here."

I open my eyes to see a pale hand reaching for mine. I grab hold, and as I'm hauled to my feet, cold mud squelches around me. My tights are muddy. My backpack, too. *Everything* is covered in the stuff.

Inside the school, the eight o'clock bell sounds—a cheery *ding-dum-ding*.

And outside? I'm a total mess.

4

"**THANKS,**" **I WHEEZE** to the person who hauled me up.

Then I see who it is.

I know this girl. Three months ago, she wrote *Wish I knew you better!* In my yearbook. It's Gemma Cohen, one of Amberleigh Allen's best friends.

And she's staring at me in horror.

"Are you okay?" she asks.

"Y-yeah," I manage, wincing at the pain in my tailbone. "Fine."

Gemma arches an eyebrow at me, like I'm a total liar and most definitely *not* fine.

I gulp. "Why? Do I look bad?"

"Uh." Gemma gestures at my tights.

I look down. The cheery daisy print is splattered with muddy goop and bits of grass.

"Your mascara is kind of all over the place," she adds.

I feel like burrowing into the muddy lawn of Bluebonnet

Middle School and living there the rest of my days, like a human toad.

But the thing is, I'm talking to *Gemma Freaking Cohen*, right-hand girl of Amberleigh. My plan has been wrecked so far, but Gemma? She could be my key to getting back on track.

"We're late," Gemma says, glancing at the school entrance. "We can go in together, though, if you want. I've got makeup wipes to help with your—" Gemma motions at my face.

"S-sure," I say, dazed. "That'd be nice."

'Cause I can't just give up. If Gemma's offering me a chance to turn this morning around, I'm taking it.

You happen to life, I remind myself, heading into the school with her.

We hurry down the hallway, and when we get to the auditorium, I tiptoe after Gemma into the darkened room. I'm scanning the seats, trying to spot Amberleigh's high ponytail, when a hand lands on my shoulder. I turn to see Mrs. Campos, my sixth grade math teacher, looming over me.

"Take a seat, girls," she whispers, motioning us to a row of empty seats.

I wait for Gemma to say something like, "I've got a spot saved over there." She doesn't, though. She just nods at Mrs. Campos and heads to the nearest seat. I follow, sitting my damp butt on the edge of the ratty purple upholstery.

Gemma waits until Mrs. Campos is looking the other way to dig into her backpack. She pulls out a small plastic package and hands it to me.

Right. The makeup wipes. I take one out and swipe it under my left eye, then my right. Nervously, I turn to Gemma, awaiting her assessment.

"It's hard to tell in the dark," she says, squinting, "but I think you got it all."

I hand the package back, but I don't give Gemma the used-up wipe, because that would be gross. I shove it into my jacket pocket, and when I do, my knuckles encounter . . . mushiness. I freeze. Oh my god. The bag of Trixie's poop. I'd meant to toss it in the outside garbage bin when Arlo and I left the house. Now, I'm sitting in school with a pocketful of poop.

So, that's a thing.

It's hard to concentrate on anything onstage. Opening assembly only happens on the first day of school. It's a quick fifteen-minute program before we're dismissed to first period. The principal makes a big speech, and then it's tradition to show a music video made by the teachers, where they swap out words from a famous song to make it, I don't know, *educational*? This year, the song is the old Whitney Houston hit "I Wanna Dance with Somebody," only the teachers have changed it to "I Wanna *Learn* with Somebody." It's cheesy, but kids cheer whenever their favorite teachers come on-screen.

I don't do any cheering. I'm too busy wondering how I'm going to impress Alex when I'm covered in mud.

Dirt is kind of rocker chic, right?

Yeah.

I can pull it off.

Next thing I know, the music video is ending and the lights are coming on. Students get up, crowding into the aisles. I'm glancing at the closest set of doors, wondering if I should make a run for the bathroom, when a voice shouts, "Gemma! Where *were* you?"

I turn around. Amberleigh Allen is only a few feet away, strolling down the aisle with her group of friends. I notice that she's holding hands with someone.

With . . . *Alex*.

My brain blows a fuse.

Hang on. Amberleigh and Alex. They're friends, right? So they're hanging out. While . . . holding hands.

Then Amberleigh leans in and plants a whopping kiss on Alex's neck—his *neck*!—and just like that, I know that the worst is true.

Amberleigh and Alex are *dating*.

"Was your mom late again, or something?" Amberleigh asks, stopping a foot away from me.

I gape so wide that I must look like a dead fish. At first, I think Amberleigh is talking to me. Then I remember who I'm sitting next to.

"Yeah," Gemma tells Amberleigh. "There was traffic, too."

Gemma crosses her arms as she looks—okay, maybe *glares?*—at Amberleigh. She seems mad about something.

Amberleigh lets go of Alex's hand to smooth down her ponytail, even though there's not a single flyaway. Then she glances my way.

"Oh wow. What happened to *you?*"

I glance at my muddied outfit.

"Uh," I say.

My brain fuse is still blown. All I can think is, *Alex and Amberleigh are a THING.*

It must've started this summer. Didn't I see a TikTok of them together at Myrtle Beach? Their families went on a joint vacation in June. Did Alex and Amberleigh have a whirlwind tropical romance I knew nothing about?

Just then, my stomach practically *howls*, reminding me that I haven't eaten breakfast.

Amberleigh laughs in surprise. "Oh my god. Are you okay?"

Tate—Amberleigh's other best friend—sniffs the air. Her face contorts, and she giggles. "Something smells like caca." She locks her eyes on me. "Or some*one*."

Oh no. Trixie's poop. *Nooo.*

Neil cackles. "Jeez, Vivian. Do your parents feed or bathe you?"

I stammer, and Amberleigh shoots Neil a dirty look. "Rude," she says, before telling me, "Mud is a bold choice. Very . . . uh, punk. Not a lot of people can pull that off."

So Amberleigh gets it. Punk *is* pretty close to rocker chic.

"Thanks," I say.

Then I rethink it. I know that Tate and Neil are poking fun at me, but I'm not sure about Amberleigh. Technically, everything she's said is nice, but what if she's being sarcastic?

I notice that Alex is biting back a grin. Does he think me smelling like poop is funny? My face burns like the boiling lava of Mount Marladia, but lucky for me, Amberleigh returns her attention to Gemma.

"You're not going to be late *tonight*, right?" she asks her.

Gemma's eyes narrow. She still looks pissed about something.

"It's raining," she says dully.

"Oh, that doesn't matter!" Tate chirps. "Dad got sunshades installed over the pool. They're water resistant."

"Anyway," Amberleigh says, "it's tradition."

Now everyone—Amberleigh, Tate, Alex, and Neil—is looking at Gemma.

All she does is shrug and say, "I guess."

"Cool." Amberleigh keeps on smoothing her smooth hair. "You got Lally first period?"

"Yeah," Gemma says.

"That's too bad."

Then Amberleigh grabs Alex's hand, which makes me want to puke.

"See you!" she calls, heading for the auditorium doors.

Tate and Neil follow her, cracking up about something, and my heart sinks as I wonder if that something could be *me*.

I turn to Gemma, and maybe I'm seeing things, but I think she's about to cry. She looks even worse than I feel. When she catches me staring, she quickly brushes a hand under one eye.

"Gonna head out," she says.

But I'm not ready for Gemma to go.

"Y-you're in Ms. Lally's math class?" I ask cautiously.

Gemma nods.

"Me, too," I say, gaining confidence. "Guess we're on the same class rotation."

Gemma's wet eyes brighten a little. "Oh," she says. "Cool."

"Wanna walk there together?" I ask.

And that's how we end up leaving the auditorium side by side.

We stop at Gemma's locker first, then mine, where I

unload my backpack. I peel off my rain jacket, relieved to find that most of the mud splatter missed my shirt. I shove the jacket into my locker, *very* aware that there's a poop bag in the left pocket.

*Something smells like caca. Or some*one.

Ugh.

That's a crappy problem—literally—for another time.

Right now, there's a more pressing issue on my mind.

"So, uh, Tate is having a pool party today?" I ask Gemma.

Instantly, I regret it. Will Gemma think I'm trying to invite myself?

If she thinks that, she doesn't show it. All she says is, "Yeah. We've been doing it since fifth grade."

"Must be nice," I say, and I want to kick myself. Everything coming out of my mouth sounds desperate.

Calm down, Vivian. Stay cool.

"Honestly?" Gemma says, watching me click my lock into place. "It's gotten old."

I frown. "What, like, you don't wanna go?"

Gemma shrugs—the same shrug she gave Amberleigh earlier. "I mean, we're in eighth grade. Maybe it's time for something new, you know?"

I think I *do* know. Gemma is saying what I've been thinking for the past few weeks: eighth grade means a fresh start. Only, if I'm hearing Gemma right, her fresh start involves *not* going to the pool party. I think about the way Gemma glared at Amberleigh earlier. Are the two of them . . . fighting?

That can't be right. Even if it is, I bet they'll work it out in a day or two. Every fight I've had with Cami hasn't lasted more than a weekend, tops.

"By the way," Gemma says, "what Neil and Tate said? The 'caca' thing? That was mean."

"O-oh," I say. "Yeah, it's no big deal."

Gemma's right: what they said was sort of rude. But there's no way I'll get into Amberleigh's group by bad-mouthing Tate and Neil, so I pretend it doesn't bother me. Water off a duck's back.

Gemma and I walk the rest of the way to room 1067. I take a seat in the second row, and I'm kind of surprised when Gemma sits next to me. When I look her way, she's biting her lip, revealing the baby pink bands on her braces. I had to wear braces all sixth grade, and I didn't look anywhere near as cute as Gemma does. I wonder if she even planned for her outfit—a scalloped pink sundress—to match her teeth.

Probably. She's that cool.

Ms. Lally starts class by taking attendance, and I flip open my notebook to the first page. On the top line, I write, *Vivian Mare Lantz, Eighth Grade*. I take a deep breath. I say "here" when Ms. Lally calls my name. Then? I stop paying attention. I'm stuck in my head, and all I can see is Alex and Amberleigh. Amberleigh and Alex. Holding. Hands.

It doesn't make sense. They have nothing in common. Alex loves soccer and has a great sense of humor. Amberleigh hates sports—I've heard her say so a billion times in PE—and from what I can tell, her idea of "funny" is making off-key TikTok sing-alongs.

It's only as Ms. Lally draws a parabola on the board that I have a revelation: Amberleigh and Alex *don't* make sense. And that means that they can't possibly last. Maybe they fell for each other in Myrtle Beach, but they're back in the real world now. No way they'll stay together for more than a month or two. He's meant to be with me—*his hero*. So I don't need to go erasing goal number three from my Master Plan.

Yeah. Alex and Amberleigh will see that they're wrong for each other and break up, and then Alex will notice me. By then, I'll be in Amberleigh's group, so we'll be hanging out all the time, and he'll see what he's been missing. Soon, *we'll* be the ones holding hands. I'll go to his soccer games and hold up a big poster board that says, *Fernandez #17*, and I'll make him laugh so hard that his 7UP shoots through his nose, and then . . . I'll get my first kiss. I bet that Alex's lips will be warm, and they'll taste a million times better than rocky road ice cream.

I can hold out for that kiss.

I've been doodling spirals in my notebook as I daydream. Now, feeling bolder, I draw an "A" connected to a "V." Together, they form a sparkling diamond. *A and V.* Alex and Vivian. Meant to be.

My gaze drifts across the aisle to Gemma's desk. She's drawing in her notebook, too, only her doodle is an actual picture: a girl in a flowy dress, with wavy hair drawn in purple ink. She has long lashes and looks dreamy with her chin propped in one hand as she stares out an arched window. I keep watching as Gemma adds details to the girl's dress: a sash around her waist and buttons down the bodice. Then Gemma writes something beneath her drawing. *Princess Ruth*, it says in a loopy purple scrawl.

Princess? Color me intrigued. I wonder if Gemma likes fantasy books, like me. Books like the Relevane series. I file that away as something to ask her—the next step of my plan to befriend Gemma and thereby infiltrate Amberleigh Allen's group.

After pre-algebra, I run to the bathroom, where I empty a whole paper towel dispenser wiping the mud off my tights, skirt, and shoes. Then I put on fresh coats of lipstick and mascara so that by my next class I look like an actual human. I wolf down a s'mores Pop-Tart so that my stomach won't rumble through physical science, and by the time I'm in language arts, I feel fed, clean, and confident. That's a good thing, because the key to goal number two is impressing my new teacher, Ms. Rose.

I'm laser focused in class. I take three full pages of notes, and when Ms. Rose asks for someone to explain the difference between a simile and a metaphor, my hand shoots up. Ms. Rose calls on Jordan Gilday instead of me, but, hey, I made the effort—unlike, say, Amanda Cravens, who I'm pretty sure has fallen asleep with her eyes wide open.

After class, I walk up to Ms. Rose, who's sprinkling fish food into the aquarium of Virgil, a crowntail betta fish and our unofficial class pet.

"Class pets are for kindergartners," Lewis Marks said when Ms. Rose introduced Virgil.

"Well, I got special permission to bring him in," Ms. Rose replied. "He'll be our literary guide throughout the year, just like Virgil was Dante's guide through hell in *The Divine Comedy*."

Lewis guffawed and pointed at Ms. Rose. "You said 'hell.'"

"I did," Ms. Rose said calmly. "Now, for anyone who's curious, Virgil's favorite snack is brine shrimp. He's also partial to mosquito larvae."

Some of the kids made grossed-out noises, but I made a

mental note. The next time I go to the pet shop with Pop, brine shrimp—whatever the heck those are—will be on the list. But today I have no offering for Virgil. It's just me and my charm.

"Ms. Rose?" I say, standing before her with excellent posture, hands clasped behind my back.

"Hello, Vivian," she says, setting the bottle of fish food aside.

Inside his aquarium, Virgil swishes in and out of a plastic turret, fringed tail aflutter.

"Vivian?" Ms. Rose prods. "Is there something you want to ask?"

Whoops. I got distracted.

I look up at Ms. Rose, and she smiles encouragingly. I go over the line I've rehearsed for the past week: *I'd like to work on the* Jaguar Gazette. *Is there a reporter spot open?*

Here it goes.

"I'd like to work on the *Jaguar Gazette*," I recite. "Is there a purporter spot open?"

Wait. No. *Purporter?*

"Uh, *reporter*," I correct, tingling with insta embarrassment. "Purporter—like, where did that come from? I promise, I write better than I talk."

I laugh nervously, sure that my face is Hot Tamale red,

but Ms. Rose smiles, like she's telling me not to worry about the flub.

"I'd love to have you aboard the *Gazette*," she says. "I've heard great things about your writing from Mr. Garcia."

Mr. Garcia was my seventh grade language arts teacher. Hearing that he's talked to Ms. Rose about me turns my cheeks hot, but for a different reason than before. At last, something today is going *better* than I'd planned.

"Do you have particular interests?" Ms. Rose asks. "Topics you'd like to cover?"

Topics? My mind goes blank. Virgil looks over at me with curious black eyes.

"Uh," I say. "I like . . . newspaper stuff. You know, reporting. Getting the hard-hitting stories out there."

I wince. That "hard-hitting stories" thing is just a phrase I heard once on a goofy local news commercial. It sounded better in my head.

"General enthusiasm is great," Ms. Rose says, "but would you be interested in covering, say, school sports? Or clubs? Interviewing students for our Shining Spotlight column?"

Oh. That's what she meant by "topics."

The truth is, I haven't read much of the *Jaguar Gazette*. I didn't even know that there was something called "Shining Spotlight." Now that I do, I wonder what answer would sound the most impressive to Ms. Rose.

I don't want to come across as too picky, so I end up saying, "Any of it. Whatever you need me for, I'll do."

Ms. Rose wrinkles her nose. I feel like she gave me a test just now, and I flunked it.

But then she tells me, "I think you'll like the *Gazette*. You'll learn all about journalism. Figure out what you're passionate about. Really hone those skills."

I nod eagerly. "For sure. They will get *honed*."

Ms. Rose goes on to tell me details about the paper—how the first meeting is tomorrow, after school, and I should bring a notebook designated solely for reporting. I nod, committing what she says to memory. I've replaced the blush on my face with a beaming smile.

Bam. I've done it. I've taken my first step to becoming a professional writer. Years from now, when I've made it big, I'll tell folks that I got my literary start on my middle school paper, just like my hero, Q. S. Murray. Today may have started out crappy, but I've officially turned it around. The Master Plan is working after all.

"See you tomorrow, Vivian!" Ms. Rose tells me.

"See ya!" I call back. "You too, Virgil!"

Then I set off running. I still have to get in good with Amberleigh's group, and for me to do that, I have to make it to their lunch table with plenty of time for a good *second* impression.

I'm practically leaping out of the classroom when my shoe catches on something, and I lurch forward, losing my balance. I've only got time to think, *Not again*. I pinwheel my arms so hard that I end up stumbling forward, finally catching myself on the edge of a desk.

Whew. This time, I saved myself from a wipeout. *Victory*.

But then I hear Ms. Rose shouting behind me, and then? I hear an almighty crash.

I look back, taking in three things at once. First, I see what tripped me: a long electric cord running along Ms. Rose's desk. Second, I see what that cord was connected to: the light at the top of Virgil's aquarium. Notice I say "was connected," because third? I see the source of the crash. It's *Virgil's freaking aquarium*, smashed into dozens of glass shards.

I stand stock-still as water gushes out on the classroom floor. Virgil's little turret lies broken in two at the foot of Ms. Rose's desk, and Ms. Rose herself is crouched on the ground, trying to catch hold of Virgil, who's frantically flopping on the linoleum.

"Vase!" she shouts. "The vase!"

I look to where she's pointing—the vase of sunflowers on her desk—and it finally clicks. I hurry to the desk, ripping out the sunflowers and offering the water-filled vase to Ms. Rose, who's managed to scoop Virgil into her hands. She plops him into the water, and for a few moments, the classroom is dead silent. Ms. Rose and I stare at each other over the vase.

"I'm sorry!" I burst out. "I'm so, *so* sorry. I didn't—"

"It's all right," Ms. Rose cuts me off, getting to her feet. "That cord wasn't properly secured, and that is my fault—not yours at all."

But it sure feels like my fault. I stand there miserably as Ms. Rose takes the vase from me, placing it on her desk.

"Watch your feet," she warns, shooing me away from the humongous mess of broken glass and rainbow-colored gravel.

"I can get a broom?" I offer faintly.

"No, no, everything's fine." Ms. Rose is trying to comfort me, which makes me feel even worse. "You head on to lunch, okay? I'll find the janitor, and we'll work this out."

"B-b-but—" I sputter.

"I *promise* it's all right," Ms. Rose tells me, smiling. "You go on to the caf."

The smile doesn't reach her eyes, though, and it's starting to sink in: I almost killed my teacher's pet on the first day of school. Way to go, Vivian.

I jet out of there before I can break anything else.

5

I'M STILL SHAKEN up when I walk into the cafeteria. The image of Virgil's little betta fish body flopping around will stay seared into my brain forevermore.

Ms. Rose told me that the accident wasn't my fault, but then, she *has* to say that. She's a teacher. I'm worried that she's actually pissed at me. And what does that mean for my future on the *Jaguar Gazette*? Does Ms. Rose think I'm a good-for-nothing klutz who can't handle responsibility?

My intestines twist up like a pretzel, and suddenly, I'm missing Cami so badly. My fingers itch, wanting to text her, but that won't make this better. Cami isn't *actually here*, to talk things over at our old table. She's not my lunch buddy anymore. I'm on my own.

I catch sight of Amberleigh across the caf. She's seated at a table, chatting with Tate. Alex and Neil sit across from them, playing table football with milk straw wrappers. Gemma isn't there, but I bet she will be soon.

Last year, there was no way I'd dream of asking to sit with Amberleigh's group, but seeing them now sparks a fire in my heart. I'm Eighth Grade Vivian, aren't I? And this is still a new first day. Forget the bad stuff that's happened. I'm going to happen to life, no matter how many obstacles stand in my way.

I ball up my fists, make up my mind, and—

"*Hellooo*, wanna sign up for the Labor Day bake sale?"

"*Yah!*" I yelp, reeling back. There's a tall kid in my face, grinning at me with shiny straight teeth. Their hair is a mop of tangerine orange, and they're wearing a shirt with a cartoon iguana on it.

"Huh," I wheeze, recovering from my shock. "Um, *what?*"

"The Labor Day bake sale," the kid repeats. "It'll be here before you know it! Can I put you down for cookies? You look like a cookie maker."

I blink at the kid. They're familiar. Definitely in my grade.

"You're Mike, right?" I ask.

"You bet!" Mike sticks out his hand for a shake, like we're at a business conference. "Mike Brot. You may remember how I got elected president of the student activities council back in May."

I remember no such thing.

"Well," Mike rattles on, "the elections take place in May because of how many activities start happening *right away*, when school starts up. Like . . . *the Labor Day Bake Sale!*"

Some of Mike's spit lands on my cheek. I take a step back, wiping it off.

"Sorry," I tell him. "I'm not much of a baker."

I move toward the cafeteria line, but Mike blocks me, smiling wide as ever.

"Okay, but what about your parents? I bet your mom bakes a mean birthday cake, right?"

I squint at Mike. I hate when people do that: make assumptions about how many parents I have, or what gender they are.

"My *dads* are both terrible bakers," I inform him. "Good luck, though!"

This time, I hurry off before Mike can get in another word. I feel kind of bad about it, but seconds later, he shouts *"Hellooo"* at someone new. So, I don't think I've dampened his spirits.

Even though I'm late to lunch, there's still a line. I wait my turn for a glop of tuna salad, an apple, and banana pudding. As I grab a jug of orange juice, I give myself another pep talk. I've cleaned up since Amberleigh's group last saw me. No mud, no poop, no growling stomach. This time, I'll make a good impression. Maybe I'll even get an invite to that pool party.

Lunch is where this whole day turns around.

I set my sights on Amberleigh's table and, most importantly, *Alex*. Alex with his warm brown skin and depthless eyes and the donut-hole-shaped mole beneath his lip. Alex, who looks especially nice in his gold and black uniform as he runs across the soccer field, sweat trickling down the back of his neck . . .

I heave a wistful sigh.

Yeah. Time to make this happen.

"Oh my *god*," says a girl passing by. She whispers to her friend, and both of them look at me, giggling.

Panicked, I glance down, wondering if I missed a spot of mud on my clothes. Okay, there's a *little* splatter on the hem of my skirt. But that's nothing to laugh about. Jeez.

I walk on toward Amberleigh's table, and I hear another snicker. This time it's coming from a whole table of kids. They're looking at me—and then, very quickly, *not*. More whispers and giggles swirl around me, like a growing cyclone. I catch shreds of whispers: "*so* embarrassing" and "she doesn't know."

Is this really over a speck of mud? I roll my eyes, acting like the whispers don't bother me. They do, though. My veins are sizzling, and I feel my heartbeat all the way up in my ears.

"Vivian?"

I whirl around to see Mrs. Campos. *Again*. She looks uneasy—kind of like how I feel.

"Hey," she says very softly. "Would you come with me?"

I don't get what's going on, but I follow Mrs. Campos to

the caf doors. On the way, I hear more whispers and laughs. By the time Mrs. Campos and I reach the hallway, I'm gripping my lunch tray hard enough to bruise my fingertips.

Even so, I'm not prepared for what Mrs. Campos says next.

"Vivian," she tells me, "I think you've started your period."

I stand in the bathroom of the nurse's office, facing myself in the mirror. I have officially tried every thinkable way to undo the last fifteen minutes of my life.

I've pleaded with God, in case they exist. I've wished for mutant time-reversing powers. I've promised Mother Earth that I will spend my twenties in the Peace Corps. I've even tried saying "Bloody Mary" three times, because I figure if anyone understands my predicament, it's a girl who has the word "bloody" in her name, and even if she *is* an evil ghost, I've made my peace with her scratching out my eyes and transporting me to a dark dimension. Anything is preferable to my present reality.

But it's no use. Nothing's worked.

My first period. On my first day of school.

Turns out the thing kids were laughing about in the caf wasn't the mud. It was the blood seeping through the back of my skirt. What I want to know is, how did I not feel anything? It's my period. Shouldn't I be aware of my *own body* releasing its *own blood*? Why did I have to be the last person at Bluebonnet Middle to figure that out?

"You all right in there, hon?" Ms. Wendy, the school nurse, raps on the bathroom door.

Nope, Ms. Wendy, I am *not* all right.

"Fine!" I call back, looking at the gym shorts Ms. Wendy gave me to change into. My skirt, tights, and underwear sit crumpled on the edge of the sink. Ms. Wendy gave me a pair of cheer shorts to use as underwear, as well as a pad, but now that I'm changed, I don't know what to do with my bloodied-up clothes.

Staying in the bathroom longer won't make things any better, I know. I've got to face the music, since I'm not getting any help from Bloody Mary. I wash my hands and open the door with the pile of clothes under one arm.

"Oh!" says Ms. Wendy, backing away. "Don't worry. I've got something for those."

She opens a cabinet and tugs out a mini trash bag. Shaking it open and holding it out, she says, "Go on and dump them in there."

I do, watching miserably as Ms. Wendy knots the bag and sets it on her desk.

"We'll leave that till after school," she tells me. "You can stop by afterward to pick them up. And of course, I have a nurse's note for your current class."

Wait. I'm supposed to go back to class like *this*? I stare down at my ugly gym shorts, bare knees, and sockless shoes. I look like a total weirdo. If the entire eighth grade doesn't already know about my period, they'll know *now*.

I start to cry. Really cry. Like, a waterfall of snot and tears.

Ms. Wendy kneels in front of me, placing a hand on my shoulder.

"Hey," she says. "Why don't we talk for a minute?"

She motions to one of the stiff-cushioned chairs along the office wall, and as we sit, I wince at the weird feeling of the pad in my cheer shorts.

"I'm sure that getting your period like this was difficult," Ms. Wendy tells me. "If it makes you feel better, you're definitely not the first case to walk through my door."

"I'm not?" I whisper.

"Mm-hmm. Your period is totally normal. Even if you're feeling awkward about it today, believe me, everyone's bound to have one bad first day of school."

My bottom lip wobbles. Then there's no stopping it: I burst into tears all over again.

"You don't get it!" I wail. "*Every* first day is a bad day! *Every. Single. One.*"

I could tell Ms. Wendy about the preschool glitter incident, or "Deep in the Heart of Texas," or my appendix bursting. I could tell her about my Master Plan, and how it's been officially thwarted one time too many. Instead, I just cry for what feels like ten minutes straight.

It's only when I let up that Ms. Wendy asks me gently, "Would you like me to call a parent to pick you up?"

I manage a heavy nod.

Ms. Wendy has to leave the room to make the call. The door clicks shut behind her, and I wipe the tears from my face. I hope Pop has his phone on him, because Da always shuts his off during the workday. Maybe I should have given Ms. Wendy the number to Be Kind, Rewind. Or maybe I shouldn't have asked her to call my dads at all. Maybe I should suck it up, even though the thought of going back to class makes me want to hurl.

"Knock, knock?"

I look up, expecting Ms. Wendy to be in the doorway.

Instead, it's Gemma Cohen.

"U-u-uh," I choke out. "Ms. Wendy's not here. She'll be back soon."

Gemma shuts the door, nodding. "Okay, cool."

She crosses the room and plops into the seat right next to me. I catch a whiff of a fruity scent, like strawberry Jell-O, and I tense up. I'm a bigger wreck now than I was this morning, when Gemma ran into me. I probably look like a freaky, bedraggled raccoon. Gemma, on the other hand, is a vision. Her curly brown hair is pulled back, and she's wearing cute knee-high boots. Her eyes glint as she looks me over. Which gets me wondering . . . why is Gemma here?

"Are you feeling sick?" I ask.

Gemma smirks. "I faked a stomachache in Mx. Ramani's class."

Whoa. "You lied to a teacher?"

Gemma narrows her eyes at me. That's when I realize how judgy I must sound.

"Not that I think that's *bad*," I tell her.

Gemma shrugs. "It's the first day of class. I'm not missing anything. Anyway, I emailed Mx. Ramani a week ago to ask for more outside reading, since I've done all mine. I'd say I'm in good with them."

I blink at Gemma. I've never heard someone talk about teachers this way. Like they have an *understanding*. And how the heck has Gemma already done all the outside reading for social studies? There were, like, twenty-five books on the list we got over summer break. She must be some kind of genius.

"So, wait," I say. "*Why* did you fake sick?"

Gemma's expression softens. She casts me a tiny smile, like *we* have an understanding, and says matter-of-factly, "I wanted to check on you."

I stare at her, knowing I must've heard wrong. Why would Gemma care how I'm doing? She barely knows who I am.

"I heard about what happened at lunch," Gemma explains,

"and the thing is, I'm the reason you fell this morning and messed up your look. Then Amberleigh was a jerk to you, and now *this*? You've had a majorly sucky day, and . . . well, I feel like it's partly my fault."

I give Gemma a weirded-out look. What she's saying makes zero sense.

"You didn't give me my period," I point out.

"Sure," Gemma says, "but I feel bad about the stuff that happened before."

"It's not like you knocked me over on purpose."

"Well, *okay*," Gemma concedes. "But I'm the one who's friends with Amberleigh. I should've said something when she was being ugly to you."

So Gemma *does* think that Amberleigh was being sarcastic earlier. That doesn't feel great.

"It's fine," I tell her, not so convincingly.

She motions to my clothes. "Well, look on the bright side? You got a free pair of gym shorts out of it."

I squint at Gemma. She squints back at me. The corners of her lips lift, and mine do, too. Then both of us are laughing. It's like all the jittery energy I couldn't cry out can be *laughed* out instead: a tumble of ha ha has that feel wrong but so right. As Gemma laughs, I notice a dimple on the left side of her smile. Seeing that makes my chest get warm. It gets *extra* warm when our laughs die down and Gemma rests her hand on the chair, her pinkie finger brushing my knee.

"I'm sorry you had a bad day," she says. Looking thoughtful, she adds, "I'm glad we ran into each other, though."

"*Literally*," I say.

"Yeah." Gemma's dimple reappears. "Literally."

The door swings open, and Ms. Wendy bustles in. "All settled!" she announces, before noticing Gemma. "Oh. Hello, hon."

Then she's back to telling me, "I got a hold of Diego. That's your—"

"Pop," I supply.

"Yes. He says he'll be here in ten minutes, so you hang tight a little longer, okay?"

Gemma looks at me in surprise. "You're not sticking around for the rest of school?"

"No," I admit, hunching my shoulders and wondering if I *should* suck it up. The day isn't over yet. I could keep working on the Master Plan. I could—

"Good for you," Gemma says emphatically. "I wouldn't, either."

She hops off her chair, and I watch in awe as she sweet-talks Ms. Wendy, complaining about indigestion and asking for a cup of Pepto Bismol. Gemma gulps down the stuff, but when Ms. Wendy asks if she wants to lie down, she cheerily shakes her head.

"Just needed a quick checkup, is all," she says, shooting me a wink on her way out the door.

Afterward, Ms. Wendy takes a seat at her desk, and as her nails clack against the computer keyboard, the good feelings Gemma brought with her begin to fade.

I thought it was bad last year when Posey McCowen dropped a box of tampons from her backpack on a field trip, and some of the eighth grade guys started calling her Plug-Up Posey. What's my name going to be? *Bloody Vivian*?

Oh my god. Would Amberleigh call me that? Would Alex? Would *Gemma*?

I shift my left knee—the one Gemma's pinkie touched.

No. I don't think Gemma would, at least.

There's a knock on the door, and I look up to see Pop's bearded face peering through the window. Relief breaks over me like a tidal wave.

"Oh!" says Ms. Wendy, glancing my way. "You ready to go?"

I really think about that. I'm used to cursed first days. I've always muddled through them in the past. But *this* first day—it's got me down, more than all the rest. Today, I tried to happen to life, but life just happened to me *again* and *again*, in all the worst ways.

So, am I ready to go?

I sigh, feeling the crushing weight of defeat.

Yeah, Ms. Wendy. I sure am.

6

IT'S QUIET AS the ancient tombs of Elystria on the drive home.

In the nurse's office, Pop asked how I was; and when all I could do was sniffle, he patted my back and told me it'd be okay. He took me by my locker, where I grabbed my stuff, and on our way out, I tossed Trixie's poop bag in a hallway trash can.

When I caught Pop staring, I muttered, "Don't ask."

"Not gonna," he replied. "Let's blow this Popsicle stand."

Now, in the car, I clutch my bloodied clothes on my lap. The garbage bag is scented, and the smell of fake citrus fills my nose. KXAN radio is playing, but Pop turns it off when he pulls into the back lot of Be Kind, Rewind. He shifts the car into park as I stare blankly at the *Reserved for Our Far-Out Customers!* sign.

I don't want to talk about this. I want to bury myself in bed, where I can drift into a hundred-year slumber. But Pop's got different plans. We head inside, where Pop takes my clothes to soak them in the washing machine. Dads have finished cleaning up the back room and opened the shop, and Da's talking to a customer up front. When Da's through, Pop pulls him aside—filling him in on my Great Humiliation, no doubt—and flips the *Open* sign to *Closed*.

Pop suggests we "talk about things," and before I know it we're in my room, Dads sitting on the edge of my bed and Da holding a box of maxi pads.

I. Am. Mortified.

A few weeks after I turned ten, Dads sat me down to tell me about the third shelf of the linen closet, where they'd stocked the things I might need when I got my first period: pads, panty liners, and tampons. I could take my pick when the time came, they said. Once Arlo caught wind of that, he went around calling it "the menstrual shelf," like it was a big joke, and the name stuck.

Ever since, my period's been looming over me, like a giant thundercloud filled with gallons of blood. I know periods are normal. People get them everywhere, all over the world. I'm sure that once I get the hang of it, life will be dandy. It's just my first period that I've been nervous about. It's the uncertainty—not knowing when it's going to strike. Cami got hers a year ago on a Sunday, when she was at home. I wasn't sure I'd be that lucky, though.

During the summer, especially, when I sweated through my shorts on extra-hot days, I'd freak out that maybe some of that sweat was blood. But those were all false alarms. This one time I needed to be prepared? I wasn't. I hadn't even thought about packing a pad in my backpack this morning. Much good the menstrual shelf did me today.

"I get it," Pop tells me, reaching across the bed to squeeze my hand. "You don't feel like talking, and that's okay. I only want to say that, believe it or not, you will recover from this."

I don't want to talk, but I can't let *that* go.

"Everyone was laughing at me!" I burst out. "People are going to call me Bloody Vivian for the rest of my *life*."

Da raises an eyebrow. "That would be unoriginal."

"It's not funny!"

"No," Pop says gently. "It's not."

"It wasn't supposed to go like this!" I keep wailing. "It's the absolute *worst* of my worst first days. And it won't just be today. It'll be my whole *year*, and people won't forget in high school, either. I'll *always* be the girl who had her period in front of the whole school!"

In the midst of my wailing, a new solution pops into my head.

I clasp my hands in front of me, begging. "We could move! We could go back to Chicago. Or *Siberia*. Anywhere but here!"

"We're not moving," Da says firmly.

Dejected, I grab Mistmorrow and prop him under my chin.

"If you need another day off school," says Pop, "that's okay."

The room goes quiet, and I peer over Mistmorrow's ears to see Da and Pop swapping looks.

Da's look says something like, *We didn't discuss that.*

Pop's says, *It's the right thing to do.*

Take *another* day off school? It was bad enough conceding defeat in Ms. Wendy's office. Then again, I don't know if I can ever show my face at Bluebonnet Middle again.

"I gotta think about it," I mumble into Mistmorrow's fur.

Dads back off after that. Da hands over the pads, and Pop tells me that if I don't feel comfortable talking about this stuff with them, I can always call Aunt Ximena. Finally, they leave the room, and the second Pop closes the door, I bury my face in Mistmorrow's mane and let out a pent-up scream.

"He still won't answer."

I'm in the kitchen, sitting at an oak foldout table set for four. There's a problem, though: only three of us Lantzes are here. Even after Da's closed the shop for the day and Pop has nudged veggies around and around on the griddle, saying we can wait another five, ten, fifteen minutes; even after Da has called Arlo three times—he's a no-show.

"Band practice?" Pop suggests, as he sets a tangerine poppy seed salad on the table.

We all know that isn't it, though. Arlo's practices are after dinner, at eight o'clock. Who knows what he's up to? Maybe it's not practice, but I bet it has *something* to do with "band life."

Over dinner, Dads talk about the news and boring shop business while I pick at the grilled veggies and cheese on my plate. I'm grateful that Dads haven't brought up school or my period again; I sure don't want to think about either of those things. Right now? I'm trying not to think, period.

I'm chewing a soggy green pepper when a melody floats into the room from down the hall. It's the main theme of the first Relevane movie—a special ringtone on my phone that can only mean one thing: Cami's calling.

Cami. That's exactly who I need at a time like this.

I look up from my plate, which is practically empty. "Can I get that?" I ask fervently.

Dads exchange a look over their glasses of wine, and eventually Pop nods at me. *Permission granted.*

I leap from the table and tear down the hall. Once I'm locked in my bedroom, I dig the phone out of my backpack.

"Hello?" I yelp, picking up.

"Dolphin *Priiide!*" Cami squeals. "Vivian! Today felt like it was a whole *week*."

She can say that again.

"But . . . it was good?" I ask, trying to sound upbeat.

"*So* good," Cami gushes. "Kind of overwhelming at first. I'd gone to that new student orientation, so I knew where my classes were, and I still got lost by second period. But this really nice girl named Fatima came to my rescue, and we got to talking afterward, and she lives two streets down from me and has a *pool*. So we're going swimming this weekend, and she's going to introduce me to some of her friends. Uh, and then I decided to . . . try out for the dance team?"

"Whoa."

"Yeah, I know. I wasn't planning on it, but Fatima's on the team, and she was telling me how fun it was, and I thought, why not?"

"That's super cool," I say.

I'd never pictured Cami on a dance team before, but now I can. In fact, I can envision a lot about her Floridian future: hanging with her new friends, swimming at Fatima's pool, cheering on the Dolphins with the dance team. Life's going great for Cami, the way I hoped it would.

So why do I still feel so crappy?

"What about your day?" Cami's tone has changed. She's quieter. *Concerned.* I know she's waiting to hear about the curse—if it still plagued me today and just how bad it was.

Oof.

Dinner churns in my stomach, and I start to feel so queasy that I have to lie down on my crescent moon–shaped rug. If Cami were still living in Austin, I know she could've saved me from today's fate. I would've walked into school with her, rather than falling butt-first into the mud. She would've noticed the blood on my skirt before the entire cafeteria did.

I needed my best friend today.

I know it's not Cami's fault that she's on cloud nine, while I had the worst first day of my life. But it feels like there's distance between us tonight—and not just the miles from Orlando to Austin.

I thought today would go so differently. I thought that my Master Plan would work and that I'd surprise Cami with my success. I would finally tell her about Q. S. Murray's advice and how it had changed everything. Now? If I start telling Cami about today, I'll dissolve into an ocean of tears.

So, I make a decision: I'm *not* going to tell Cami.

It takes every last shred of my energy, but I force a smile and say, "You know what? I'm *great*. Classes were good, and I hung out with this new girl named . . . uh, Breanna. And they had banana pudding at lunch."

Well, one of those things is true.

Cami squeals. "Really? A *good* first day?"

"Yeah!" I strain to keep my voice chipper. "Can you believe it? The curse has finally been lifted."

"That's the *best* news!" Cami sighs dreamily into the phone. "We're living the life, huh? I have a really good feeling about eighth grade."

"Mm-hmm." I shove away the sick feeling in my gut.

We talk a little longer, mostly about Cami's day. It's not that she doesn't ask about mine; I just avoid the subject when it comes up.

Afterward, I can't bring myself to go back into the kitchen. I don't even tell Dads good night. I bring my hyacinth journal to bed, and I ask myself how it all went wrong. One goal I sure didn't write in here: *Suffer a crushing social defeat that will haunt me the rest of my days.*

This isn't Q. S. Murray's fault, of course. She is the creator of the greatest fantasy world of all time. She is my oracle, and the curse-breaking advice she gave me was solid. Maybe it's just that my curse is *too strong*.

My phone lights up with a text from Cami: *HOPE TOMORROW'S AS GREAT AS TODAY.*

That puts a giant lump in my throat.

The truth is, I had the worst day of my life.

The truth is, I don't ever want to go back to school.

But staring at Cami's text, I have a sudden thought: tomorrow can't be any *worse* than today.

I look back at my journal:

VIVIAN LANTZ'S FOOLPROOF PLAN
FOR THE PERFECT FIRST DAY

Struck by inspiration, I jab my pen onto the page. I cross out the two final words and, in their place, I write new ones. Then I sit back and read my new creation:

VIVIAN LANTZ'S FOOLPROOF PLAN
FOR THE PERFECT ~~FIRST DAY~~
SECOND CHANCE

I close the journal, breathing deep with fresh determination. I trace my fingers along the golden hyacinths on the cover, and the slightest tingle shoots up my fingertips.

I can't undo today, but I can hope for a tomorrow that's *greater*. A second chance. For a moment, I feel like that's possible. I feel *okay*.

But when I put the journal away, that feeling fizzles out. I can hope for a second chance, sure, but I wish I didn't *need* it. I wish that today had just been good. *Easy*.

I turn off my lamp, and as I lie in the darkness, I whisper a desperate thought aloud: "I wish I could do today all over again."

A girl can dream.

So I hug Mistmorrow to my chest and try to dream for real.

7

"WHOA, WHOA, WHOA!"

I wake to the sound of rain on the roof and Arlo's voice shouting from downstairs. Rolling over, I grasp at the sheets in search of my phone, but it isn't there. I sit up, finding it on my nightstand instead.

Groggily, I pick up the phone, checking the clock.

6:13 a.m.

I groan. What is Arlo shouting about this time?

"Dads. Get down here quick!"

I frown. Last night, over dinner, Da said he'd boarded up the back-room window and we wouldn't have to worry about more flooding. It was only drizzling by the time I went to bed, so I assumed the worst of the storm was over. But now the rain's back to pouring—hitting the roof as hard as marbles—and it sounds like we've got another problem on our hands.

I want to yank the covers over my head and go on snoozing.

I could always pretend I didn't hear Arlo. But we Lantzes are a team. It wouldn't be right to leave Dads and Arlo alone with whatever new mess is downstairs. So I lurch out of bed and make my way down the hall. Arlo is at the bottom of the stairs, his hair sopping wet.

Wow. I had my own bad day, but two mornings in a row of floodwater hair? That's rough. I wince at Arlo in sympathy. He grimaces back.

"Where's Dads?" he asks.

Right then, Da and Pop come barreling down the hallway. Trixie skitters behind them, barking like there's no tomorrow.

"The damage?" Da demands.

"My whole bed," Arlo replies.

Pop rumples my hair as he and Da pass me on the stairs.

"Morning, Viv," he says with a wink.

Whoa.

I've got major déjà vu.

It's not just the flooding. I've lived this *moment* before: these words, that hair tousling, the wink. All of this happened yesterday.

I shake my head. No, something *like* this happened. Dads and Arlo are just being Dads and Arlo, same as always.

When I get downstairs, Da's in the back room, cussing again about our house's crappy gutters.

"Arlo, get rags from the laundry closet," he shouts. "Diego, the water drum from out back. Vivian, I'll need you here."

Arlo and Pop get a move on, and I head to the back room. Da is cramming rags against the rotting window above Arlo's bed. Right smack under the flood, there's a shelf of inventory boxes.

I stare. The same window is leaking—the window that Da said he boarded up.

And those boxes—we moved all of them yesterday. They shouldn't be there.

This isn't déjà vu. It's something else. Something . . . *impossible.*

"Here's the plan," Da's telling me, hauling down one of the dampened boxes. "Move all of these from point A—"

"I—I'll be right back!" I interrupt.

I don't wait for Da's reaction. I take off, ripping through the shop and nearly toppling a jade-knobbed curio cabinet. I charge up the stairs as a rumble of thunder shakes the house, making Trixie howl. Then I careen into my bedroom.

I stop dead in my tracks, staring in shock at the clothes hanging on my closet door. Because they're not *today's* clothes. They're a jean miniskirt, a yellow ringer tee, and a pair of daisy-printed tights.

This isn't right. I tossed that shirt on the floor last night. The skirt and tights were in the washing machine.

One moment, I'm made of marble. The next, I'm made of wind.

I whoosh across the bedroom, picking up my phone. I suck in a massive breath, steeling myself for what I might see. Then I turn on the screen and look.

Monday, August 22.

My knees go soft like butter. I sink onto the bed in a woozy daze.

Monday. That was yesterday.

It's yesterday *today.*

I pinch my arm hard. Harder.

Nothing happens. I don't wake up, so this isn't a dream.

A girl can dream.

The memory of last night hits me. I wanted so badly for yesterday to have never happened. I whispered, "I wish I could do today all over again."

Was my wish . . . granted?

I cross the room to my desk. My backpack hangs from the chair, and there's not a speck of mud on it. It's like my entire bedroom has reset to twenty-four hours ago.

I race to the bathroom. No pad. No period.

I check my phone again. Yesterday's date glows up at me above a photo of me and Cami at the Relevane midnight premiere. We're both dressed as Sage Miriel, wearing emerald eyeshadow and purple velvet robes.

Cami. Code Unicorn. We promised we'd tell each other about real-life magic. But is that what this is? Have I been given a magical second chance at my first day of school?

Another peal of thunder shakes the house, jolting me out of my thoughts. Dads and Arlo. They're still downstairs, dealing with the back-room flood. Whatever's going on, one thing's for sure: my family needs me.

I return to the back room, my head a swirling storm. Da's still at work, moving inventory out of the flood zone. He sets down a box when he sees me.

"Everything all right, Viv?" he asks.

"Y-yeah," I say, taking a box. "Just, uh, had to pee."

Arlo comes in with a handful of rags, and he and Da get to blocking up the window. Pop drags in the water drum to catch the rest of the leaking water. I go through yesterday's motions, hauling boxes across the room. Pop sorts through their soggy contents, complaining that he's going to have to wash and line dry the clothes. Meantime, I feel like my brain's been zapped by lightning. I can't make sense of the *how*.

I'd be lying if I said I hadn't pretended that magic is real. I've daydreamed about walking in the shoes of Sage Miriel, facing down mythical creatures and conjuring spells.

Well, what if this *is* the real deal? Real-life, touch-it, see-it, taste-it magic?

I'm in a daze when Arlo tells Dads, "I could stay home from school to help."

Da tells him, "Nice try."

"Plus," says Pop, "I don't think Vivian would appreciate her chauffeur bailing on her."

"You wouldn't mind, would you, Barficorn? Eighth grade's a joke, anyway."

I stare at Arlo. I've heard his question before. I've heard *all* of this before.

He nudges my shoulder. "Hey. You can afford to miss your first day."

It really is my first day *again*.

My gaze drifts past Arlo to the clock over the door.

It's seven twenty.

Seven twenty.

Something bursts inside of me, deep down in my gut. It's an almighty revelation, like the way I felt when I watched Q. S. Murray's message for the first time. Last night, my high hopes for eighth grade felt like a dying flame. Now, they're being fanned back into a fire.

Somehow, some way, I'm living Monday again.

"Arlo!" I yelp. "Be ready to go in ten!"

I take off. I race from the back room and up the stairs. I'm not asking any more questions; I'm just taking this second chance. I can think about the *how* later.

I throw on my clothes, swipe on my makeup, and grab the Pop-Tarts from the kitchen. When I clomp downstairs, Trixie is waiting for me, whimpering.

Oh no. The accident.

I stare at the unholy sight of poop and pee on the vintage rug.

Then Tate's voice is in my head, saying, *Something smells like caca.*

I can't let that happen again. Not to mention, there's no time.

"Sorry, Trixie," I whisper, scratching her ears and racing past the mess.

Arlo is in the back room, right where I left him, and this time, everyone's looking at me kind of funny.

"Sure you're all right, Viv?" Da asks.

I nod emphatically. "I just lost track of time."

Pop places a hand on my shoulder. "It's normal to be a little stressed on your first day of school," he says. "Especially without Cami. But you're going to be all right."

"Mm-hmm, I know."

I force a smile at Pop. Then I turn to Arlo.

"Sure about this?" he asks, with an arched brow. "Eighth grade sucks. Better to take a break until high school."

"Arlo," Da says warningly.

"Telling it like I see it," he replies.

But I'm way too antsy for Arlo's philosophizing.

"I'm ready to go," I tell him.

Arlo shrugs, like, *Your loss.*

I don't bother asking about his clothes, but Arlo explains anyway as he slips on his flip-flops: "The rest of my ensemble is in the back seat. Band life."

Yeah, I think distantly. *I've heard that before.*

"Happy first day, kiddos!" Pop calls as we head out.

"Love you!" Da adds.

"Love you, Dads!" I say. Then, super quick, I add, "Trixie had an accident in the shop!"

Arlo whistles lowly as I slam the door shut. "Cold-blooded, Barficorn."

I grimace. I know it's not cool of me to leave Dads with Trixie's mess, but what else can I do? I can't show up late to school again with a pocketful of poop. I've been given a second chance, and I'm taking it. This time, today will be *perfect*.

But as I step into the rain, I realize that I'm missing one majorly important wardrobe item: my rain jacket. I've been so distracted by the, uh, *freaking magic* that I forgot to grab it on my way out.

I can't very well go back inside now, after dropping my poop truth bomb on Dads. Nope. I decide to book it, racing across the parking lot and flinging myself into the passenger seat of the Civic. I try to ignore the corn chip stench as I pull down the visor and rake my fingers through my rain-spattered hair. This is fine. A little wet hair is totally rocker chic. Right?

"Someone to impress?" Arlo asks.

The same rock song from yesterday—*today?*—is playing on the radio. Arlo turns it down as he pulls out of the back lot.

"Just trying to be presentable," I tell him.

Actually, I've got a ton of people to impress: Alex and Amberleigh and Tate and Neil and Ms. Rose and . . . my heart thumps a few extra beats at the thought of seeing Gemma.

But Alex, mostly. It's mostly thumping for him.

"Uh-oh. This doesn't look good."

I look out the windshield. Glaring red taillights are strung out in front of us.

The traffic jam. How'd I forget? If I hadn't been so distracted by my wet hair, I could've warned Arlo. We could've taken a shortcut by turning on Mary Street. Now, it's just like before: we're packed into traffic on South First.

"Must be a wreck." Arlo gestures ahead of us.

"Yeah," I say hazily.

I tell myself to get it together. I can't waste this second chance. I have to stop making the same mistakes, and that starts here and now, in the car.

It sucked that Arlo wasn't at dinner last night. I know that it hurt Dads' feelings, and I sure would've appreciated having him there after my bad day. So this time? I'm going to convince Arlo not to bail on us.

I start by keeping things casual.

"How's it going with the band?" I ask.

Arlo doesn't reply. He frowns ahead at the traffic, and I decide he must not have heard me.

I switch off the radio and ask again, "How's the band?"

Arlo looks my way. He seems chill enough, but his knuckles have whitened around the steering wheel—like yesterday. "We're fine. It's . . . band life."

"But, like, do you have any shows coming up?"

"Sure. Plenty."

"Where at?"

Arlo looks at me again. There's a steeliness in his eyes. The *off* look. It's back.

"Did Dads put you up to this?" he asks me.

I make a face. "What?"

"Did they ask you to fish around for details?"

"Of course not. *I* want to know, that's all."

What a weird question. It's like Arlo has selective amnesia about how I've supported his dreams. Like he doesn't remember how he practiced his bass solo from the Who's "My Generation" a bajillion times in front of me, before his audition for the Neon Spurs. I even made him a homemade good luck card on the big day.

Arlo heaves a sigh. "Look, Viv, I'm sorry. I guess I'm paranoid about Dads these days. Especially Da. He's always looking for a reason to tell me I'm doing life wrong."

"Like how you don't want to go to college?"

Oops.

I slap a hand across my mouth. I'm not supposed to know that. *Yesterday's* Arlo brought up college. Today's hasn't.

Arlo looks startled. "Who told you that?"

You did.

But I can't say that.

"Uh." I flounder. "I dunno, I just thought that maybe you'd rather be doing stuff with the band. Real-life sound engineering instead of going to school for it, right?"

Now that I've put it that way, Arlo's plan makes more sense to me.

He doesn't buy my answer, though.

"Where would you . . . Have you been snooping on my phone?"

"*Pfrsh.*" I throw a hand in the air, like Arlo's the one who is out of line.

"God, Viv." He groans. "It's bad enough, dealing with Da."

I stare out through the pouring rain at the Starbucks parking lot. I don't see why Arlo and Da can't agree to disagree about the Neon Spurs. They've been fighting so much lately. I'm starting to see why Arlo might be skipping dinners.

That thought makes my insides feel like decomposing matter.

"I didn't go through your texts," I tell Arlo. "For real. I'm not a snoop."

"Yeah. It's whatever."

Arlo doesn't sound convinced, so I decide to be honest about something else.

"I think you should ditch college, if you want," I say. "I just don't like when you blow off family stuff to hang with the band. Sometimes it feels like . . . like *they're* your new family."

I poke at the door handle, swallowing an ache in my throat. I've never said something like this before. I haven't let myself *think* it. But lately, I've been feeling insecure. Arlo's bandmates do stuff with him that I can't, like stay out late and play at cool venues downtown. I'm thirteen, and they're, like, *adults*. How am I supposed to compete with that?

Arlo doesn't answer me—not right away. The traffic lets up, and we ride in silence the rest of the way to school. It's only when we pull up to the awning that Arlo reaches across the console.

"Viv."

That catches me off guard. Arlo's nickname for me is Barficorn. He only calls me Viv for serious stuff—like the time he broke the news to me that Uncle Declan had died.

I grow still, hoping that Arlo will do something to make this right. He looks me straight in the eye, and I stare back expectantly.

Then he says, "You're my little sister. You'll always be that to me."

I nod haltingly. What's that supposed to mean? Of course I'm Arlo's sister. That's just a practical fact.

"So, I'll see you later at dinner," I say. "You'll be there?"

I can't read the look in Arlo's eyes, but I know that if he planned to come to dinner, he'd say yes. He doesn't, though. It's clear that whatever plans he's got with the band, he's not going to cancel. So much for *that* second chance.

I shake my head in disappointment, getting out of the car and shutting the door with a heavyhearted thud. Rain splatters onto my bare head, and I'm making a run for it when Arlo rolls down the window.

"Hey," he calls. "Barficorn! I love you, okay?"

I stop, turn, and give a half-hearted wave. "Yeah," I call back. "Love you, too."

Arlo drives off, but I don't watch him go. I'm too bummed, and I'm getting more soaked by the second. I run for the cover of the awning, and as I do, something catches my eye: Gemma Cohen is at the front doors, steps ahead of me.

"Hey!" I call after her. "Gemma! Wait up!"

I MIGHT BE running late again, but the way I see it, I've got a whole day left of second chances. I can still fix the rest of yesterday's mistakes. For instance, I can make friends with Gemma without landing butt-first in the mud.

"Hey!" I gasp, catching up to her at the school entrance.

She's giving me a weird look. Almost like yesterday didn't happen.

Because it didn't. *Duh.*

If it's Monday all over again, then I'm starting from scratch with Gemma. We didn't run into each other yesterday, so she didn't give me a makeup wipe, and we definitely didn't talk in Ms. Wendy's office. As far as Gemma's concerned, the most we've said to each other is "hello" and "Will you sign my yearbook?"

Gemma already has one hand on the door.

"Is . . . something wrong?" she asks. She squints at me. "You're really wet."

"Oh! Yeah. Forgot my rain jacket. *Whoops.*" I laugh, and it's the most awkward sound a human being has ever made.

Ugh. What if Gemma thinks I'm a freak? I start to lose my nerve.

But then I remember Q. S. Murray telling me, *You have to happen to life.*

Right. The thing about magical second chances? You've got to *take* them.

So I gather my courage and ask, "Want to walk in together? It'd be way less awkward showing up late if I wasn't alone."

At first, Gemma's expression is blank. I start to worry that she'll say no. Maybe she only walked in with me yesterday because she felt bad about knocking me down. Maybe I got this all wrong, and Gemma doesn't want to be friends. Maybe—

"Sure," Gemma says. Then she smiles at me, and that dimple appears in her left cheek.

My "maybes" flit away.

We head inside, sprinting down the hall. That's when I notice—*really* notice—how cute Gemma's dress is. It's printed with strawberries, and even Gemma's backpack has a sparkly strawberry charm. Guess she's as wild about berries as Cami and I are about hyacinths.

Principal Liu is still giving his welcome speech when Gemma and I sneak into the auditorium. When a hand touches my shoulder, I know who it's going to be.

"Take a seat, girls," Mrs. Campos whispers, waving us toward the empty row of seats.

Gemma and I do as we're told *again*. We sit side by side in the dark as Principal Liu introduces the music video. As it plays, I carefully lean toward the empty seat on my left and wring out the ends of my sopping hair. I can't do anything about my clothes, but at least they'll dry in an hour or two. Right now, I've got to focus on what's next. When the video ends, Amberleigh will head our way. She'll be holding hands with Alex, but I'm prepared. I might be soaked, but at least I'm not covered in mud, and that's an improvement. Plus, I don't smell like Trixie's poop.

Sure enough, when the houselights turn on, Amberleigh walks up to me and Gemma. It's still not easy watching her smooch my two-year crush on the neck, but at least I'm not taken by surprise. This time, I'm going to speak before Amberleigh gets the chance.

I sprint ahead of Gemma, getting to Amberleigh first.

"Oh, I *love* your shoes," I say loudly, pointing. "Louboutins, right?"

I know this because Pop has an affinity for vintage designer shoes. He stocks them regularly at Be Kind, Rewind, and there's a list of repeat customers he calls whenever we get a new pair. Once, this seventy-year-old lady name Marguerite paid a whopping $200 for a pair of 1997 Louboutin heels, even though their soles were worn out.

Well, I bet a million dollars that Amberleigh's soles aren't worn. Those silver-studded white suede sneakers look brand spanking new.

She stops in her tracks, glancing down at the shoes. "Uh, yeah. My dad got them for me on his last trip to New York."

"He's got great taste," I say.

Then, oh so suavely, I run a hand through my wet choppy bangs and turn to Alex. "This weather is brutal, huh? Like, I got totally soaked."

Ha! I've used my lack of rain jacket to my advantage. I'm a second chance genius.

And it *works*. Alex actually looks at me. He cracks a smile and says, "Yeah, it's like the freaking apocalypse out there."

Then he frowns and asks, "You're, um . . . who?"

My heart cracks.

Amberleigh pushes Alex's shoulder. "Oh my god, don't be rude. She's Vivian Lantz. You remember, right?"

Then Amberleigh does the worst possible thing. She bursts into song: "*The stars at night! Are big and bright!*"

Neil and Tate are just walking up, and Neil, catching on, plants his feet in the aisle, bellowing, "*Deep in the heart of Texas!*"

This just goes to prove my point: people *don't* forget your bad first days. But this is eighth grade, not third, and the new Vivian Lantz is turning things around. The new Vivian is cool, and cool kids? They don't let a little teasing bother them.

That's why I laugh when the gag is over and say to Alex, "That's me!"

"Oooh, yeah," he says. "I remember now."

My smile falters. Alex called me his freaking *hero* a mere two years ago. How could he have forgotten who I am? Unless . . . that fateful moment didn't mean as much to him as it did to me.

Ow. My heart cracks some more.

"So, where were you?"

Amberleigh turns from me to Gemma, who's got a ticked-off look on her face. I'm sure of it now: she and Amberleigh *must* be in a fight.

"Mom was running late," Gemma says.

"You're not going to be late *tonight*, though, right?"

Gemma frowns at Amberleigh. "It's raining."

"Oh, that doesn't matter!" Tate cuts in. "Dad got sunshades for the pool. They're water resistant, so we're, like, fine."

"Anyway," Amberleigh adds, "it's tradition."

All eyes turn to Gemma, and I get uncomfortable. I don't like the way everyone is piling the pressure on her.

Gemma doesn't seem fazed, though. She shrugs and says, "I guess."

Right then, my stomach howls like a ravenous wolf.

Whoops. Forgot to eat breakfast again.

This time, Amberleigh doesn't seem to notice. She doesn't even comment on my rain-soaked clothes. Instead, she looks me over and says, "You could come, too, if you want. It's, like, a chill pool hangout we do."

My hopes soar like Mistmorrow when he leapt—against all odds—across the Celater Gorge. Gemma must've had it wrong about Amberleigh yesterday. I mean, Amberleigh wouldn't be inviting me to the party if she didn't *like* me. Just goes to show where the right shoe compliment can get you.

"Uh . . . yeah," I say, reminding myself to breathe. "That sounds fun."

Amberleigh turns to Tate. "That's cool with you, right?"

"Sure!" Tate chirps. "I just wish we were inviting more *guys*."

She bursts into feathery giggles, like she's scandalized by her own words. I've noticed that about Tate: she giggles a lot.

Amberleigh nods like everything's settled and smooths a hand over her ponytail. "You got Lally first period?" she asks Gemma.

Gemma, who looks like she's gritting her teeth, just nods.

"Shame." Amberleigh sighs. "Well, see you!"

She grabs Alex's hand—which only *slightly* makes me want to vomit—and heads for the exit. Tate and Neil follow.

They're not laughing, so I think it's safe to say that I am not the butt of anyone's joke this time.

Score. Class hasn't even started, and I've got a party invite. Perfect first day of school, here I come. Well. Perfect *second* first day? Whatever. Point is, it's going to be perfect. Everything that yesterday *wasn't*.

I turn to Gemma, fired up, and say, "The party sounds great."

"Does it?" She narrows her eyes at me.

"Um . . . yeah?"

I think back to what Gemma said about the party yesterday: *It's gotten old.* I wonder what would make her say that?

"Okay, give me your number." Gemma pulls a phone from her backpack, and I nearly choke in surprise.

"Wh-what?" I say.

"So I can text you the address."

"*Oh*. Um, yeah!"

Keep it cool, Vivian.

I do the best I can. I tell Gemma my number and take out my phone to add hers. That's when I see the text from Cami: *Hope it's a good day!*

Quick as I can, I shoot back, *GO, DOLPHINS!!!!!!!*

"Ladies."

I look up. Mrs. Campos is back, looming over us. I know the rule: we're not supposed to have our phones out in school unless we're making an emergency call. But nobody *really* follows that rule. Not that I plan on pointing that out to Mrs. Campos. I tell her a heartfelt "sorry," hoping she won't take my phone away, and when she doesn't, I quickly tuck it into my backpack, out of sight.

It's only as she's walking away that the terrible memory hits me: Mrs. Campos pulling me out of the caf to tell me I'd gotten my period.

Crap. I forgot to grab something from the menstrual shelf.

"*Vivian.*"

I shake myself. Gemma's looking at me expectantly.

"Sorry," I say sheepishly. "What?"

"I was saying I'll text you later." Gemma's words are short. It's almost like she's . . . pissed off?

"Y-yeah," I tell her. "That sounds good."

Then I make a run for it.

I don't want to ditch Gemma, but I've got to get to the restroom before first period.

Ha, I think bleakly, hurrying down the hall. *First period.*

I grab a pad from the nearest restroom—I'm lucky that we've got working, stocked dispensers at Bluebonnet Middle— and lock myself in an empty stall. At first, I panic. There's already blood. But when I wiggle my skirt and tights around to check, I don't find any stains on my clothes.

Whew. Got here in time. *Another* first-day crisis averted.

I'm still getting used to wearing a pad. I feel like a kid in a diaper leaving the stall, but Cami told me that, after a while, you pretty much forget it's there. Here's hoping.

When the school bell sounds, I'm still two halls away from room 1067. I pick up the pace and practically slam into the classroom door. Ms. Lally looks up from calling attendance.

"Trouble finding us, Vivian?" she asks coolly.

"Sorry," I whisper.

My seat from yesterday is taken, but there's one free right behind Gemma. I give her a small smile as I pass. She doesn't smile back.

Okay. Now I'm *positive* that Gemma is pissed at me.

I get it. It was rude of me, running off and leaving her in the auditorium. Plus, if Gemma's in a fight with Amberleigh, she probably didn't appreciate me cozying up to her, talking about Louboutins. Not that Gemma and Amberleigh will be fighting for long. I've just showed up in the group at an awkward time, is all.

My eyes drift, and I watch as Gemma sketches the purple-ink Princess Ruth. Today, she's adding details that I didn't catch before. A delicate circlet of flowers and jewels rests on the princess's head. A chubby bird sits on the windowsill, and Gemma adds a speech bubble above its head, scribbling in all caps, "*CHIIIRP!!!*"

A giggle escapes me, and Gemma's shoulders stiffen. I

squeeze my lips together, holding in my laugh until Gemma eases up and starts sketching again. Turns out she's talented *and* funny, and that makes me all the more bummed that she's mad at me.

But, hey! Today isn't over yet. I bet that at tonight's party, I can get on Gemma's good side. I *can* make this the perfect first day that I wished for. And once I do, who will need to know about yesterday but me? No one.

Yesterday won't exist.

Today in language arts, when Ms. Rose asks the class about metaphors, I feel too jittery to raise my hand. Not that it matters. Jordan Gilday answers, explaining that it'd be a *simile* if you said someone's smile was *like* sunshine, but a *metaphor* if you said someone's smile *was* a blazing supernova.

My chest sure feels like an exploding star. I have to get things right with Ms. Rose. No flubs. No aquarium smashing. Just journalistic finesse.

When class is over, I walk up to Ms. Rose's desk. She's sprinkling fish food into Virgil's tank, and I feel sweaty as I get a flashback of Virgil flopping across the linoleum, on the verge of death.

"Hello, Vivian," Ms. Rose says.

Virgil's staring at me with one black eye, and I get this

creepy feeling like he knows what I did yesterday. He knows, and he's sending murderous fish vibes my way.

But that's silly. Virgil is just a fish, and this time, I'm watching my feet. I make note of the cord running down from the aquarium light, around Ms. Rose's desk, and up to the outlet beside the poster that says *Reading! A Passport to New Worlds*.

Accursed cord. No way am I tripping on *you* today.

I focus instead on Ms. Rose and say the lines that I've rehearsed: "I'd like to work on the *Jaguar Gazette*. Is there a reporter spot open?"

Nailed it. No *purporter* flub here.

"Really?" Ms. Rose sets down the bottle of fish food. "I'd love to have you aboard the *Gazette*. I've heard great things about your writing from Mr. Garcia."

Now it's showtime. I'm ready to wow Ms. Rose. No stammers or blanking out, because I'm prepared. I wrote down my ideas during physical science.

"I've been thinking of topics I'd like to cover," I tell her. "I think I'd be great at sports coverage—especially soccer games. Or I could do an exposé on the abysmal funding for the arts program."

Ms. Rose quirks a brow. "Abysmal, huh?"

I freeze. *Abysmal*. That's the word Arlo used when he told me about the Bluebonnet music program a few years back.

It means "bad," right? I should've looked it up beforehand, to be sure. What's Ms. Rose going to think if I can't use the right word? That's the last thing she'd want in a reporter. It'd be almost as embarrassing as—

"You're right." Ms. Rose cuts into my thoughts. "The funding *is* abysmal. I do already have Uma Foster on the soccer beat, but I love where your head is at. These are great ideas, and I'm all for a new reporter who's given the job some thought."

I congratulate myself. Way to go, Vivian—for real this time.

"I think you'll like the *Gazette*," Ms. Rose tells me.

"Yeah. I *know* I will."

Ms. Rose goes over the details of the paper, same as before, and I grin thinking about how good tomorrow's meeting is going to be. No aquatic accident to recover from. Just me and a big, blank paper to fill with stories. *Possibility.*

That's what I envision as I steer clear of Virgil's aquarium cord—*win!*—and head to lunch. Possibility is what I love most about writing. You've only got twenty-six letters to work with in the English language, but somehow, there are *endless* arrangements to make. Scintillating sentences and punchy paragraphs—a whole realm of unwritten ideas, awaiting fresh ink to bring them to life.

I don't know much about newspapers, but I'm going to give it my all. And in return, the *Jaguar Gazette* will teach me to be a better writer—just like Q. S. Murray.

My Master Plan is back on track. Now it's time to ace the rest of this magical second-chance day.

9

I STOP BY the bathroom on my way to lunch. The whole period thing is going okay. Yeah, it's weird to see blood and not freak out. Three years ago, I would've assumed I was dying of a mortal wound, like when Sage Miriel only discovers she's been hurt in the Battle of Brawn when she takes off her rose-crested armor and *gush*.

Boy, Sage Miriel, do I commiserate.

After washing my hands, I linger in front of the mirror. My rocker chic outfit has dried out, and I touch up my makeup until it's A+. Even my hair is impressive, considering it got the rainwater treatment this morning. My hopes are sky-high as I strut into the cafeteria. I know precisely where Alex and Amberleigh are sitting, and I plan to make an unforgettable appearance.

But first? Food.

The line is short, since I'm later to lunch than before. I grab the usual, but somehow it looks yummier today. The tuna salad is almost appetizing.

"*Hellooo*, wanna sign up for the Labor Day bake sale?"

I just about throw my tray of tuna in the air.

Mike Brot stands before me, fists on his hips and teeth bared. Sunshine gleams off his pearlescent smile.

"You *have* to stop doing that," I wheeze, recovering from the Great Scare of My Life.

"Stop what?" Mike asks cheerily. "Fighting for the cause of baked goods? *Never.*"

Maybe I should've expected Mike's attack, but I assumed I'd avoided him, thanks to my change in schedule. Turns out, a bathroom stop means nothing to this guy; he's been lurking in the cafeteria shadows, waiting to pounce. I scowl at his goofy iguana shirt.

"Sorry, I can't make cookies," I say, and I cut him off when he starts to protest. "Or cakes, or muffins, *or* pies."

Mike is undeterred. "What about your parents? I bet your mom—"

"Don't have one of those," I interrupt. "Good luck!"

I whisk past Mike, making it clear that the conversation is over. I feel a twinge of guilt, but how can I be expected to care about Labor Day bake sales when I've got a true love to woo? Would Torin the Rogue be caught dead baking gingersnaps at a time like this, if it were *Sage Miriel's* heart on the line?

No way.

Alex sits at Amberleigh's table, laughing so hard at one of Neil's jokes that his brown curls practically vibrate. They look so soft, and his eyes are impossibly deep. If you stared into them for too long, you'd straight-up drown.

That's why I'm careful to look only at my tray as I walk up. I tell myself, *Be confident.* It's a lot easier to do now that I've got an invite to the pool party. It would be weird if I *didn't* sit with the group, right?

"Hey!" I say. "Can I sit here?"

I point to any empty chair at the table. There are two empty chairs, actually, and I know who should be in one of them. Same as yesterday, Gemma isn't sitting with the group.

Amberleigh glances up. "Oh. Hi, Vivian."

She waves limply at the seat. She's not exactly exuberant, but she's not unfriendly, either. So I sit, sliding my tray next to Tate, who gives me a sort of half smile. I remember what she said yesterday about me smelling like poop, but I can let that go. If I'm getting a second chance, then Tate can have one, too.

Across the table, Amberleigh says, "Vivian, don't your parents own a store?"

I nod enthusiastically. "Be Kind, Rewind. On South First."

"Hmm," she says. "It's secondhand stuff, right? Junk that people don't want anymore."

Irritation prickles my skin. I'm sure that Amberleigh didn't mean "junk" in a bad way, but it feels kind of demeaning, all the same.

"It's a vintage store," I explain. "So, they're, like, nice things from the past. Da focuses on furniture—especially mid-century modern pieces. Pop is more into fashion and knickknacks: old records and photos and . . . well, shoes." I nod at Amberleigh. "Last month, he got a pair of Saint Laurent heels from the seventies. You might like them."

Amberleigh screws up her eyes. "I don't know. I buy my things new."

Neil guffaws. "Your *parents* buy them, you mean."

"I get an allowance," Amberleigh corrects him. "But my parents say you should always buy new. They haven't ever bought a used car, because can you imagine? You don't know what's gone on in there. There could be old coffee spilled on the upholstery or baby barf."

"Or people had sex in the back seat," offers Neil.

"*Ew*," Tate says, giggling.

Amberleigh rolls her eyes but says, "Exactly. It's gross."

I don't say that both Dads and Arlo bought their cars used. I especially don't say that Amberleigh's parents sound like out-of-touch snobs. I'm trying to make a good impression here, so I change the topic.

"Is Gemma sitting with you?" I look around the caf, expecting to see her coming toward us with a drink refill.

There's got to be an explanation for why she isn't around.

When I look back to the table, though, I get a sudden chill. It's like the temperature's dropped a full ten degrees, thanks to an icy look in Amberleigh's pale blue eyes.

Whoops. Turns out that wasn't a good topic after all.

"Who knows where she is." Amberleigh sighs. "She's been acting weird lately. Hasn't she, Tate?"

Amberleigh turns expectantly to Tate, who's taken a big bite of tuna salad.

"Urgh," Tate says around the food. "Yeah, I guess."

"*So* weird." Amberleigh points her fork at me. "You were sitting by her in opening assembly. Didn't she seem weird?"

Everyone at the table looks at me, including Alex. This time, I can't help myself. I stare into his deep brown eyes and start to float off to sea. . . .

"Uh, Vivian?"

I snap my attention back to Amberleigh.

"S-s-sure," I splutter.

Amberleigh has pulled out her phone, and it looks like she's reading a text. After a moment, she glances up at me. "Sure, *what*?"

"Uh," I say slowly. "I mean, it's kind of weird that she doesn't want to go to the party."

Amberleigh makes a face. "She said that to you?"

I tuck a strand of hair behind my ear, heat filling my

face. This is . . . not great. I like Gemma. Amberleigh must like her, too, or they wouldn't be friends. But it's clear that Amberleigh's not happy with Gemma *right now*. She obviously wants me to say more.

What do I do? If I leave it like this, Amberleigh might get bored with me. Maybe she'll go back to talking about how uncool it is for my dads to sell used stuff. Or what if she disinvites me from the party? Tells me it was all a big mistake? That would mean no more chances to make friends. No chance to hang with Alex and his deep-sea eyes . . .

I catch myself. I did it *again*—got lost in those shimmering pools of goodness. I clear my throat and refocus. Then, sneaking another glance at Alex, I make my decision.

I go on talking.

"Yeah," I say. "Gemma told me the party's gotten old. Like, you all should grow up and do something more exciting."

Okay, I added a *slight* embellishment, but that's more or less what Gemma told me yesterday.

Even though Amberleigh's phone is still out, her eyes are fixed on me. I wait for her to say something, but the table stays silent. That's when I realize I have to *commit*. I keep going.

"Which is, like, a weird thing for *her* to say, right? She's the one who draws those goofy cartoons in class. I mean, drawings of princesses—isn't that, like, total third grade stuff? It's pretty embarrassing. Who'd want someone that immature at a party, anyway?"

Nobody at the table replies. Neil is blowing into the straw of an empty Capri Sun. Alex and Tate are looking at Amberleigh, like they're waiting for her to answer first. But Amberleigh seems distracted. She's brought her phone close to her chest, tapping away. There's a *swoosh* sound—a sent text message. She looks up solemnly.

"Wow," she says. "I didn't know you thought Gemma was so *immature*."

I feel raw, like I've peeled off a layer of skin. My head spins as I catch up with the words I just spewed. Why did I bring up Gemma's drawing? That seemed personal to her. Not to mention, I don't *actually* think there's anything embarrassing about drawing princesses. I read about princesses, don't I? I even dress up like them for Relevane events. So why did I say all this stuff I don't mean?

I feel like crap, and the way Amberleigh's glaring at me doesn't help matters. She looks grossed out, like I'm a hairball some cat has chucked up on the lunch table.

She taps her phone, a regretful look on her face. "If I were Gemma? I'd be *so* pissed at you right now. Like, how awful to get a video of you saying those things about her."

Like that, my hearts stops beating.

"Wh-what do you mean, *video*?"

I stare at Amberleigh in disbelief. She shakes her head back at me.

"Sorry, girl, but Gemma is one of my best friends. I think she deserves to know when people are talking behind her back."

The truth crashes in on me. I understand now why Amberleigh was holding up her phone during my Gemma speech. All this time, she was *recording me.* And now? She's sent that recording to Gemma's phone.

No. *No.*

"That's not okay!" I yelp.

"Yeah," Amberleigh agrees. "It's *not* okay to talk crap about someone you don't even know. You're, like, a really mean person, Vivian."

My face catches fire. I look around the table, horrified. Amberleigh, Neil, Tate, *Alex*—they're giving me the same dirty look. Like they think I'm a living, breathing monster. A monster who shouldn't be sitting with them.

I thought I was giving Amberleigh what she wanted. How could she trick me like this? Now everyone here thinks I'm mean, and Gemma? My stomach hollows out at the thought of Gemma seeing that video. Oh my god. *No.*

I've made a huge mistake. I have to find Gemma and apologize—or better, stop her from ever opening that video. There's still a chance she hasn't seen it. There's a chance to save my perfect first day.

I grab my lunch tray and get to my feet.

"Mmm, yeah," Amberleigh says, yawning, like she's bored. "You'd better go."

And right then, right there, I know: this was Amberleigh's plan, all along. This is why she's been nice to me. It's why she invited me to her party. That was all to lure me in, get me comfortable. Then she took that video on purpose. She wanted to get everyone mad at me. So . . . what? She could end whatever fight she's having with Gemma?

It's *unjust*. Torin wouldn't stand for something like this. He'd rage like he did before the Council of Seven, when they voted to banish his younger brother Jerrod from court. But I'm not Torin of Marladia. My rage stays stuck inside, held down by a lump in my throat. Mainly, I'm trying not to cry as I step away from the table, heading for the tray conveyor belt.

It's as I'm passing Amberleigh that I feel a sudden whack. I glance down, startled, to see my tray smushed against my chest. When I look up again, I see Amberleigh's arms in the air—stretched up high for an "innocent" stretch. She timed the collision perfectly.

"Oh gosh," she says, wincing. "Sorry, did I do that?"

I peel the tray from my chest. My ringer tee is covered in banana pudding. Glops of it fall to the floor, splattering onto my shoes, and it's official: I'm a banana-scented disaster.

"*Wow.*" Amberleigh's voice booms from the table. "That's so embarrassing for her."

Around me, kids are pointing and snickering. Neil is laughing so hard that he starts to cough. And Alex? He holds a hand over his mouth, curls vibrating.

Alex Fernandez is laughing at me.

My vision tilts, like I'm aboard an unseaworthy galley on the Tempest Sea. Everybody's laughing at me *again*.

I run. Past Alex. Past tables of giggling kids. Past a concerned-looking Mrs. Campos.

"Vivian!" she calls after me.

But I don't stop. I keep running—past classrooms, around corners, down hallways—until someone else shouts my name. It's a voice I recognize—and the last one I want to hear.

I stop in my tracks, horror stricken, and slowly turn around.

There's Gemma Cohen, standing in the empty hallway, near the east stairwell. I wish the earth would open up like the Chasm of Celater and swallow me whole.

I'm in no such luck.

"Vivian?" she says again.

Her cheeks are as red as the strawberries on her dress. She steps closer, and I notice the phone gripped in her right hand.

It's too late. She's seen the video. Gemma has heard every

horrible thing I said about her. I wish I could take it all back. I wish I could do over this do-over. I *wish*, but it's not doing me any good.

"Why would you say those things about me?" Gemma's question is threadbare.

"I shouldn't have," I say, desperate. "It was—"

"Like, what is *wrong* with you?" Gemma's voice is stronger now, a mix of fury and hurt in her brown eyes. "I never told you the pool party had gotten old. Why would you lie about that?"

She's right. Gemma told me that *yesterday*. In this version of Monday, I'm lying. Even if I weren't, there's no excuse for everything else I said.

"I'm sorry." I press my hands together, pleading. "I swear, I never wanted to hurt your feelings."

Gemma snorts loudly, folding her arms. "Know what's messed up? I actually thought you might make a good friend. But now I get it: you're like them—Tate and Amberleigh."

"N-no," I say. "I promise, I'm—"

Gemma holds up her hand. "Whatever, Vivian. Save it for your *mature* friends."

She turns away, but I see the tears spilling down her cheeks.

Guilt washes over me so fast, I think I might drown in it.

I feel like I'm falling, falling, *falling*—and then? I hit the cold, hard ground of reality.

What have I done?

I turn and run again. I run, and this time, I don't stop until I reach the nurse's office.

I burst inside, causing Ms. Wendy to shout, "Good lord!"

But I don't apologize. I don't even stop to think.

I blurt, "I got my period, and I want to go home *now*."

❦ ❦ ❦

I sit alone in my bedroom, bemoaning my folly.

You would think that for such a big fan of the Relevane series, I would know that magic comes with risks. When Princess Dexalva made a deal with the Amethyst Mage to make her the most cunning warrior in battle, she accepted the consequences of their pact: in return for her military prowess, she gave up half the years of her life. The mage warned her, "Magic comes at a price."

So I should have known that this second-chance magic would come with strings attached. I had the chance to make things right, but choosing wrong—bad-mouthing Gemma— has made my first day even worse than before.

Sure, I didn't get mass humiliated by my period, but I'm beginning to think that Amberleigh Allen is a fate ten times worse. Secretly videotaping me. Saying Dads' shop is full of junk. Smashing banana pudding onto my shirt. Who does that girl think she is?

I've always thought of Amberleigh as kind of unreachable—rich, popular, maybe a little snooty. But I never thought she could be so *mean*. I figured there was a reason why people wanted to be her friend. Now I know the truth: Amberleigh is not to be trusted. She used me to make Gemma feel bad. She humiliated me in front of everyone, including Alex. She's a backstabber, plain and simple.

But more terrible than that—what's got me really torn up—is that *I'm* the worst, too. I stabbed Gemma in the back first.

How could I do that? What kind of person am I? When I shut my eyes, Gemma's face is there—every detail etched onto my memory. She looked so hurt. So *sad*. And I did that to her. I made fun of something super personal. I sold her out, and for what? Amberleigh's good opinion? A chance with Alex Fernandez?

Even if I'd gotten what I wanted, I know now that I wouldn't have been able to live with myself.

Pain, sharp and unexpected, blooms inside me. I had no idea I could feel this bad—so absolutely, completely rotten.

I deserve way worse than a banana pudding to the chest.

After Pop drove me home from school, I listened dully to what he and Da had to say. They told me the usual: I can take off tomorrow if I'm still not feeling good, they're around for questions, and Aunt Ximena is, too. I didn't breathe a word about what Amberleigh did to me. As far as Dads are concerned, my misery is due solely to period woes.

I want to keep it that way.

Now that they're gone and I'm burrowed in bed, my brain throbs with a hundred "shoulds" and "shouldn't haves." I should've remembered my period. Should've remembered the traffic jam. Shouldn't have trusted Amberleigh. Shouldn't have talked crap about Gemma.

Now? There's zero chance of me getting into Amberleigh's group, let alone winning Alex's heart. Now Gemma—a girl I actually like—hates my guts. And as for the *Jaguar Gazette*—what if Amberleigh ends up sharing that video of me with the whole school? Who would want to interview with me after seeing something like *that*?

At least yesterday I had potential with Alex. I had a journalistic career before me. I was making friends with Gemma. It wasn't so bad. Not compared to social ruination by Amberleigh.

I glance at my nightstand, where the hyacinth journal sits, its gold blooms shimmering in the low light of the room. I didn't bring the journal to school today, but it's not like that would've made a difference. I don't need to read over my plan *again* to know how badly I botched it.

Who messes up a magical second chance? Me, apparently.

Brava, Vivian Lantz. The medal of Elystrian Honor goes to *you*.

I flop onto my back, feeling more dejected than ever. I can't keep thinking like this. So instead, I think about . . . *the magic*.

That's the only word I have to describe what's happening to me. It's my one explanation for this impossible day. When I whispered that wish into my pillow last night, someone— or *something*—must have been listening.

But who? Who has the magic to turn back time?

I concentrate, staring at my nightstand, where my Relevane books are propped between dragon bookends.

Then thunk. It hits me like a flaming arrow.

Q. S. Freaking Murray.

I think back to what she told me in her MeetNGreet:

I'd like to help.

That's how you break curses.

I'll be sending you all *the good magical vibes.*

Oh. My. God.

Q. S. Murray said that she wanted to help me. She said that she'd be sending me magical vibes. Before, I figured she meant that, you know, metaphorically. But *no*. She meant it *for real*.

People say to write what you know. Well, what if that's

actually what Q. S. Murray has been doing all these years? What if she's like the mages of Marladia herself—*magical*? If that's the case, she could've been keeping tabs on me with her magic ever since she sent her MeetNGreet—through a seeing stone or a tracking spell, the way the Marladia mages keep in touch with their wards in the books.

And if Q. S. Murray's magic is real, then . . . what if my *curse* is real, too? Not a "curse" in the way I've meant it all these years, but an actual *supernatural, powers-of-evil curse*? I mean, it sure fits the description.

So Q. S. Murray recognized that I was under a curse, and then, when she saw that said curse was too strong to break through my pitiful mortal effort alone, she sent magic my way. She heard my wish for a do-over and she granted it. Vivian's First Day of Eighth Grade 2.0.

I know, I know. It sounds totally out-there. But magic is staring me right in the face. There's no denying that I'm reliving my *second* first day of eighth grade. Either that, or I've been hallucinating for twelve hours straight.

I like the magical explanation better.

I don't join Dads for dinner. I tell them I've got cramps (my stomach *does* hurt), and Pop brings me a plate of food in bed. He tells me that Arlo hasn't shown up, but that's no surprise to me. Arlo as good as told me he wouldn't be at dinner.

Whatever. I don't care about Arlo right now. I'm way too

lost in my thoughts, more convinced by the minute that Q. S. Murray's behind all of this. She *has* to be.

So I decide to test my theory.

I lick my lips and cautiously whisper, "Q. S. Murray, can you hear me?"

At that exact moment, my phone starts blasting the Relevane theme song. I scream, knocking the phone from where it's been resting on my bed. It smacks Mistmorrow in the face and clatters to the ground.

Is this *happening*? It's a magical sign from Q. S. Murray. It's—

Then I remember: *Cami*.

"Crap," I say, scrambling across the bed and grabbing the phone from the rug below.

"Dolphin *Priiide!*" Cami cheers when I answer. "Vivian! Today felt like it was a whole *week*."

Woof. She has no idea.

But this is it! My chance to fill Cami in on what's happening.

Another thing I've learned from the pages of Relevane is what happens when you share a powerful secret too soon. Prince Lorace thinks he's doing the right thing when he shares one of the secret prophecies of the Relevanian Council. He stands bravely before the Celaterian Court and tells his fellow Celaterians that they will suffer ten years of famine.

But what do the people end up doing? They *drive Prince Lorace out of his own freaking country.* They claim that he's been corrupted by dark magic—all because they don't want to hear the truth.

Secrets are dangerous things. People can treat you differently once you share them. That's why I wouldn't dream of telling a soul about the second-chance magic—*except* Cami. If anyone would believe me, it'd be her. We agreed to Code Unicorn.

But where do I even start?

I clutch my phone, thinking through my options. Should I start by telling Cami about the secret advice from Q. S. Murray? Or my secret Master Plan? Or my secret bad first day?

My throat dries up. I've been keeping a *lot* of secrets from Cami lately. I mean, I've had good reasons. I didn't tell her how bad yesterday was because I was too worn out. I didn't tell her about Q. S. Murray's advice or the Master Plan because I was waiting for everything to work out first.

But the Master Plan *hasn't* worked out. I've only ended up making things worse.

So do I want to tell Cami the truth? *Can* I? Everything's just so fresh right now—I don't think I have the strength to explain.

"Uh, Vivian? You okay?"

I startle at Cami's voice.

"Y-y-yeah," I stammer.

Then I decide: I'm going to lie again. It's just . . . *easier* this way. For now.

But if I'm going to lie, I'll need to be more convincing.

"*Yeah*," I say again, this time with confidence. "It was great, actually. Classes went well, and I made a friend named Jenna, and they had banana pudding at lunch."

My big lie sounds even more convincing this time around.

Cami squeals. "Really? A *good* first day?"

"Yeah!" It's sort of scary how easily the lie comes out now. "Can you believe it? The curse has finally been lifted."

"That's the *best* news!" Cami sighs happily. "We're living the life, huh? I have a really good feeling about eighth grade."

I listen as Cami tells me about getting lost in second period and trying out for dance team with her new friend Fatima. I listen, but I'm distracted. I tell Cami "uh-huh" and "yeah," and I laugh when she tells a joke, but all I can think is *magic, magic, MAGIC.*

After we hang up, I look around my bedroom and breathe in deep. I've got unfinished business, and now that I've had time to think about it, I know exactly what I want to say.

I clear my throat. Then I say, out loud, into my empty bedroom: "Hello again, Q. S. Murray. So, I don't need a sign. You don't even have to say you're there. However you've been following me—seeing stone or tracking spell—I've just gotta trust that you still are. The only thing I'm asking is . . . will you give me another chance? A, uh, *second* second chance. One more day to get everything right."

I know I just told Q. S. Murray that I don't need a sign, but I'd be lying if I said I don't wait around, hoping for one.

In the end, there's no mysterious fragrant breeze or whisper on the wind, the way there was when Torin received his first vision from the Relevanian Oracle. I hear no faint pluck of a lyre—the telltale sound of magic in Marladia.

I sigh in defeat. I've got no guarantee that Q. S. Murray heard me, or that she'll even grant another wish. But practically speaking? I'm gonna act like she did, and she *will*.

Sinking into my pillow, I reflect on the Master Plan.

My style remains killer, so first up on my list of goals? It's *Join the school newspaper*. This time, I'm joining with zero hiccups. No aquarium accident. No ruined reputation. I will become a star student journalist, like Q. S. Murray was before me.

Then there's goal number three. Alex laughed at me in the caf, and I'm peeved about that, but he *had* just watched me be a huge jerk to Gemma. So honestly? I don't blame him. I *know* that Alex is a great guy, and tomorrow, I will make sure that he sees how great *I* can be.

I've watched Q. S. Murray's MeetNGreet a million times,

but tonight, more than ever, I need a pep talk from the world's best author.

"Here's what's up, Vivian," she tells me, from her Bostonian office. "Big breakthroughs don't come from sitting around, letting life happen to you. *You* have to happen to *life*. That's how you break curses: you take the power into your own hands. So, start happening! Try something new."

I absorb Q. S. Murray's words into my very pores, and later, with the lights turned off, I make a vow to the plastic constellations above my bed. I've learned from my mistakes. I know where I went wrong. If Q. S. Murray grants me this third chance, I swear I can make tomorrow *actually* perfect.

My phone lights up with a text:

HOPE YOUR TOMORROW'S AS GREAT AS TODAY.

Here's hoping, Cami.

I'm still dressed, down to my daisy tights, but I curl up in bed all the same, and the last thing I think before drifting off is that I *still* smell like banana.

10

"WHOA, WHOA, WHOA!"

I wake to the sound of rain on the roof and Arlo's voice shouting from downstairs.

I don't move—not for a whole ten seconds.

Then I sit up. I breathe in.

There's not a whiff of banana in the air.

I look down. I'm not wearing my ringer tee and daisy tights. I'm in the same sleep shirt I've woken up in three mornings in a row.

"Dads. Get down here, quick!"

I look at my closet door. My ringer tee is on its hanger, fresh and clean.

I grab my phone from the nightstand and check the time: *6:14 a.m.*

There's a commotion in the hallway. Dads' footsteps thump past my door, followed by Trixie's yips.

"The damage?" Da yells.

"My whole bed," Arlo shouts back.

Dads' feet clomp down the stairs, and I'm left staring at my phone. Beneath the time is today's date: *Monday, August 22*.

It *worked*. Q. S. Murray granted my wish! Again!

I jump out of bed and run for the door, but when my fingertips touch the knob, I freeze.

What am I doing? I made a vow last night. I've been granted one more second chance. A chance to get everything right. The perfect first day. No more mistakes.

So I don't open that door. I whirl around to face my desk mirror, and I point at myself.

"You *got* this, Vivian Lantz," I whisper.

Then there's no more wasting time.

I plop down at my desk and crank up the heat on my curling wand. Today, I'm actually going to style my hair for the optimal first impression. I curl each strand and pin back the one weird cowlick that won't lie flat with my bangs. I take my time with the lip gloss and mascara. I even add the smallest dab of blush to my cheeks, the way I learned on YouTube.

Next, it's wardrobe time. I take a big sniff of my ringer tee. No banana. No trace of yesterday. On it goes. Today, I add a silver bracelet with a ruby charm—my birthstone—that Dads gave me three Christmases ago. Turns out, it's the perfect match to my red backpack. You *see* these things when you have time to spare.

Do I feel bad about leaving Dads and Arlo downstairs to clean up? Sure. Then again, if the magic works the way I think it does, this is only their first time cleaning, while it would be my third. I think I've earned a break.

Dads must not be too overwhelmed, because no one comes upstairs for me; they probably think I'm still fast asleep. That's why I'm careful about sneaking out of my room and down the hall. I step over the floorboards that I know squeak the loudest, and I open the creaky linen closet door at sloth speed.

There's no way I'm forgetting the menstrual shelf this time. The pads Dads bought for me are way nicer than the school ones. They're thin and smooth where the school's are thick and cottony, and they don't make me feel like a thirteen-year-old baby. Instead, I feel prepared. Empowered. Like I'm about to do some life happening.

I pack the hyacinth journal, too, wedging it between books in my backpack. Having it there is like a reminder: *You've got a Master Plan, and you're gonna see it through.* Those golden hyacinths shimmer, giving me a botanical boost.

This morning, I'm the one to text Cami first.

GO, DOLPHINS!!! I write.

As I do, I get a prickly feeling. Every time I text Cami this message, the words mean less. Every time, Cami feels farther away. But I can't think like that. I push the feeling down till it doesn't prickle anymore.

In the kitchen, I take the time to toast and butter my Pop-Tarts. I eat them sitting down, like a proper lady. Then, at last, I make my way downstairs.

Trixie is at the shop's front door, whimpering to be let out.

The accident. I'd almost forgotten. Lucky for everyone, I got here in time.

"Trixie's gotta pee!" I shout to the back room. "Be right back!"

I hook a leash to Trixie's collar and step out into a gust of rain-spattered wind. Trixie takes a few unwilling steps into the rain and dejectedly does her business before scampering to the shelter of the porch. I keep my distance as she shakes herself out, and my daisy tights get hit with only minimal splatter.

"Crisis averted," I say, as we head inside.

No poop pocket for me. No accident cleanup for Dads. If today's second chance were a test, I'd be acing every question.

"Morning, everybody!" I announce, bursting into the back room.

Dads and Arlo look up from their work, hunched over dampened boxes. That's when I remember that I'm supposed to be shocked.

"Oh . . . uh, *wow*," I say, pointing to the leaky window. "What happened?"

Da mutters an explanation, while Pop shoots me a wink across the room.

128

"Thought we'd let our eighth grader snooze," he says. "Beauty sleep's important for middle school."

Arlo snorts. "Real subtle about playing favorites, you two."

"Come on," Da tells him. "If Viv had woken up with us, we'd have put her to work. No favoritism about that."

"I'm not so sure," Arlo mutters.

It's nothing new, Arlo fighting with Da, but this time, he is *way* off base. I know for a fact that I would've helped out, because I did. *Twice.* I'd like to tell Arlo as much, but how does a person bring that up? "By the way, I'm in a magic do-over day. So *there*"?

"What time is it, even?" Da asks, checking the clock over the door.

"Seven twenty-five," I inform him. "Time for me to leave."

Arlo looks peeved. "Why do you want to get to school *early*?"

"I have my reasons," I say airily, fetching my rain jacket. (There's no way I'm forgetting it *this* time.) "Anyway, there could be traffic."

I'm starting my day in a good mood, and no one—especially not a grouchy brother—is going to take that away from me.

"Eighth grade sucks," Arlo informs me. "Better to take a break until high school."

"Arlo," Da says warningly.

"Telling it like I see it," Arlo retorts.

I roll my eyes cheerily. Eighth grade does suck if you do it wrong; I'll be the first one to tell you that. But not if you do it *right*, which I *will* today.

Arlo puts on his flip-flops, and I zip up my jacket, carefully tucking my hair beneath the hood. No frizzy roots or smeared mascara for me. Still, I double-check in the visor mirror once I'm in the Civic.

Arlo's giving me major side-eye as he pulls out of the parking lot. He's playing his rock station loud—louder than the last two rides, that's for sure.

"Someone to impress, huh," he says.

"Don't know what you mean," I say, as airily as before. I turn down the radio and add, "You should take Mary Street."

Arlo quirks a brow. "Why is that?"

"First South gets trafficky around now." I try to sound casual, like I'm *not* an all-knowing mage from the future.

I'm not even sure we need to take Mary Street. We're leaving home earlier today, so it could be we'll miss the traffic altogether. Better safe than sorry, though.

"Anything for you, Barficorn." Arlo grunts, taking the turn and putting his rock music back on full blast.

I guess hauling boxes alone with Dads put him in his bad mood. If I'd been around to help—like I was the last two days—he wouldn't be this pissy. But if I hadn't spent all that time getting ready, I wouldn't feel this confident, and I *need* confidence for a perfect first day.

Sorry, Arlo. That's the way it's gotta go.

Technically, Mary Street is the longer route to school, but at least it's a guarantee I'll get there on time. No collision with Gemma. No racing to opening assembly. I can enact my original plan to infiltrate Amberleigh Allen's group.

Here's the decision I made over breakfast: Amberleigh is awful—there's no mistaking that. But that doesn't mean I can't still try to win my way into her pack. I want to be friends with Gemma, after all. I want to *date* Alex. Neil and Tate could be nice, too. It's not their fault that they're friends with a jerk. Amberleigh's so two-faced, they probably don't even see the bad side of her. So Amberleigh is the only one I need to steer clear of. This time, I won't take her at her word. I won't answer leading questions. And I absolutely will *not* bad-mouth Gemma.

Once, I went camping with Cami and her mom in Big Bend. It's a national park in West Texas with craggy limestone cliffs that are split in two by the winding Rio Grande. Cami and I pretended we were on the Delwindian Plains, foraging for food to sustain us, like Sage Miriel does when she's exiled in book three. While we were playing, I stuck my hand in a shrub, acting like I'd found edible berries.

"Behold!" I shouted. "We shall live another day!"

But Cami tensed up, taut as one of Arlo's bass strings.

"Move slowly," she said. "*Slowly*. Pull your hand out."

I did. It was only afterward that I saw the scorpion through the pale leaves of the shrub. It skittered away, its stinger pointed downward, like a poisonous talon. Afterward, Mrs. Ruiz told us not to touch *any* plants we found on our hikes.

Amberleigh is like that scorpion. She's dangerous, but if you move slowly, and luck is on your side, you can get away from her unscathed. It's a tricky game, but I'm willing to play it if it means getting to know Alex better. Gemma, too.

Gemma. Guilt squeezes my heart. Today is my second chance to make things right with her, even though she doesn't know I made them wrong before. I tap at the rivulets on the passenger window, filled with resolve.

Arlo pulls the Civic up to Bluebonnet Middle. The entrance looks totally different this early in the morning. Kids are hanging out, gathered in tight bunches beneath the overhang. Amberleigh's group isn't in their usual spot, thanks to the rain, but I spy them soon enough, sitting together on one of the turquoise benches near the entrance.

I grab my backpack and turn to Arlo, who's been jamming with the radio, oblivious to me. I think of the two nights in a row that he hasn't shown at dinner—not even yesterday, after I asked him to. But maybe, if I put it another way . . .

"Hey, Arlo?" I say. "Could you come to dinner tonight?

132

Please? It'd mean a lot."

Arlo makes a face, like I expected he would.

"What's that supposed to mean?" he asks.

I can't answer that question. I don't want to repeat what I said yesterday, about the band being Arlo's new family. I don't want to get sad again, or—worse—get into a fight.

Instead, I step out of the car, and before I shut the door, I tell him, "Just *come.*"

Then I turn toward school and don't look back.

I've got a scorpion to handle.

She's sitting beside Alex, of course, their hands intertwined. I set my jaw, reminding myself that their relationship is temporary. I've got to focus on the long game. That's why I can smile as I stroll up to the group.

"Oh, hey." *Alex* notices me first. I wonder if, this time around, he remembers who I am: the girl who saved his phone from destruction. His hero.

"Hey," I say, and now my smile is for real.

"Your tights are cute, Vivian," says Tate. She sounds sort of shocked, like she can't help but let the compliment slip.

"Thanks." I push back my rain jacket hood, shaking out my perfectly styled hair. Judging from the looks on everyone's faces, I'd say it has the desired effect.

"Oh, wow," says Amberleigh. "You got bangs, huh?"

At last, the scorpion speaks. It's an innocent enough

question, but this time I can see the stinger, and I'm not reaching for it.

"This rain is out of control," I say instead.

"For real," says Tate, clutching her bare, shivering arms.

"It sucks," Alex agrees. "The field is a mud pit. Coach has had to cancel practice for a week, and we're supposed to play Murchison next Sunday. All the guys are pissed about it."

Neil grunts in agreement, but I've only got eyes for one member of the Jaguar soccer team. Alex answered my question, and even though he seems more irked by the rain than interested in me, it's a start.

"Hey," Tate says to me. "Don't your dads own that shop on South First? Rewind whatever?"

I nod, waiting for Amberleigh's stinger to emerge again. What'll it be this time? A sweet-as-sugar comment on how "cute" and "little" my dads' business is? Another jab about how she only buys new stuff?

But Amberleigh keeps her mouth shut.

"My mom got something there last week," Tate says. "This gold mirror with glitter roses on it for our living room. Dad think it's disgusting. He keeps calling it 'Janice's folly,' but she says it's vintage, or whatever." She giggles. "I dunno, I think it's kind of cool."

"My da found that one," I tell Tate. "He's picky about the furniture he buys, so we end up with really unique stuff."

"Ooh, yeah. Seems like it."

I grin. Tate and I are having an *actually good conversation*. It just goes to show what a second—uh, *third*—chance will do. I was right to think that Amberleigh's friends could be nice, even if *she's* rotten.

"We should head inside," Amberleigh says, checking her phone.

She's right. Kids around us are shuffling toward the doors, and it's only a matter of time before the first bell rings. I take a few steps back, like I plan to let them go on without me. Like I'm totally chill on my own.

Amberleigh doesn't let go of Alex's hand—not even once they're on their feet. The two of them head for the doors, Neil and Tate trotting after them, and just when I think that my chance might be slipping away, Tate turns and says, "You coming?"

"Oh!" I say, like she caught me off guard. "Sure, I guess."

I walk behind them, playacting that I could take or leave the invitation. It's only as we're heading down the hall that my palms start to sweat. Silently, I repeat Q. S. Murray's words: *Start happening. Try something new.*

Check, and check.

Amberleigh sits where I knew she would, in the back left-hand row of the auditorium. Alex files in after her, and before I can lose my nerve, I jump ahead of Neil and Tate to take the seat on Alex's other side.

My heart thumps in my ears, but I play it cool, like I was meant to sit here. Like it's my birthright, same as it was Torin's to claim the Elystrian throne. This close to Alex, I can hear his shallow breathing. I can smell . . . well, a little too much musky body spray.

Tate takes the seat on my other side, and as the auditorium lights start to dim and Principal Liu walks onstage, I hear her and Neil whispering. One word catches my ear: "Gemma."

I perk up.

"Don't think she's texted Amberleigh since camp," Tate is telling Neil.

"They'll make up," Neil says through a yawn. "Don't they fight all the time?"

"Yeah, but why isn't Gemma here?" Tate glances furtively past me to Amberleigh. "I think she's late on purpose. I don't even know if she'll come to the party."

I'm hanging on to Tate's every word. I *really* want to know what's going on between Gemma and Amberleigh. What did Amberleigh *do* to make Gemma stop texting her?

I drift out of my thoughts, only to realize that Tate is looking at me. I smile at her, but she narrows her eyes. Uh-oh. What'd I do wrong? Tate suspects something. Maybe the do-over magic is fading, and she's remembering the past two days. Maybe it's coming back to her, how I smelled like poop and said awful things about Gemma.

But before I can freak out, Tate leans in and says, "There's a party at my house today. You can come if you want. It's super laid-back, and there's gonna be tons of food: pizza, chips, stuff like that."

Yes. A party invite, just like that!

"Sure," I tell Tate. "Sounds great."

"I'll give you my address at lunch," she whispers back.

That settles it. Everything's coming up roses.

Principal Liu begins his speech, but I'm too busy basking in my victory to pay attention. Once the rest of today goes according to plan, my great humiliations will be erased. Pop won't remember picking me up from the nurse's office. Ms. Rose won't have a clue that I toppled Virgil's aquarium. And Gemma will absolutely never know that I once talked crap behind her back. Thanks to my second-chance magic, everyone will only get the version of me that I want them to see: suave, sophisticated Vivian Lantz.

Opening assembly drags on. Principal Liu finishes his speech, and the "I Wanna Learn with Somebody" music video plays. Near the end of it, my stomach starts churning like it's making butter. It's only when the houselights come on and we file out of our row that I realize why: I'm about to see Gemma for the first time today.

Without warning, a memory hits me. It's of me and Gemma

in Ms. Wendy's office, when Gemma's finger brushed against my knee. I gulp. I've been sitting next to Alex for twenty minutes, but all that time, I didn't care if *his* finger touched my knee.

Huh.

As I follow Neil and Tate out of our row, I clap eyes on Gemma, and my insides turn to gloop.

She's cute in her pink dress—like, cuter than I remembered—and she's wearing a matching scrunchie on her wrist.

I'm so distracted with staring, Amberleigh's words to Gemma sound like a distant foghorn.

"Was your mom late again, or something?"

"You're not going to be late *tonight*, right? It's tradition."

Gemma. She's got great style—not rocker chic, but something that's entirely true to her. She's smart. She's brave enough to fake sick in class and nice enough to do it so she could check on me in Ms. Wendy's office. And I wouldn't complain if her pinkie finger brushed my knee again.

Whoa. I rest a hand on my chest, feeling the *thump-a-thump* of my heart.

Then it hits me like a boulder launched by a Celater trebuchet—*smack*.

Oh my god.

I've got a crush on Gemma Cohen.

I guess that's not a great thing to realize the day after I totally *betrayed* her.

Is that why it hurt so bad yesterday, once I realized what I'd done? Because I'd hurt someone I like? 'Cause that's the thing: I like Gemma. I . . . *like*-like her.

I can't believe it.

I've known for a while that I like both guys *and* girls. That's not what's new. It's the Gemma part. Before, my girl crushes have been on celebrities—like Lara Sebastian, star of my favorite TV show, *The Mirkwood Chronicles*. I haven't crushed on a girl IRL before. Maybe that's why I can't believe that I'm crushing on Gemma now—this girl who's been right in front of me for years.

And I'm crushing, like, *hard*.

I suck down a breath. *Steady, Vivian.*

A crush on Gemma doesn't have to be anything other than that: a crush. Alex Fernandez is my one true love. He's the Torin to my Sage Miriel. He's the one I'm destined to be with, even though plagues and wars and court politics—or, in this case, Amberleigh—stand between us.

Gemma? She's a crush, and that's fine.

It's fine.

It is.

"Vivian?"

"Hmm?" I blink, turning to Tate. "What?"

"We were saying we're headed to Ms. Bissmeyer's class."

"Oh. I'm in Ms. Lally's."

"Guess we'll see you at lunch, then." Tate waves goodbye, and she and the others head for the auditorium doors.

I rub my forehead, wondering how I could've spaced out so majorly. It's just me and Gemma now, and my stomach lurches as Gemma turns to me with a stitch in her brow.

"So, you're hanging with Amberleigh?" she asks.

"*No*," I say, so fast and loud that Gemma's eyes get wide.

"I mean, Tate and I started talking outside about my dads' shop," I blabber. "So we ended up sitting together. But Amberleigh's not . . . I'm *not* friends with her."

Gemma nods slowly. "Okay. Just a question."

I know it's a brand-new Monday. There's no video of me on Gemma's phone. She doesn't know the bad things I said about her yesterday. But I don't feel any less awful about what I did. I am determined to make today different. Amberleigh is a means to an end. Gemma is who I *want* to be friends with. *Just* friends, of course.

"You want to go to class together?" I manage to ask.

My throat's gone dry, and I'm suddenly worried that Gemma will say no.

But Gemma doesn't ditch me. In fact, she looks sort of happy that I asked.

"I'm down," she says, and so we head to room 1067.

✿ ✿ ✿

It's my third time in the same math class, but I don't know any more about parabolas today than I did when this whole thing started. Ms. Lally lectures away, and I stay fixated on Princess Ruth in all her purple hand-drawn majesty.

How could I have ever used Gemma's drawing against her? Where did I get off calling her *immature*? Today, I'm going to make up for that, big-time.

After class, I work up the nerve to tell Gemma, "You're a good artist."

She arches a brow as we step into the hallway. "You saw that?"

"Yeah. You could, like, illustrate books."

Q. S. Murray's books are the ones I have in mind.

Gemma snorts and says, "It's a hobby, that's all."

Her cheeks turn pink, though, and I feel brave enough to ask, "Are you going to Tate's party?"

Gemma frowns as we round the corner.

"Well," she says, "we've been doing it since fifth grade."

"Oh," I say. Then I just blurt it out: "Are you and Amberleigh fighting?"

Gemma chews her bottom lip. She's wearing a peach-colored lip gloss that reminds me of a sunset.

"I don't want to talk about that," she says.

"Got it."

If Gemma doesn't want to talk, that's fair, but now I'm more curious than ever.

"Are *you* going to Tate's?" Gemma asks.

"I'm planning on it," I say, like I'm confessing something bad. "It seems like it'll be fun. And Tate's dad got new sunshades, right? So, the rain won't be a problem."

Gemma says nothing—not until we reach our next class and take seats beside each other.

"I guess I'll go," she says, centering a pencil on her desk. "Why not, right? It's tradition."

It seems like she's talking more to herself than to me, but my heart takes flight. I grin, even as Ms. Gustafson drones on about the periodic table.

11

IT'S FUNNY HOW you can live the same day over and over again, and you only notice certain things the third time around. Like Gemma's pink scrunchie.

Or how mesmerizing Virgil's tail is.

I don't mean to get distracted in language arts. Virgil is whisking to and fro, circling a pink pumice stone, and as I study the quivering strands of his red and blue tail, I get to wondering how long betta fish live, and how long *Virgil* has been alive, and how I nearly became a fish killer two days ago, and how maybe fish have special brains, impervious to magic. What if Virgil really does remember the big accident?

I gulp as his gaze seems to pierce my very soul.

"Vivian, what about you?"

I startle at Ms. Rose's question. Uh-oh. What about me, *what*?

"Um." I rack my brain for what Ms. Rose has been

teaching the last two days. Metaphors, right? I decide it'd be worse to ask her to repeat the question, so I take a risk.

"Metaphors are when you make a direct comparison," I say. "Similes are where you use the word 'like.'"

Someone snickers two rows behind me, and Ms. Rose frowns.

"That would be the right answer if we were talking about metaphors. Which we aren't . . . *yet*."

I wince. I've got to be more careful. It's not like I think Ms. Rose would assume I'm a time traveler, but I can't be blurting out stuff that I shouldn't know—like my teacher's lesson plan.

Ms. Rose turns to the class and asks, "Anyone else? Who can tell me who Walt Whitman was?"

I nearly melt into my desk. I know who Walt Whitman was. He was an American poet. He wrote *Leaves of Grass*. Duh. But I've gone and made myself look like a bad student—one who doesn't pay attention *or* know her poets.

To make matters worse, toward the end of class, Ms. Rose comes up to my desk and quietly says, "I'd like to speak with you after class."

Crap.

I'd already meant to talk to Ms. Rose. I just hadn't planned for it to be like *this*. But everything's okay. Even perfect days have their hiccups, right? *Right?*

I keep my head held high when class ends and the other kids leave the room. I even give Gemma a smile on her way out. She smiles back, like she knows I'll catch up with her later. Maybe today, she'll even come to lunch.

For now, I've got Ms. Rose to face.

I approach her desk as she sprinkles food flakes into Virgil's aquarium. He's still staring at me with his vacant eyes. Like a *challenge*.

I'm kind of beginning to hate that fish.

"Hello, Vivian," Ms. Rose says, setting the fish food aside.

That's my cue.

"I'm sorry I wasn't paying attention," I say. "I totally know who Walt Whitman was."

Ms. Rose smiles. "I figured you might. Mr. Garcia told me what a good student you were in his class last year. I try not to put any students on the spot unless I think they'd like to answer a question. But I think I misjudged this time."

It's the fish's fault! I want to yell.

But all I say is "Yeah, I was spacing out."

Ms. Rose nods. "First days can be a lot to handle, even if it's eighth grade and old hat."

Especially *if it's eighth grade*, I think.

"I'm not mad," Ms. Rose adds. "I only asked you to stay to be sure you were okay. I never want my students to feel embarrassed."

My tensed shoulders relax. Ms. Rose seems like a good teacher, and that makes me extra glad that she's the adviser for the *Jaguar Gazette*.

"Is there anything *you* wanted to talk about?" she asks.

It's like she can read my mind.

"Actually, I wanted to ask about working for the school paper," I say. "Is there a reporter spot open?"

"Really?" Ms. Rose looks happily surprised. "I'd love to have you aboard the *Gazette*. Like I said, Mr. Garcia's told me great things about your writing."

That's a compliment I don't think I'll ever get tired of hearing. But it doesn't prepare me for Ms. Rose's next question: "Why do you want to join?"

Huh. Ms. Rose hasn't asked me *that* before.

I was ready to talk about topics and projects—how I could write that exposé. But "Why do you want to join?" That's as good as asking "Why do you want to breathe?" Who's got a good answer for that?

"Well," I say, scrounging around for words, "one of my favorite authors, Q. S. Murray? She got her start at *her* school newspaper."

"I see," Ms. Rose says slowly. "But how do *you* feel about journalism?"

I have to think about that. I'm not wild about newspaper

reporting, but considering we don't have a creative writing club, I don't have any other option. It's not about how I *feel*; it's about what I can actually *do*. I don't know how to explain that to Ms. Rose, though, so instead I just shrug and say, "I feel great."

Ms. Rose looks thoughtful.

"Do you like the idea of reporting?" she asks.

"Sure," I say. "That's why I want to be on the paper."

"Do you *love* the idea?"

Of course not. But I don't see how that's Ms. Rose's business.

"I'm only asking," Ms. Rose says, "because some writers prefer to write—oh, say, fiction. Or essays. Or poetry. What matters when it comes to writing is if it's something you love to do. Something that lights a fire inside you."

"Sure," I say. "I know that."

I *don't* say, "Sure, Ms. Rose, but who's going to teach me how to finish a whole novel without getting overwhelmed? Who's going to calm my nerves about sharing my writing with *total strangers*?" 'Cause the answer is *nobody*.

I know Q. S. Murray would understand my predicament. Ms. Rose doesn't seem to get it, though. Now I'm even scared that she might say no to me joining the *Gazette*.

But that's not what happens in the end. Ms. Rose gives

me the details about the first meeting tomorrow. Still, something's different this time. She keeps on looking like she's unsure about this. Unsure about *me*.

"We'd love to have you on board," she concludes. "I only want you to take your time thinking through your reasons for joining."

I narrow my eyes at Ms. Rose. She really *doesn't* get it. And I don't like the way she's talking, like she knows more about me than *I* do. Like she can give me better advice than Q. S. Murray.

There's no bounce in my step as I leave class, even though I have technically accomplished goal number two. I do at least remember to watch my step. No pulled power cord. No watery disaster. Really, I should be happy. *Thrilled.*

As I enter the caf, I try to shake off the funny feeling I got from Ms. Rose's speech. It's time for lunch, and I'm gonna need my wits about me. The past two days, everything's gone wrong here, in the cafeteria. If I can make it through lunch this time with zero humiliation? I'll be utterly unstoppable. This will officially be—

"*Hellooo*, wanna sign up for the Labor Day bake sale?"

"*Aaaaah!*" I screech, clutching my hands to my chest.

Mike Brot, student activities council president, has manifested before me with the swiftness of a Relevanian blood-fanged dragon. I was so lost in my thoughts about avoiding public disgrace, I forgot to gird myself against his sneak attack. This time, I'm more breathless than ever before.

"This *has* to stop," I wheeze.

Mike doesn't seem to have heard me, because he's already launching into his spiel about baked goods. This guy is unavoidable, like mosquitoes on a summer night. It takes me a full five seconds to catch my breath, but as soon as I do, I cut Mike off.

"Can't make cookies," I inform him. "Or cakes, muffins, or pies. My dads can't make them either, but I wish you all the best. Bye!"

Then I sprint away before Mike can ask any tricky follow-up questions. At least I've learned to do *that* much.

In the lunch line, I go over my game plan. Today, I'll be sitting at Amberleigh's table, but I'll be avoiding her stinger, thank you very much. I will do something that makes Alex laugh for the *right*, crush-worthy reason. Maybe I'll even get to hang out with Gemma.

But when I arrive at the table, Gemma isn't there. It's got me wondering where she *has* been the past two days. Has she been eating her lunch somewhere else, alone? That thought makes me want to punch a wall.

"Hey, Vivian!" says Tate when she sees me.

"Hey," I say, taking the empty seat beside her.

Alex and Neil are flicking a paper football across the table, and I watch dreamily. Until now, my crush on Alex has been real, but not . . . *solid*. Not sitting in front of me at lunch.

I guess that's why my first response when Alex asks me how classes went is to gawk like a stunned cockatoo. This is the same guy who, one day ago, had to ask my *name*. I'd call that progress. A real step toward crossing off goal number three of my plan.

I tell him that classes were good. I don't bring up spacing out in language arts, but I do casually mention that I spoke to Ms. Rose after class.

Neil responds to that with a grunt.

"I can't believe she brought a frickin' fish to school," he says. "His tail is all mangled and weird. I bet he's got, like, fish diseases."

"He has a name, you know," I say. "It's Virgil."

Why am I defending a fish that I hate? Maybe it's because I still feel bad about almost murdering him. Or maybe it's just that Neil is kind of being a jerk.

"It's creepy," he insists. "So is she. Archie says Ms. Rose was his worst teacher. She kept trying to force feminist crap on everyone in class. Like, she had them reading all these girl authors."

"Archie is Neil's brother," Tate whispers to me. "He's *hot*."

I've never laid eyes on Archie, but I beg to differ. Dissing Ms. Rose for teaching women writers? Nothing about *that* is hot. And Neil repeating that super gross opinion is even less appealing.

"Something wrong with your face?"

I realize too late that I've been giving Neil the stink eye. Now he's shooting a dirty look back at me, along with his question.

"Something wrong with your *opinions*?" It's out of my mouth before I can stop myself.

Neil's glare hardens. "Excuse me?"

Whoo boy.

I've got a choice. I could double down and tell Neil that he's totally wrong. *Or* I could drop this and go on eating my tuna salad. I'm at lunch with Alex Fernandez. Why rock the boat? Tate could still be nice. Gemma is great. I can put up with Neil being gross. Two jerks out of five friends isn't that bad. Right?

But I just can't let it go.

"I don't see why your brother's upset about reading women authors," I say. "Seems sexist, if you ask me."

Neil rolls his eyes. "Here we go. You sound like Gemma."

I flush. I'll take that as a compliment.

"Calm down, both of you," gripes Amberleigh, looking totally bored.

Alex doesn't say anything. He's checked out, flicking his paper football across the table—which I don't find so dreamy anymore. Didn't he hear Neil? Couldn't he say something like, "Dude, not cool"?

Tate leans in and whispers, "Ignore him. Neil only wants attention."

That's clear. But what about Alex? Why didn't he speak up? Does he *agree* with Neil?

The tuna and mayonnaise on my tongue turn to flavorless paste. I stare across the table at Alex, horrified down to my bones.

What if I've been wrong? What if all of Amberleigh's friends really *are* as bad as she is?

I'm sitting very still, lost in my thoughts, when Amberleigh turns the topic to her next choir rehearsal. She talks about trying out for the fall play—it's *Godspell* this year—and how she's owed a top role, since she's in eighth grade, and how Ms. Davis pulled her aside last year to say she *would've* given her the role of Belle in *Beauty and the Beast*, only it wouldn't have been fair to the older girls.

"Luckily, that won't be a problem once I get into professional theatre," Amberleigh concludes, like this is a totally normal segue and Neil wasn't casually sexist over lunch.

Tate doesn't mention it, either. Everyone's acting normal. Which makes me think that maybe I'm overreacting. What if I'm judging Alex and his friends too quickly—even

Amberleigh? Maybe they all deserve a second chance. I've gotten a few of those, haven't I?

Tonight, at the pool party—that's when I can get to know everyone better. I can decide if my first impressions have been the wrong ones. I can keep an open mind.

So I stick it out through the end of lunch, listening as Amberleigh goes on about *Godspell*, and on our way to the conveyor belts, I exchange numbers with Tate and tell her how excited I am for the party. I keep an eye out for Gemma, but she never shows. When I get to my next class, I find her sitting in the back row.

"How was lunch?" she asks me.

I'm too tired to lie, so I just shrug.

"Oh," she says. "You're . . . still going to the party, though?"

I think about the address that Tate texted me at lunch. That text feels like a ticket to a wondrous, unknown destination. And the truth is, I want to find out what a party with Amberleigh Allen's friends is *actually* like.

"Totally," I tell Gemma. "You, too?"

Gemma's lips tip conspiratorially. "I will if you will."

Gemma sounds the way she did in Ms. Wendy's office. It's like we're in on this together. Like she's got my back. And I like that feeling. A lot.

I tell her, "Deal."

But what Neil said—and what Alex *didn't* say—has put a weird flavor in my mouth. It sticks with me through Mx. Ramani's lecture and all the rest of my classes, lingering on my taste buds. It's there when the final bell rings, and it grows more bitter when I tell Gemma goodbye and head to the pickup line. Amberleigh, Alex, and Tate are outside, talking by the bike rack.

"Hey!" Tate shouts, spotting me. "See you tonight?"

I nod and wave, just as I notice Pop's Toyota. The rain has let up to a drizzle, but I still throw up my hood as I run out to meet him.

I did it. I got through the day unstung. I didn't make any big mistakes. And now? It's pool party time.

"I got invited to Tate's house tonight," I tell Pop, as he turns onto South First.

"Tate Matthews?" Pop asks. "Patricia in the PTA has a girl named Tate."

"That's the one," I say.

"Huh. Well, Patricia's nice."

"Mm-hmm. Anyway, Tate invited me to a pool party at her place."

"Which is where?"

"Travis Heights."

"For how long?"

"Um . . . she didn't say? But it starts at six o' clock."

"On a school night." Pop grunts. "And will they have dinner there?"

"Yeah."

Pop seems to think this over before telling me, "I don't think you should stay past eight."

Two hours. I'm okay with that. It's enough time to get answers to my most important questions. Like, is Alex really the guy of my dreams? Is Tate good friend material? Does Gemma want to be *my* friend? Is Neil a massive jerk? Is Amberleigh the actual worst?

When we get home, Da is helping a customer in the shop. The back room is under control—leaky window boarded up and two floor fans spinning, drying clothes that hang on a laundry rack. Since Dads don't need any more help, I have plenty of time to get ready for tonight.

For my swimsuit, I choose a one piece with vertical green and white stripes. It's only when I try it on that a zing of panic hits me. *My period.*

I can't show off my swimsuit while I'm wearing a pad. The sticky wings on the bottom would be a dead giveaway. I know about tampons, of course, but I absolutely do *not* want to use my first one today. They look uncomfortable, if you ask me, and what if I do it wrong?

Conclusion: there's zero chance I will be getting in Tate's pool.

It's a bummer, and on top of that, my stomach is feeling weird, which must be the cramps again. Whatever. I won't be deterred. Tonight can still be fun—the cherry on top of a perfect first-day sundae.

I pull on a pair of cute, stretchy jean shorts that look good with my bathing suit top—*not* like a fashion faux pas. If I show up with flip-flops and a towel, like I plan to swim, but I just . . . don't get around to it? I'll be fine. I can spend my time talking to people instead. People like Gemma.

It's Gemma Cohen, and no one else, who's on my mind as I get ready. When I swipe on a fresh coat of lip gloss, I remember Princess Ruth's purple-ink lips. When I pop sunglasses atop my head—even though it's still drizzly outside—I find myself thinking about how the ugly school fluorescents sparkled off Gemma's brown eyes.

By the time we leave for the party, my knees are practically knocking together. But it's not over the thought of seeing Alex, my true love. It's over my nervous hope that Gemma keeps liking me.

I really, *really* want her to like me.

"Okay there?" Pop asks, as he slows the RAV4 to a stop in front of Tate's big, two-story house. I stare up at the sloped lawn, swallowing hard.

"I'm great," I tell him, sounding a billion times more confident than I feel.

Pop chucks my arm. "You got this. Da and I are only a phone call away."

"And you'll pick me up at eight?"

"Da will," Pop replies.

This is it: the moment I've been working up to for three days in a row. It's taken three chances to land my *first* chance at a big social debut. There's no way I'm backing down now. I'm about to party with the most popular kids at school. This is what it means to *happen to life*.

Well, isn't it?

I suck in a breath and step out of the car.

12

TATE'S HOUSE IS enormous. It's a sleek, modern box made of wood and iron bars, and giant planters of succulents line the driveway. Walking up, I feel like I've arrived at a beach resort. I hear the sound of music from farther down the driveway, so I head that way, slipping into the backyard through an open gate.

Tate wasn't kidding about those sunshades her dad installed. They're strung over a giant infinity pool, alternating in white and burnt orange—the colors of the UT Longhorns. This morning's rain has petered out to mist, but it's still nice to walk beneath the cover of the shades, brushing off little droplets that cling to my arms.

Neil and a couple of guys from the soccer team are in the pool. Everyone else is laid out on deck chairs or gathered around a table crammed with pizza boxes and bowls of chips. There are more guys from the soccer team and a few other people I'm pretty sure are in choir with Amberleigh.

Amberleigh herself is sharing a pool hammock with Alex. They sit shoulder to shoulder as Amberleigh pushes her heels into the ground, sending them swinging. Alex is eating a Popsicle, the edges of his lips stained raspberry red.

I guess I should be entranced by those lips—and don't get me wrong, they're *nice*. But instead, all I can think is how Alex didn't tell Neil to stop being a jerk over lunch.

I turn away from the hammock, only to find myself looking straight at Gemma. She's sitting on a lounge chair, hugging a balled-up pool towel. Tate sits across from her, and the two of them are talking in hushed tones. When I peer closer, I see that Gemma's eyes are wet, reflecting the shimmering string lights. She looks upset, and so does Tate, and I feel like an intruder for even noticing them.

I wonder if this is about Gemma's fight with Amberleigh. They probably *will* patch it up in the next few days, all on their own, but I wish I could make things better for Gemma *now*, the way she made them better for me in Ms. Wendy's office.

Gemma glances up, and I lose my breath.

"Oh. H-hi, Vivian," she says.

Tate whirls around, instantly brightening. "Vivian! Hey!"

"Your house is super nice," I tell Tate, unsure of what else to say.

"Yeah, guess so." Tate giggles, motioning to an empty lounge chair beside Gemma. "Sit down, if you want."

I sit crisscross on the chair's vinyl slats and admit, "I might not swim."

"Oh, *same*," Tate says fervently. "You think I want in there with them?"

She makes a gagging sound and nods to the pool, where Neil is on someone's shoulders, pool noodle sword fighting with two other guys and shouting, *"Suck it, dude!"*

"Pool parties aren't really about swimming," Tate adds. "Not once you're our age, anyway."

She stretches out languidly on the chair, crossing her ankles. Whatever conversation she and Gemma were having is clearly over. Gemma has stayed quiet, staring at her bunched-up towel, and I notice the crumpled can of Dr Pepper by her side.

"Want more of that?" I ask, pointing, and before Gemma can answer, I'm on my feet.

"I could use a bottled water!" Tate calls, as I head for the snack table.

There, I find a giant cooler crammed with bottles and cans. I grab two Dr Peppers for me and Gemma and a water for Tate.

Tate cracks open the bottle as soon as I hand it over.

"Thanks," Gemma says, taking her soda. Her eyes have dried a little, and she's set aside her towel. She seems like she's more in the mood to talk.

"I love Dr Pepper," she tells me, "but my parents won't keep it in the house. My mom's a dentist, and she's basically morally opposed to soda."

"Torture," Tate says, laughing. "I've had, like, ten cavities, and I'm *fine*." Then, standing up, she says, "I gotta pee."

She heads into the house through a sliding door, leaving me and Gemma alone.

Tonight, Gemma's wearing a pair of frayed shorts and a shirt that says *Orange You Sweet*, with a drawing of a cartoon orange and a soft serve cone holding hands. It makes me smile. Her hair is frizzy with the humidity, and a stray ringlet hangs in front of her eyes. She keeps pushing it away, but it creeps back across her forehead every minute or so.

Maybe it's the fact that Gemma looks pretty, or that her shirt is funny, or that I've figured out I'm crushing on her. Whatever the reason, I decide to tell her my news.

"I'm joining the *Jaguar Gazette*," I say.

I do *not* mention Ms. Rose's weird lecture about writing lighting a fire in you, etcetera.

"Huh," Gemma says. "That's cool. Not for me, though. I can't imagine coming up with stuff every week for a paper."

"I bet you could do a weekly illustration," I suggest. "Do you draw cartoons?"

Gemma shakes her head. "Nope. I just draw for myself."

"I don't see why. You're *really* good."

Gemma smirks at me. "Amberleigh said once that her fourteen-year-old cat could draw better than me."

I look over Gemma's head to where Amberleigh is helping herself to a slice of pizza at the snack table. White-hot anger eats at my insides.

"Well," I say, turning back, "she's one hundred percent wrong."

Gemma shrugs. "I like drawing for myself. Anyway, I won't have as much time for it once I'm in high school. I want to do International Baccalaureate, which is gonna murder my schedule."

"International Bac-a-*what*?"

"It's this program for, like, nerdy kids."

Oh. I get it.

"You mean *smart* kids," I say.

"Whatever." Gemma rolls her eyes. "But I'm planning on being a pediatrician. I want to go to Vanderbilt for med school, so that means I have to think ahead, and IB looks great on résumés. Then there's PSAT tutoring, so hopefully I can be a National Merit Scholar, and I need to start shadowing doctors my sophomore year at the latest. School is basically a full-time job, you know? So I wouldn't want to get distracted with something else, like drawing."

"But you *like* drawing," I say, trying to understand.

"Well, yeah. But I like school, too. And the better I am at that, the better I can be at helping kids. I've wanted to be a doctor since, like, second grade. My mom got me this kit when I was little, and she still jokes about how I'd run around trying to listen to everyone's heart through my stethoscope. I was *super* annoying about it."

Gemma laughs. These past few minutes, she's been aglow about school, which is sort of strange to me. I get okay grades, and language arts is fun, but I don't light up like the Fourth of July when I talk about college and tests.

I've figured out something: Gemma is an *original* Master Planner. She's got her entire life planned out—not just eighth grade—and it sounds like she's been planning since she was a kid. Me? I've needed two whole magical do-overs just to work on three measly goals.

"You make happening to life seem easy," I say wistfully.

Gemma frowns. "I— What?"

"Um. Nothing."

"What I mean about drawing," Gemma says, "is that I like doing something that doesn't have a point. You know? It's not like school. Nobody's grading my drawings. I can just make them."

I have to chew on Gemma's words, but in the end, I think I get it. Writing last year's book report for *Bridge to Terabithia* felt very different from writing my Relevane stories. When I wrote for Cami, I wasn't worrying about if my spelling and grammar were perfect. I was just *creating*.

I'm still lost in my thoughts when, suddenly, I'm hit by a cold sensation. I gasp, realizing that I've been drenched by a giant splash of water. Gemma is soaked, too. I turn, and there is Alex Fernandez, laughing his head off in the shallow end of the pool.

"Sorry, ladieees," he calls, as the soccer guys around him cackle and whoop.

"Now *that* was a cannonball!" Neil shouts, slapping Alex's back.

Then the whole lot of guys start splashing water up at me and Gemma, shouting, "Get in the pool! Get in the pool!"

"*Stop!*" Gemma yells at them, rising to her feet. She storms toward the pool, and by the time she reaches the edge, she's scared the guys off.

Alex calls back, "Calm *down*. It was just a joke!"

If that's the case, Alex has a rotten sense of humor. My canvas tote is soaked, and so is Gemma's towel. Frantically, I pull out my phone from the tote pocket, relieved to see that it's stayed dry.

"Man," Neil hoots. "You girls are so freaking emotional about a little water." His face contorts, and he calls out in a high-pitched baby voice, "Is your poor wittle phone okay, Vivian?"

I glare back at him. "Yeah, *luckily*. No thanks to any of you."

He and Alex share a look. They burst into wheezing laughter.

"Whoa," says Alex, raising both his hands. "Jeez. So hostile."

"See? This is why you shouldn't invite girls to parties," Neil proclaims.

I glower at the two of them. "In case you hadn't realized, you're *at* a girl's party."

"Whatever," says Alex, waving off me and Gemma and turning to Neil. "They're probably on their periods."

Uh. *What?*

I stare at Alex, phone gripped in my hand.

He didn't say that. He couldn't have.

But the guys in the pool are roaring with laughter, like Alex just made the joke of the century.

Gemma storms past the pool to a wicker bench stacked with fresh towels. She grabs two, and then, on her way past the snack table, I hear her growl at Amberleigh, "You've got a real ass of a boyfriend."

Amberleigh's been talking with her choir friends, but at Gemma's comment, she snaps to attention.

"*What* was that?" she calls.

Gemma stops in her tracks and whirls around. "You heard me. I don't appreciate coming to a party where I have to deal with your boyfriend and the whole soccer team acting like two-year-olds." Gemma pauses. "But wait. That's *way* too unfair to two-year-olds. At least their impulse control is still developing. They've got an excuse."

Amberleigh crosses her arms. "Wow, so you've got a problem with Alex now, too? This summer really did change you."

Gemma's a few yards off from me, but I can see that her hands are shaking. She crosses the distance to Amberleigh, tossing the towels on the snack table and knocking over a bowl of Doritos. Then she says something too low for me to make out.

Amberleigh's reply is as loud as ever: "Cool. Why don't you find a new friend who will take you on spring break skiing trips to Vail. Good luck with *that.*"

Then she shoves Gemma—actually *shoves* her—away from the table. It's so forceful that Gemma stumbles a full five steps and then topples, careening into the giant drink cooler. The cooler slams over, ice chips scattering everywhere and soda cans rolling across the patio. Gemma is sprawled in the wreckage, a look of total shock on her face, and that split second feels infinite. No one moves. No one speaks. Even the party music seems to fade away.

Then it's over.

Gemma gets to her feet and hurries off—past Amberleigh and past me. She runs through the open gate, and the last I see of her is a stray frizzy curl.

I watch with an open mouth. All this time, I've assumed that Gemma and Amberleigh would patch things up. They've been friends for so long, one fight wouldn't end that, right?

Maybe I was wrong.

"What's going on?" Tate is back from the bathroom. She stands at the patio door, looking around at the tense scene. Her eyes land on me as she asks, "Where's Gemma?"

"She's gone, thank god," Amberleigh announces, grabbing the Bluetooth speaker and cranking it up till a Dua Lipa song is blaring.

I wait for Tate to say something like "That's not cool" or "Why'd she leave?" I watch as she stands motionless at the sliding door. It's like she's considering. Deciding.

Then, she moves. She walks up to Amberleigh and her friends, grabbing a handful of chips and plopping down on an ottoman. "So," she says, "what else did I miss?"

It's like Gemma has ceased to exist.

I stare in disbelief—first at the guys in the pool and then at Amberleigh, who is smugly chomping away at a piece of pineapple pizza. I feel light-headed. It's like I've imagined the past five minutes, and Gemma and I *weren't* splashed, and Alex *wasn't* a total jerk, and she and Amberleigh *didn't* fight, and the whole thing *didn't* end with Amberleigh shoving Gemma. Everyone else sure is acting that way.

But I reek of chlorine, and Gemma isn't here. I'm not the one who's got this all wrong.

Back in seventh grade, when Cami and I would hang out on the turquoise benches before school, I'd watch Alex chilling with his friends by the bike rack and wonder what it'd be like to be on the inside of Amberleigh's group. Gemma and Tate would be laughing about something, and I'd want to know what. Alex would be holding hands with Drea, and I'd want to be that close. I was curious. What was it like to be one of them? It looked so nice. It looked fun.

Turns out, it's not.

Alex's words are still ringing in my ears:

It was just a joke.

Jeez. So hostile.

Probably on their periods.

I dig my nails into my palms.

I came to this party hoping for the best. I wanted to know Alex better. I thought I'd get to know Tate. I was ready to give Neil—even *Amberleigh*—a second chance. Well, now? I'm out of chances to give.

Alex has clearly moved on from the gross stuff he shouted at me and Gemma. He's busy dunking Neil underwater, cackling hysterically. Amberleigh and Tate don't seem the least bit bothered, either. They're onto another subject, Amberleigh chatting loudly about the choir's solo auditions next week.

Then—"Vivian!"

Tate waves, motioning for me to join the rest of the girls at the snack table. For a moment, I see possibility. I picture Amberleigh's group by the bike rack—only now, where there was once Gemma, there's *me*. I'm the one sharing the joke with Tate. I'm holding Alex's hand.

Then the possibility fades, like a wisp of campfire smoke.

Why would I ever want to be friends with people who've treated Gemma like dirt?

Now that I know what it's like on the inside? I want to get out.

I ignore Tate, grabbing my sopping-wet tote and standing up. Maybe I'm ruining my social reputation all over again. Maybe I'm throwing away the perfect end to my perfect first day.

Too bad.

I set off toward the open gate, running as fast as my flip-flops will let me and praying to the second-chance magic that I can catch up to Gemma.

13

I FIND GEMMA one block down from Tate's house.

She's sitting on the sidewalk, hunched over. Tear tracks stain her cheeks, and she doesn't look my way, even when I'm right beside her, saying, "You okay?"

Gemma jolts, staring up at me.

She doesn't answer, but I don't blame her. It was a bad question.

"Can I sit with you?" I try instead.

Very slowly, Gemma nods. I plop down on the damp concrete. It's still misting, and teensy droplets have collected in Gemma's curls.

"Ta-da." Gemma's eyes are dull, but she lifts her hands, making spirit fingers. "It's me, the instant party pooper. Guaranteed to ruin your finest soirees in five minutes flat."

It takes me a second to realize that Gemma is making a joke. I decide to play along.

"It's a miracle product!" I say, in a TV announcer voice. "Just add water!"

I poke Gemma's rain-slickened shoulder, and she huffs out a laugh. Then her expression changes. She slumps her shoulders, dropping her face in her hands.

I don't know what to say anymore, but I have to try *something*.

"I'm sorry that happened," I tell Gemma. "Amberleigh shouldn't have pushed you."

Gemma peers up at me. "Yeah, well, that's not the worst thing Amberleigh's done."

The unanswered question screams inside me: *What was your fight about?* It would be rude to ask that *again*, though, and I don't want to pry.

Gemma rests her chin in the palm of her hand. "You don't have to sit with me. I called my sister. She's coming to pick me up."

"Well, you didn't have to sit with *me* in—"

I catch myself. I was about to say *in Ms. Wendy's office*. But of course, that hasn't happened in Gemma's version of Monday.

"Uh," I say. "I mean, in Ms. Lally's class."

Gemma scrunches her nose, and a dozen brown freckles collide. She looks confused, but instead of elaborating, I say,

"For what it's worth, I'd rather be having a party with you than with them."

I could tell Gemma that she was the main person I thought of as I got ready tonight. I could tell her I think it's cool that she wants to become a doctor. I could say that I'm curious if Princess Ruth has a backstory.

I could say all that, but I don't. It doesn't feel like the right time.

Quiet settles on the street—Mariposa Drive, according to the sign across the road—and Gemma and I sit silently in the dusk. There's a purply glow around us as streetlights buzz to life, and I look up, tracing the swoop of power lines.

"It wasn't always this way," Gemma mutters. "I mean, yes, Amberleigh was prickly. When we were little, I was scared to touch her Play-Doh, because she got *so* pissed if you mixed the tiniest bit of two colors together. I knew she was mean to other people, but she wasn't too bad to me. Not till this summer."

Gemma's eyes flit to me. "You have two dads. So . . . you're cool with that, right?"

"What, being queer?" I say, surprised. "Of course."

My heart is pounding in my ears. I have a feeling that Gemma is about to share something important. Something big.

"Last November," Gemma says, "I told Tate and Amberleigh I'm gay."

Gemma's voice catches. There are new tears on her cheeks.

This *is* big, but not the kind of big that topples me over. Instead, I feel stronger—strong as the marble columns of the ancient Elystrian Temple. I want Gemma to know that she's okay. That's why I reach out and squeeze her hand.

Gemma's gaze flicks up to mine, but she doesn't pull her hand away. Our palms stay clasped as she goes on talking.

"I thought things were fine. She and Tate both said they supported me, and we were cool. They even said it would be fun to go on triple dates together one day. But then in July, we went to camp together in Dallas. It was Amberleigh's idea. She's been dying to go to a performing arts camp, but she didn't want to do it alone. Tate and I just thought it'd be fun to get away for a month. There's a big musical you rehearse for all camp-long and perform at the end for the parents. We all auditioned, but I got cast in one of the lead roles instead of Amberleigh. She was *pissed*. At first, she said it wasn't fair because I'm not even into music, and then she said that the part would be too hard for me, because I don't have the vocal range."

My hands are forming fists for the hundredth time today. I imagine the scene—Amberleigh raising her scorpion's stinger, aiming for the heart. Going in for the kill.

"Then," Gemma says, "after campfire session one night, Amberleigh pulled me away from the others and said she knew for *real* why I'd been cast. She said the director had found out that I was a lesbian, and she was afraid that if she didn't cast me, she'd be called discriminatory. Amberleigh said the only reason I got the role was for 'diversity.'"

New tears gather in Gemma's eyes. I squeeze her hand again, and this time, she squeezes back.

"Tate heard us talking," she says unsteadily. "At first, she took my side. She told Amberleigh that she was just jealous. But then Amberleigh said . . . she said I was probably *pretending* to be gay to get attention."

I stare at Gemma. *"What?"*

Amberleigh Allen has said some real crap in the past couple of days, but this? *Pretending to be gay?* Where does she get off telling Gemma that?

More words rush out of Gemma: "It was a bad fight, but the next morning, Amberleigh acted like nothing had happened. She never apologized. Tate didn't bring it up again, either. Sometimes even *I* think it was a dream."

"But it wasn't," I say.

"No." Gemma shakes her head. "It just feels that way, because it doesn't make sense. I'm not *out*. The only people at camp who knew about me being gay were Amberleigh and Tate. So there's no way the director would know unless one of them told her. And why would I *want* the attention for that? Like, I think my family would be cool with it, but I don't want them or anyone else making it a big deal. It's just who I *like*. Amberleigh's the one who turned it into something."

I study the concrete, shaking my head. "That is so messed up."

Then I feel a jab of guilt. I'm remembering the mean things I said about Gemma yesterday, at lunch. *You're like them*, she told me. *Tate and Amberleigh*. Now her words have a whole new meaning.

"I've been mad at her since camp," Gemma says. "She's gone on acting like she didn't say this horrible thing. Now I don't trust her. I'm worried that if she gets mad enough, she'll tell anyone she wants about me liking girls. I don't want to be around her anymore, and I'm mad at Tate, too. But losing my friends in eighth grade? That'd be the worst. Everyone's already found their crowd at Bluebonnet. Who am I going to make new friends with—the sixth graders?"

I crack a smile. "Definitely not them."

"I know, they're like *toddlers*." Gemma chokes out a laugh. She sweeps a hand beneath her eye, leaving a mascara trail behind. "It'd be easier to stick with Amberleigh, the way it's always been. But I don't think I can do that for a whole year. I hate the way she makes me feel. It's like Amberleigh is this giant star, and no one else can shine as bright as her. If you do?"

Gemma lets go of my hand, pushes her fingers together, and spreads them apart like an explosion: *pow*.

I nod. "I get that. I get what you mean about starting over, too."

Gemma toes a patch of crabgrass poking through the sidewalk. "I heard about Cami Ruiz moving. I'm sorry. You two seemed really close."

I'm surprised. I never thought that someone like Gemma noticed what people like me and Cami were doing. Now I'm starting to see that I haven't had *any* idea who Gemma is.

"I can't wait for middle school to be over," Gemma concludes, heaving a raspy sigh. "I wish I could just move to Boston."

I scrunch my nose. "I thought you wanted to go to Vanderbilt?"

"Oh! That's for med school," Gemma explains. "Brandeis for undergraduate. That's my dad's alma mater."

I'm awestruck. "You've got it all planned out."

"Well, plans don't mean much compared to reality," Gemma says glumly. "I know what I want for my future, but I don't know what I'm supposed to do right *now*, in eighth grade."

"Tell me about it," I mutter.

"Vivian?"

I look up. The gleam of a streetlight catches on Gemma's face, and suddenly all the breath leaks out of me.

"Y-yeah?" I manage.

"Thanks for listening. I kind of word vomited on you."

"Oh. Uh, vomit away!" I say, which . . . sounded a lot better in my head.

Gemma looks down. "I knew how mean Amberleigh could be to other people. We've been friends for so long, I guess I learned to make excuses for it. I didn't do anything when she talked crap about someone else. But now I see Tate acting that way—like it's more important to suck up to Amberleigh than stick up for me, and . . ." Gemma sighs. "What I'm saying is, I should've stood up to Amberleigh before, when she was treating other people the way she's treating me now."

I smile ruefully. "I guess she's said some mean stuff about me."

"Actually?" Gemma says. "Amberleigh's pretty jealous of you."

I balk. *"Me?"*

Gemma nods. "I don't know if Cami ever told you, but Amberleigh was, like, dead set on making Cami part of our group. She invited her to the pool party the first day of sixth grade, but Cami said she already had plans with you."

I remember. That was the day that Cami invited me to hang out at her place after school. Cami never told me about the pool party invite, though. Or that she turned it down.

"After that," Gemma says, "Amberleigh would go on about how you 'stole' Cami from us. And you two seemed to always be having fun together. It was like you didn't care what anyone else thought."

Gemma's right: Cami and I didn't care what other people thought. We were Relevane nerds and outsiders together. But I never would've believed that someone like Amberleigh was paying attention to us, much less being *jealous.*

"I'll be real," Gemma says, picking at her thumb. "I used to wish *I* could be friends with you. Guess I still do."

Am I hearing right? Gemma *does* want to my friend.

"I'd . . . like that, too," I say. "I've felt that way all week."

Gemma's freckles collide in another frown. "All *week*?"

Whoops. I say, "I mean, we could be friends *now*. Eighth grade doesn't have to suck so bad if we do it together."

Gemma's wearing a strange smile, like she might not believe me. Then headlights illuminate her face. A little red car is pulling up to the curb.

"My sister," Gemma explains, scrambling to her feet.

I get up, too. There's a girl a few years older than me and Gemma behind the wheel of the car.

"Hey," she calls through the open window. "You all right?"

"A little better now," Gemma tells her, glancing at me.

We share the tiniest smile, and then Gemma brushes past me to open the car's back door. Her fingers skim my elbow, and like *that*, a thousand nerves light on fire, up and down my arm.

"Hannah, this is Vivian," Gemma tells her sister, gesturing toward me.

"Hey, Vivian!" Hannah waves. "Do you want a ride?"

Oh. I hadn't considered that. I take a quick look at my phone and see that it's barely past seven o'clock. Da's not supposed to pick me up for another hour.

"That'd be nice, actually," I tell her. "I live on South First."

"Not a problem," says Hannah. "Pile in."

Gemma and I slide into the back seat of the car. The leather seats are cold to the touch, because Hannah's got the AC on full blast.

"Address?" she calls back to me.

I tell her, adding, "It's a shop. Be Kind, Rewind."

Hannah shifts the car into gear, and we're off. I sink into my seat, feeling suddenly exhausted, like I might as well have swum five hundred laps in Tate's pool.

Gemma and I don't speak on the drive to my place. We listen to Hannah's music—pop songs with bass notes that thump in my collarbone. The back seat feels dark and safe, like a cozy cocoon, and it smells of sugary-scented perfume.

My chest is crammed with feelings. Anger at Amberleigh and Tate. Irritation at Neil. Massive disappointment over Alex. But so much *hope* about Gemma.

Maybe this new crush—the one that's been growing day

by day—doesn't have to stay a crush. Maybe there's a chance that Gemma could like me back.

Maybe I really *want* her to.

Dads and Arlo know about me liking both guys and girls. Cami does, too; I told her in seventh grade, when I realized that the way I felt about Lara Sebastian during a kissing scene on TV? Yeah, it was more than me *admiring her talent*.

I was worried about one thing, though: How come I hadn't realized that I liked girls earlier? Eventually, I brought it up to Pop.

"Did you know you liked guys when you were little?" I asked.

"I did," Pop said. "Guys, girls, everyone. I didn't think it was wrong until I started hearing things from my papa and guys in school. Even when I told my friend Roger, who was gay, he told me, 'You're either straight or gay. You can't straddle the fence.'" Pop threw up his hands. "Whatever that *fence* is. But later, I saw things differently. Liking all genders doesn't mean you're confused, or too much, or not enough. It simply means you're being *you*."

"You knew all that about yourself when you were *little*, though, right?" I asked, still uncertain. "Like, kindergarten, basically?"

Pop laughed. "I didn't know *all* of that. And there are plenty of folks who don't know those things when they're young. Figuring out that you're queer when you get older doesn't make your queerness any less real."

I thought about what Pop had told me for a while. Then I decided he was right: my queerness *was* real. I could crush on Lara Sebastian on TV, and I could also think that Alex Fernandez was my one true love. Both of those crushes were normal, and one crush didn't make the other one less true.

I haven't seen a reason to bring up who I like to kids at school. Now, though, I feel like, at some point, I could work up the courage to tell Gemma about my crush on her.

Definitely not *this* point, though.

Hannah pulls up to Be Kind, Rewind, and as I'm crawling out of the back seat, I feel pressure on my arm. It's Gemma again—her fingertips practically sparking against my skin. I have to catch my breath as my feet hit the pavement outside the car.

"Maybe we could eat lunch together tomorrow?" she asks.

"Yeah," I tell her. "I'd like that a lot."

When Gemma smiles, it's brighter than a sunrise.

I wave goodbye as Hannah drives off down South First. Then I head around the shop, to the back entrance. I notice on my way in that Arlo's parking spot is empty. No Civic. Just the *Reserved for Our Far-Out Customers!* sign. I sigh. So Arlo didn't listen to me. *Again.*

I let myself in with my latchkey and find the back room

empty. The only sound is the gentle hum of the two floor fans. Sequined dresses and bell-bottom Levi's flutter in the electric breeze. I duck beneath a houndstooth shawl as I make my way to the shop and up the stairs.

It's late. Not *late*-late, but late by Vivian's First Day of School standards. This time yesterday, and the day before, I was finishing dinner with Dads. Any minute now, I should be getting a call from Cami to ask how my day went.

I don't know where to start with that question any more than I did on my first bad day.

Today, I followed my Master Plan to the letter. I fixed my past mistakes. I finally made it to the pool party. Technically, today was pretty close to perfect.

So how come it doesn't *feel* that way?

When I reach the top of the stairs, the answer smacks me in the face. The trouble is, my goals have changed since that first Monday night. I've learned stuff. I've had revelations. And that means my Master Plan is in need of adjusting.

I should tell Dads that I'm home, but I figure that can wait five minutes. Right now, I've got a fire under my butt. I slip into my bedroom, turn on a lamp, and sit at my desk. I pull out the hyacinth journal from my backpack and open it to the first page. There, in bold letters, is goal number three:

3. Make Alex Fernandez my boyfriend

Ugh.

It's safe to say my crush on Alex has been . . . well, *crushed.*

Vivian from a week ago would've been gutted over that. *This* version of me—Second Chance Vivian—is still super disappointed. But also? I'm kind of glad that I've finally seen Alex for who he is, up close.

Without a second thought, I cross out the goal with two heavy strokes of my pen.

That feels *good.*

Then, just as quickly, I write a new goal in its place:

3. Make Gemma Cohen my friend

I stare at the words on the page and swallow hard. What I've written feels like a big deal.

Just then, the Relevane theme blasts from my phone. I don't have to look at the screen to know it's Cami calling. But I just can't answer. Not now. I grab the phone, muting the ringtone, and look back at my journal.

Before, I hadn't considered making a goal about friends in my Master Plan. Cami has been my best friend for two years solid, and me trying to get that close to someone else? I guess I would've felt like I was betraying her somehow.

Now I'm thinking that through. These days, Cami and I are living 1,127 miles apart (yeah, I checked), and I haven't been able to tell her what's *really* going on in my life here in Austin. Meantime, she's making new friends in Orlando, like Fatima and the girls on the dance team.

Maybe I should be doing the same thing.

And Gemma sure seems like she could be a great friend.

I add an explanation to my goal:

(Because I <u>need</u> one.)

Writing it down like that, I know for sure that it's true: I *do* need a new friend. A real friend. Someone to talk to and share secrets with, the way I have with Cami. And as for my *crush* on Gemma? I'll . . . save that topic for another day. One big change at a time.

Tomorrow—*Tuesday*—I won't waste my time with Amberleigh or Alex. I'll get to know Gemma better. I'll start work at the *Jaguar Gazette*. I'll keep on rocking my rocker chic style. Master Plan 2.0.

I've got this.

I'm finally ready for a new day.

Muffled voices reach me from down the hall. I frown, setting down my pen. Dads are in the kitchen, talking, but something isn't right. Da's voice sounds strained—almost like he's crying.

I shut the journal and make my way down the hall. Right

outside the kitchen door, I catch Arlo's name. I stop in my tracks and listen as Da speaks:

"It's my fault. No, don't try to—it is. You've always handled it better than me. You told me I should ease off the pressure. I thought my approach was more direct. But now . . . and the band . . . I did everything wrong."

I clutch the doorframe. Da *is* crying.

I'm in a predicament. I don't want to barge in, but I need to let Dads know I'm home safe. I settle on a plan: I'll backtrack to my bedroom and shout from down the hall, like I just got home. But when I take my first step back, the ancient floorboard creaks beneath my shoe.

Trixie gives a warning bark from the kitchen. Seconds later, Pop peeks his head out the open door.

"Hey, Viv," he says. His eyes are red and damp.

"Uh . . ." I take another step back. "The party ended early, so I got a ride back with a friend."

I guess that's partly true.

Pop nods. "That was kind of them."

"Yep. Well, I was just heading to my room. Homework, you know!"

I'm ready to flee the scene, but Pop stretches out a hand.

"Why don't you come into the kitchen?"

I'd rather do anything else. Still, I follow Pop into the room. As I take a seat across from Da, I realize why I don't want to be here. It's not that I'm afraid of my dads crying; I'm afraid of what's *making* them cry.

I've got a queasy feeling that something bad is about to happen—like the time I freaked out on the diving board at Barton Springs Pool, and Arlo shoved me off into the freezing cold water. It's *that* feeling: the moment before the shove.

Pop sits beside me at the table. He nudges aside the salad bowl between us and tents his hands beneath his chin. I can tell he's working up to say something, but I don't want to hear it. I don't want the shove.

"We just got a text from your brother. He told us that he's left home."

I keep my eyes on Pop, not moving a muscle. I don't even blink.

"He's with the band," Pop says. "Apparently, they've been planning a Southwest tour for months. Arlo informed us that he's been studying for the GED this summer. He claimed he had our permission and passed the test in July. Now he's dropped out of school, all so he can play music full-time."

I still don't move an inch.

Pop sighs, running a hand through his short, dark hair. "We had no idea what Arlo's plans were, and I can't say that we agree with them. At the same time, he turns eighteen in November. He'll be a legal adult, and we're not sure it'd be helpful to go after him now. This is upsetting for me and

Da, but we've decided to give our consent to this GED plan of Arlo's. Get things sorted out. Let Arlo be his own person."

Pop is talking calmly. That doesn't matter, though. No amount of calm can change the truth: Arlo has left home. Just *left*. And he didn't even think to tell me, his only sister.

I'm so sad I could burst into tears. So mad I could scream for an hour straight.

But I just grit my teeth as I tell Pop, "Okay."

Pop looks confused. I guess he was expecting the tears or the screaming. He glances at Da and back at me. "We know this a lot to absorb, Viv. Da and I are still processing it ourselves. But if you want to talk this through, or—"

"Nope!" I cut Pop off, throwing him my brightest fake smile. "I'm fine. Just, uh, gonna get to that homework!"

Da looks up. "Vivian," he starts to say, but I wave him off.

"Love you!" I chirp, overloud.

Then I'm off like a bullet train.

I only let myself cry once I'm huddled in bed, under the sheets. I hug Mistmorrow so hard that his sparkly eyes nearly pop off.

Arlo's gone.

It all makes sense now. There were a hundred little clues scattered across the last three days. I ignored them, but now they're flash flooding my memory. I think of the boxes packed in the back seat of Arlo's car. It was always a mess back there, but it was especially bad this morning. Now I know why: those boxes were packed with the stuff that Arlo's taking on tour. I think of the *off* look on Arlo's face, and how it appeared whenever I mentioned the band. I think of how he didn't show up for dinner the past two nights. Turns out, if I'd stuck around a little longer at those dinners, I would've been there to see Dads get Arlo's goodbye text.

This wasn't a spur-of-the-moment thing. Arlo's been planning to leave home for—how long did Pop say?—*months*. All without breathing a word to me.

I *hate* him.

I hate Arlo with every bone in my body. Every freaking freckle on my skin. Yesterday, he had the nerve to tell me, "You're my little sister," like he actually *cared*. Well, what's that good for? What's the use of being family if he won't tell me important stuff, like, I don't know, that he plans on *leaving home for good*?

I check my phone, but there are no notifications. I sure didn't get a text. No goodbye. No explanations. No *way* am I forgiving Arlo for this.

I dig my fingers into Mistmorrow's matted fur. Rage courses through my veins. The way I feel now, I could yank up every floorboard in the hallway and nail them all down again till not a single one of them squeaks.

The past three days, my head has been crowded with thoughts of Alex and Gemma and Amberleigh. I've been worried about my period. I've been trying to avoid humiliation of monumental proportions. That's why I didn't notice that Arlo wasn't just late to dinner; he wasn't coming *home*. By now, he's miles away on his Southwest tour, headed to Phoenix or Las Vegas, or maybe as far out as California.

"Who cares," I seethe.

Forget Arlo. If he couldn't be bothered to tell me his plans, then I won't be bothered to miss him. He can leave on his precious little tour. I've got eighth grade to worry about, and that starts tomorrow, with a brand-new day.

Thanks for the second chances, Q. S. Murray, I think. *I've got it from here.*

Anger roils in my gut as I bunch the pillow under my head and wish for unconsciousness.

This day can't be over fast enough.

14

"WHOA, WHOA, WHOA!"

I wake to the sound of rain on the roof and Arlo's voice shouting from downstairs.

I blink blearily, wishing that Arlo would just shut up.

Then my eyes snap open.

Arlo.

He's home.

I jolt up in bed, grabbing my phone from the nightstand and checking the screen:

6:13 a.m.

Monday, August 22

Wait. *What?*

"*Dads. Get down here, quick!*" Arlo screams from downstairs.

No way.

This . . . doesn't make sense. It's like yesterday never happened. *Again.*

Panic squeezes my chest. This isn't the way it's supposed to go. Yesterday was the Monday I wanted to keep. Now? It's like none of those moments ever happened. All my progress—*erased*. Worst of all, last night's talk with Gemma is gone, too. She won't remember all the important stuff she told me, or how we said we'd be friends. I'm back to freaking square one.

I thought I had this figured out. I assumed that if I wanted another chance at Monday, I'd have to ask Q. S. Murray for more second-chance magic. But I didn't ask for *anything* last night, so how is this happening?

I turn to face the Relevane books lined up on my night-stand, desperately thinking through everything I've read about magic in the series.

There *is* this part in book three, when Sage Miriel consults with the Mage of Fairwood. She's trying to master the art of small magic, frustrated by her inability to move a simple pile of stones. That's when the mage gives her this advice: "Magic is a force of nature. You are not *conjuring* it; you're tapping into the flow. Building dams. Diverting paths. Working with a power that's already there."

Oh man.

Of course.

Just like Sage Miriel, I've been thinking about my magic the wrong way. What if this magical time loop is like a flowing stream? What if this loop will keep on looping—propelled by magical momentum—until I build a dam? Or . . . you know, ask Q. S. Murray to build the dam for me.

I get it now. The magic works by me telling Q. S. Murray that I'd like the loop to *end*. I've had the answer all along, within the pages of Relevane. I just had to consult the Mage of Fairwood.

So I've figured out the magic—for real this time. But that doesn't make today any less terrible. How am I supposed to live through *another* first day of eighth grade?

And how am I going to face *Arlo*?

I can't believe he had the nerve to act normal this morning. He knew, even when we were cleaning the back room and when he was dropping me off at school. He knew that he was leaving me without saying goodbye. I can't look at him the same way ever again.

Well, I don't *have* to look at Arlo's traitorous face. Not right now, anyway. Dads don't know that I'm up. I can pretend again that I'm still asleep.

So I don't go downstairs. I stay in my bedroom, planning for a *fourth* first day.

I glare at the clothes hanging from my closet door. They've gotten old. I need something *fresh*. I fling open the closet door and fish out the boldest of my rocker chic outfit combos—the one I was planning on working up to debut on, say, Friday.

Well, it's *basically* Friday today.

I go for a pair of black jean shorts, plus a fringed leather vest that Aunt Ximena gave me last year, when I turned twelve. She told me that it had been her favorite possession when she was in middle school. Today, I swing the vest over a black camisole, and I add the finishing touch: a pair of black heels that I've only ever worn to a couple of holiday parties.

I do my hair and makeup, and this time I go all the way. I open the sealed stick of eyeliner that I've been too nervous to use, drawing thick streaks across my eyelids. I add mascara and coat my lips with a bright red gloss. Then I separate my hair into dozens of strands, curling the crap out of every one, and hair-spray my bangs till I'm coughing from the fumes.

At last, I stand in front of the mirror, taking everything in. I look *good*, and older, too. I could convince anyone that today was my first day of high school, not eighth grade.

I figure, why stop there with my change of plans? I move to the kitchen, where I treat myself to a leisurely breakfast. I make buttered toast, plus a side of scrambled eggs. I cook the eggs to perfection, with a splash of milk and a sprinkle of cheese. They taste like clouds of fluffy protein heaven on my tongue.

I remember to use a pad, and I toss a couple of extras into my backpack. I don't forget Trixie, either. The first thing I do when I get downstairs is take her out before she makes a mess.

I didn't ask for another chance, but at least I've got this Monday down to an art. In fact, by seven twenty-five, I'm actually in a good mood.

I can get through this day one more time. I *can*.

I walk into the back room, and my eyes clamp on Arlo first thing. He looks so smug in his Aerosmith tee, moppy haired and barefoot.

"Finally decided to grace us with your presence, Barficorn?" There's actually a *sneer* in Arlo's voice.

The nerve. Like he's got a right to be ticked off with *me*.

"Slept through my alarm," I lie.

"Yeah, and that's why your hair's done perfectly," Arlo scoffs. He's in a worse mood than all the Mondays before.

Fine by me. I'm not going to let my traitor brother get me down.

Ignoring his comment, I turn to Dads in total fake shock and say, "What *happened* here?"

Somebody hand me an Oscar.

Da explains the situation, and Pop adds, "Thought we'd let our eighth grader keep snoozing. Beauty sleep's important for middle school."

"Real subtle about playing favorites," Arlo grouses.

This time, I can't keep my irritation at Arlo to myself.

I roll my eyes and tell him, "Duh. I *am* the favorite."

"*Vivian*," says Pop, looking scandalized.

"Just kidding!" I laugh it off—*kind* of convincingly—and head for the door. "Come on, Arlo. Time to go."

By now, Arlo's royally pissed off. He glares at me, not budging an inch.

"So, what, I'm your chauffeur now?" he asks.

That's *it*. Arlo's got a lot of nerve treating me this way when *he's* the one in the wrong.

I look him straight in the eye, meeting his glare, and say, "Don't worry. You're only doing it for a day."

Arlo frowns, looking suddenly uncertain. *Good.* Let him wonder if I know his secret. He can sweat it out.

"What's that supposed to mean, Viv?" Pop asks from across the room. "You're not planning on ditching school, are you?"

"What?" I blink innocently. "Oh! No. It's just an inside joke between me and Arlo." I glance back at him. "Right?"

Arlo shakes his head at me. "Whatever. I can't take you seriously when you look like a clown."

"Arlo," Da calls warningly. He's perched on a stepladder, measuring the leaky window.

"It's true," Arlo mumbles, slipping on flip-flops. "She's got all that makeup on."

Da snaps up the measuring tape and looks my way. "Do you feel comfortable in your makeup, Vivian?"

"Yes."

"Well, that's what matters. As long as we're not sending you to school naked, everything's copacetic. Isn't that right, Diego?"

Pop gives me a thumbs-up. "Xime would be proud, seeing you in that vest."

I beam as I grab my rain jacket. Arlo: zero. Vivian: a trillion.

Arlo must know he's beat, because he doesn't speak again—not even once we're in the car.

"You should take Mary Street," I tell him, as we pull out of the parking lot.

Arlo doesn't answer. He turns up his rock station, playing the same screechy guitar solo I've had to endure for days.

"I mean it!" I shout over the music. "There's going to be traffic on the main road."

"So you're a psychic now?" Arlo scoffs.

That's the way he wants to play? Fine. Whatever attitude Arlo dishes out, I'll dish it right back.

"Yeah," I tell him. "Maybe I am."

My blood is simmering, its temperature rising with every word Arlo says. I'm mad at him for ditching me. Mad at him for not telling the truth.

As we get closer to Mary Street, I shout, "Turn left!"

He doesn't.

"Ar*lo*!" I wail, as the street sign flies past.

"What, you want to drive?" Arlo demands.

"I'd do a better job than *you*."

"Sure." Arlo turns to me. "Why don't I pull over, then, and you—"

"*Watch out!*" I screech.

Arlo slams on the brakes, but it's too late. There's a metallic crunch, and I lurch forward, tightened seat belt smacking me in the chest.

"Oof," I grunt, my skull thunking back against the headrest.

I blink, taking in the scene through the windshield. The front of the Civic is smushed into the back bumper of a station wagon.

The station wagon, I remember. It's the same one that cut off Arlo on my first Monday. Arlo said that it had almost caused another wreck. Well, today, it *has*.

"You okay?" Arlo asks, looking me over.

I nod, in a daze.

The driver of the station wagon opens the door and steps out. They're in a suit and tie and look like they're in their fifties. They squint through the pouring rain in our direction. Arlo unfastens his seat belt.

"Stay here," he orders, getting out of the car and slamming the driver's door shut.

I watch through windshield wiper swishes as Arlo talks to the driver. They look over the damage, and then Arlo pulls out his phone and starts tapping. The driver does the same thing, so I guess they're exchanging numbers. Behind us, a line of headlights stretches as far as the eye can see.

My intestines twist as I wonder how this will mess up the rest of my day. What if I don't catch Gemma before opening assembly? What if we don't sit together in Ms. Lally's class? This could ruin *everything*, and the kicker is that it wouldn't have happened if Arlo had just listened to me.

By the time Arlo gets back in the car, my blood is at an all-out *boil*.

"Fender bender," he mutters. "Nothing major. It's whatever."

It's obviously *not* whatever to Arlo, though. He looks shaken up, and his hand trembles as he tucks his phone back in his pocket. I could almost feel bad for the guy.

But I don't. He brought this on himself.

Ahead, the station wagon is moving forward. There's a screech of metal as its bumper pulls away from ours. Arlo shifts us into drive, and we follow the station wagon as it straightens onto the road and lurches toward traffic—which has only moved, like, a block.

I glare out the rain-spattered window at the Starbucks parking lot. It's gross out there, like someone's blotted a watercolor, mixing the colors till they turn brown. And *inside* the car, there's the blaring rock music, pounding against my skull.

As the traffic starts to let up, I tell Arlo, "Your music sucks."

He clicks off the radio. "That better for you?"

I clench my jaw. On another day, I'd keep it clenched. Any other day, I wouldn't speak words that I can't take back. But today? I'm going to give Arlo a piece of my mind.

"I mean, *your* music sucks," I say venomously. "The Neon Spurs—you sound like amateurs. Like a bunch of screeching hamsters. Even if you went on tour? I bet people would boo you off the stage."

The car gets super quiet. Arlo doesn't speak, but I've got plenty left to say.

"It makes zero sense why you'd want to drop out of school for your crappy band. But obviously, they're *way* more important than me and Dads. They're your real family. So that's why you decided to give up on ours, huh? Why you couldn't take *five seconds* to tell your own sister that you were going to leave town?"

Arlo pulls up to Bluebonnet Middle and its empty front lawn. I'm not thinking about how late I am. I'm way too amped up on telling off the world's worst brother.

Arlo puts the car into park. Slowly, he turns to me.

"Vivian," he says. "How did you find that out?"

I stare at him, dumbfounded. *Wow.*

"That's the takeaway?" I shout. "*How did I find that out?* Not, like, 'Sorry for lying to your face'?"

Arlo stares blankly at me. He looks like he's going to be sick.

Well, he can do that on his own time.

"Have *so* much fun on tour," I growl, getting out of the car.

I slam the car door, and then? I shoot Arlo the bird. It's something I've seen him do lots of times with his friends, but it's a first for me. And it feels . . . *great.* I make sure Arlo sees my middle finger—really sees it—before I whip around and stomp toward school.

I am electrified, like someone's zapped a lightning bolt through my spine. This must've been how Sage Miriel felt when she defeated the Prince Philosopher in a battle of wits. I feel zero remorse. Zilch. It felt magnificent, getting that off my chest.

That's when a thought springs up in my brain. It's big. It's bold.

I'm almost positive I've figured out how the magic *really* works: I'm in a loop, and it'll keep on looping until I ask Q. S. Murray to make it quit. Well, if that's how the magic works, why shouldn't I take advantage of its . . . magicalness?

Why shouldn't I go on feeling this good? I want to get *everything* off my chest.

Tomorrow, I can focus on creating another perfect Monday. But today? Screw it. I'm gonna say what I feel. I'm gonna do what I want. No holding back.

First things first.

I whip out my phone and text Cami, *GO, DOL-PHINS!!!!!!!!!!!*

This time I add the extra exclamation marks, plus five dolphin emojis, for fun. Why not? I feel like it. Then I turn my attention to Bluebonnet Middle School. I interlock my hands, pushing them out and cracking each knuckle. I stretch my neck from side to side. Then I stomp up to the front doors, confident in my leather vest and killer attitude.

Let the freaking games begin.

I know exactly where to find Amberleigh. She and the others are sitting in their usual spot at the back of the auditorium. I head that way, expertly avoiding Mrs. Campos, and creep into the empty row behind them. I take a seat behind Amberleigh, who's busy whispering to Alex. No one notices me, which is how I want it.

I stay perfectly chill as Principal Liu concludes his speech.

I cross my legs and fold my hands in my lap. I'm a model student—that is, until the music video starts. The peppy eighties tune blasts through the speakers, and the audience begins to laugh and cheer. That's when I get to work. I made this plan on the fly, as I stomped my way to opening assembly. Now I mean to savor every minute of it.

I slide out of my seat, pulling a Sharpie from the front pocket of my backpack. I keep it in there for doodling, but today? It serves a single purpose: to ruin Amberleigh Allen's fancy new shoes. There's a risk, sure. Amberleigh might feel the pressure of the marker tip on her heels. That's why I have to be careful, drawing lightly onto the fabric of her Louboutin sneakers. I take my time, connecting lines and loops. It's dim, but not so dim that I can't watch with satisfaction as black ink bleeds into the pristine white suede.

When I'm through, I carefully scoot out from under Amberleigh's seat, my bare knees skidding against the linoleum. I sit back down, and when the houselights come on, I admire my masterpiece in all its glory. Across the backs of Amberleigh's shoes, I've written the words "THESE ARE FAKE." I even finished the sentence off with a cute little heart.

I've asked myself what Amberleigh Allen hates most in the world, and the answer is clear: anything she can't brag about. Well, who can brag about fake Louboutins?

I'd like to stick around and gloat, but I'm smarter than that. If Amberleigh sees I was sitting behind her, she'll put two and two together when she discovers my . . . *artistic touch*. So I make myself scarce, skipping down the opposite aisle—the one she and Alex won't take. Once I'm out the back doors, I giggle so hard that my eyes start to water. By the time I stop by my locker, kids are giving me weird looks.

When I catch Jacob Eisley staring, I shout, "Take a picture, my dude. It'll last longer!"

Another guy—Ethan Sysmanski—calls out "Dope vest!" as we pass in the hall.

By way of reply, I primp my excellent hair. I *do* feel cool in Aunt Ximena's vest. Confident, too—in a ready-to-burn-down-the-world kind of way.

I don't get out my notebook in pre-algebra. What's the point of taking notes that'll have disappeared tomorrow? No, the *new* point of math class is this: seeing Gemma Cohen walk through the door.

When she does, I swear, a fragrant strawberry breeze wafts my way. The classroom turns a hazy pink, and the sound around me gets sucked into a void. All that's left is the sight of Gemma taking the seat beside me and uncapping her violet-colored pen.

"Hey," I say, across the aisle.

She looks up in surprise. "Oh. Hey."

Like that, my chest explodes with pain. I press a hand to my heart, wincing at the aching sensation.

"Are you okay?" Gemma asks.

I nod, but I don't speak. I *can't*. Gemma frowns. Then, after a couple of seconds, she turns away and heads the top of her paper with today's date: *August 22*.

That's the problem. That's why I'm feeling this sudden, terrible ache. For Gemma, August 22 is a once-a-year kind of date. It's the usual twenty-four-hour deal. In Gemma's timeline, she doesn't know about our conversation in Ms. Wendy's office. She doesn't remember last night's party or what she told me on Mariposa Drive.

I learned so much from my talk with Gemma last night— about what she wants to do with her life, and how she likes girls *and* wants to be my friend. But now that's all forgotten. I've lost our perfect moment together, and that hurts.

I keep my hand on my chest, pushing against the pain as Ms. Lally starts her talk on parabolas. I like Gemma a lot. That's why I'm feeling the way I do. But I can't let the ache get the best of me.

I've got more damage to do.

15

"**HELLOOO, WANNA SIGN** up for the Labor Day bake sale?"

You'd think I'd be expecting Mike Brot by now.

You'd be wrong.

This morning, I've been an eensy bit . . . distracted. I've been hatching my next plot against Amberleigh. I didn't even talk to Ms. Rose after language arts. There's no need if I'm just going to *re*-perfect today tomorrow. The *Jaguar Gazette* isn't my priority; beating Amberleigh at her own game *is*.

But I've been so dead set on revenge, I forgot what horrors await me inside the cafeteria. That's why, when Mike jumps in front of me, sounding off like an air horn, I jump straight out of my skin. I don't even scream. I'm too shocked.

After what feels like an eon, my senses return, and I wheeze, "You *have* to stop."

Mike just gives me his same old goofy grin. I glare at his iguana tee.

Frankly, I've had enough of Mike, with his pearly whites

and sneak attacks. This is my cafeteria, too, and I should live without fear of bake sale ambushes. No more fleeing the scene. Today, I will face down the dude.

No. Better than that. I will *mess* with him.

"*Wow*," I say, faking excitement with those Oscar-winning chops of mine. "Man, I'd really love to help out. My peanut butter cookies are legendary."

Mike's eyes light up. "Really?"

"Mm-hmm." I nod vigorously. "But you shouldn't be asking me."

"Why not?" Mike hasn't stopped smiling. He's about to, though.

"Oh," I say solemnly. "No one's told you?"

"Told me what?"

I stare at the floor, as much to be dramatic as to keep from smiling at my own bogus story. "Well, in sixth grade there was this . . . incident. Look, it *wasn't* my fault! I must've mixed up the ingredients somehow. I take a more relaxed approach to baking. Like, who needs measuring? It's not an exact science. Only, I must've gotten something wrong, because those cookies? They, uh . . . well, they made some people sick."

On cue, Mike's big ol' smile disappears. "W-what kind of sick?"

I lean in close and whisper, "The poop kind, Mike. Poop

everywhere. So many girls on the volleyball team ate those cookies? They had to cancel their trip to the regional tournament."

Mike looks uncertain. He takes a step away from me, but I'm not through.

"I didn't *mean* to, Mike," I say pleadingly. "It was a baking mishap, is all. But then people were saying stuff like, um . . . 'eternal ban on bake sales'? And 'hazard to the community'? But if you'd like to give me a second chance, I'd—"

"*Nope!*" Mike practically bellows, backing up. "Nope, nope, that's cool! Thanks, though! Have a good day!"

He turns heel and flat-out runs away. Victorious, I watch him go. That'll teach him to scare kids half to death when they're on their lunch break.

When I reach the dessert pan in the cafeteria line, I ask Ms. Maffett, one of the workers, "Is it normal to taste-test the utensils? Because that's what Jacob Eisley is doing."

I point to the start of the line, and Ms. Maffett, looking horrified, abandons her post to run and investigate. In a flash, I reach across the pan, grab the ladle, and scoop out a whopping five helpings of banana pudding onto my plate.

"You're not supposed to do that," whines some kid behind me.

"It's August twenty-second," I tell them, flashing a smile. "Don't you know? That means I get to do whatever I want."

I don't wait for the kid to reply or for Ms. Maffett to return. I skip off with one destination in mind: Amberleigh Allen's table. As I get close, I can tell she's pissed off about something. So, she's finally found out about her shoes. Perfect timing.

"Something wrong?" I ask cheerfully, plopping my tray down at one of the empty spots.

Tate looks up in shock.

"Wh-what are you're doing?" she squeaks.

I blink innocently at her. "This seat is free, right?"

Tate looks mystified, like she'd never expect me to be so bold. I get it: I *wasn't* this bold three days ago. Second chances sure can change a girl. Plus, I haven't forgotten what Gemma told me last night about Tate backing up Amberleigh. After what I saw of Tate for *myself* last night—the way she pretended like Gemma had ceased to exist—I'm pretty convinced she'd help Amberleigh hide a murdered corpse.

So, yeah. I don't need to play nice around Tate.

"I mean . . . um, sure?" Tate motions weakly at the chair, and the moment my butt hits plastic, she leans in to whisper, "Just watch it. Amberleigh's in a bad mood."

Like I needed someone to spell that out.

There's a feral glow in Amberleigh's eyes. Alex sits beside her, one hand resting on her shoulder, and I guess he's trying to comfort her, but it looks like he's scared to make any sudden moves.

Scorpions and their stingers, I think. *You gotta watch out.*

But today, I'm equipped with my very own stinger. Here's what I plan to do: the moment Amberleigh starts to complain about her shoes being labeled fakes? I'll stand up and announce, "You know what's *really* fake at this table, Amberleigh? *You.*"

Then I'll do it. I'll pick up my plate, piled high with banana pudding, and I'll smash it on top of her head. Sweet payback—literally—for what she did to me *and* Gemma. Sure, I'll get sent to Principal Liu. Heck, I'll probably get a suspension. But none of that matters, thanks to the second-chance magic. Tomorrow, my record will be wiped clean, but I'll get to treasure my memory of banana-flavored justice forever.

That's how I'm expecting this to go.

What I *don't* expect is for Neil ask me, "Yo. Why do you have so much dessert?"

He sounds impressed.

I look down at my mountain of pudding, trying to think up a good explanation. I blurt out the first one that comes to me: "It's my birthday."

That gets everyone's attention—even Amberleigh's. It wasn't the best line, in retrospect. I've gone to school with everyone here since third grade, so one of them might know I'm lying. But my lie is close enough to the truth; my actual birthday *was* last month.

"Whoa, so you get extra dessert on your birthday?" Alex asks.

I squint across the table. Alex Fernandez, the *former* boy of my dreams. I'd be happy to dump my pudding on *his* head, too. But I've got to keep my eye on the prize, and for now? That means playing nice with these jerks.

"It's a new policy," I lie, smiling at Alex with utmost civility.

I'm cool as ice on the outside, but I'm starting to feel nervous. I don't like how much attention my banana pudding is getting. My plan relies on the art of surprise. Plus, Amberleigh still hasn't mentioned her shoes. She's staring across the table at me, a heavy stitch in her brow.

"So, what, you're fourteen?" she asks.

"Thirteen," I correct.

"Oh, wow. I thought you got held back a grade."

Sting. The scorpion strikes.

"Nope." I smile sweetly. "But there wouldn't be anything wrong with that if I was."

"Yeah," Tate says, her voice sharper than usual. "I got held back in first grade, Amberleigh. It's no big deal."

"You did?" Amberleigh looks surprised. "Oh my god. I forgot."

I've guessed the truth: Amberleigh didn't forget about Tate; she just doesn't care. I think Tate knows that, too, because she's giving Amberleigh the evil eye. Abruptly, she turns to me and says, "That's a cool look, by the way. I love the vest. It's bold but not *too* in your face. Shows you put real thought into it. Like, *some* people spend wads of cash on their outfits without actually *styling* them, but just because it's designer doesn't mean it's *cute*."

"Oh," I say, shrugging. "Thanks."

I might've been fooled a few days ago, but now? I know Tate's compliment is fake. It's obvious she's just trying to get back at Amberleigh for her dig.

Serves you right, I think smugly. *That's what you get for staying friends with scorpions. Sometimes they turn the stinger on you.*

"I'm having a party at my place tonight," Tate adds. "Want to come? We could celebrate your birthday, too."

Then—there's no mistaking it—she smirks across the table at Amberleigh.

I'm kind of impressed. I didn't know Tate had it in her.

I guess I could be mad that Tate is totally using me to piss off Amberleigh. But then I think of something I heard Da say once, when he was watching the news: "The enemy of my enemy is my friend."

"We won't have, like, a cake," Tate tells me, "but it'll be fun."

She's talking to me, but her eyes are still locked on Amberleigh. Meantime, I'm deciding what to say. I hadn't planned on this. I just wanted to dump banana pudding on

Amberleigh's head and call it a day. But pudding dumping would get me disinvited *instantly*.

"I'll have to think about it," I say slowly, concocting more lies. "My dads have a birthday dinner planned, but . . . maybe we could do that early."

"Sure." Tate nods. "Give me your number, and I'll text you the address. If you make it, you make it."

I can't exactly tell Tate that I already know her address, so I go through the motions. When I pull my phone from my backpack, my hyacinth journal topples out. I forgot that I'd stashed it in there this morning. Force of habit, I guess.

Tate picks up the journal, turning it over.

"This is *gorgeous*," she gushes—more fakeness for Amberleigh's sake. "What sort of flowers are those?"

"Hyacinths." I feel a jab between my ribs as I'm reminded of Cami and how I didn't answer her call last night.

"So, it's your journal?" Tate asks.

"Huh?" I look up distractedly from my phone, where I'm punching Tate's name into my contacts. "Oh, yeah."

Tate and I swap numbers. Across the table, Alex is howling at something Neil's said. Suddenly, his words from last night are throbbing in my ears: *They're probably on their periods.*

The memory of stinky chlorine from Tate's pool tickles my nose and I wonder why I *ever* wanted to be Alex's hero.

I jab at my food. I'm so sick of tuna, I could go a whole decade not eating another bite. Amberleigh still hasn't complained about her shoes, and my giant glob of banana pudding sits untouched on the plate. Sure, I could just drop the pudding on Amberleigh, without explanation, but that wouldn't be nearly satisfying enough.

I think over Tate's invitation to the pool party. I hadn't planned on going, but now I'm reconsidering. Why dump pudding on Amberleigh when I could, say, *dunk her in a pool*? Yeah. *Way* better. I've made up my mind.

There's a new pep in my step as the group of us leave the caf.

"So, see you tonight maybe?" Tate asks, as we head out to the hall.

She says it super loud, for Amberleigh to hear, and I answer just as loudly when I tell her, "You bet."

I'm switching out books from my locker when I spot Gemma down the hall. I've wondered for days now where she slips off to during lunch. The bathrooms, maybe? An empty stairwell? Anywhere she doesn't have to sit with Amberleigh? I don't blame her.

"Hey!" I say, shutting my locker and falling into step beside her.

Gemma startles. "Um . . . hey?"

"I looked for you at lunch," I say. "I was at Amberleigh's table."

"Uh-huh." A V-shaped dent forms above Gemma's nose.

It's not that I *want* to bring up Amberleigh around Gemma, but I can't hold in my curiosity about tonight. I go ahead and ask, "Are you going to Tate's party?"

"Oh." Gemma shrugs. "Yeah, probably."

"Same!" I wince, wondering if I sound overexcited. Gemma sure doesn't seem hyped.

I think back to what she said about the party on our first day. Then, acting more nonchalant, I shrug and add, "It's gotten kind of old, though, right?"

Gemma turns on me, right outside Mx. Ramani's door. She looks annoyed.

"How would you know if it's gotten old?" she asks. "You've never been."

"Right! I know." I rub my neck, wondering how to talk my way out of this.

This isn't the version of Gemma I'm used to. She's distant, like she's weirded out that we're having this conversation. The ache from earlier is back in my chest, and I suddenly realize that I'd be happy to wreck all of my plans—even my plan to enact sweet revenge on Amberleigh—if it meant I could hang out with Gemma the way we did last night. I want Gemma to know that I'm *not* a weirdo. Even if this day doesn't count for anything, I can't stand the thought of her not liking me.

"What if you hang out with *me* tonight, instead?" I blurt.

Gemma's expression doesn't change. I blather on.

"Like, at my place? My da's making this great dinner, and . . . well, I think you're really cool, and I thought that maybe we could get to know each other this year. You know, like, what you wrote in my yearbook, about wishing you knew me better?"

What am I *saying*?

Shut up, Vivian. Shut up.

I shut up.

Gemma looks confused. Maybe even *sorry* for me? It's a fate worse than death.

"Uh," she says, eyebrows bunching. "That's nice of you to offer. But we've been doing this party since fifth grade. I can't bail on my friends."

"But you bailed on them at lunch!" I yelp.

Gemma narrows her eyes at me. She's definitely annoyed.

"You know," she says, measuredly, "it's kind of a big deal if you got invited to the party. Tate and Amberleigh don't ask a lot of new people. If you don't want to go, that's fine. But, like, sorry. *Me* going isn't any of your business."

With that, Gemma heads into class, leaving me behind.

I watch in silence as she takes a seat at the back of the room.

So, that was a failure. A big freaking flop.

I trudge into the room, taking a seat far off from Gemma, and tell myself not to get worked up. I can redo this day. I *plan* to redo this day. The only thing I should be focused on is getting back at Amberleigh.

I replay the moment from last night, when Amberleigh shoved Gemma and yelled, "Why don't you find a new friend?"

At least I can stop that from happening again. I can keep Gemma from getting hurt *and* I can make Amberleigh pay. At tonight's version of the party, I'll make sure *we* get the last laugh.

🌷 🌷 🌷

"Okay there?" Pop asks, as he slows the RAV4 in front of Tate's house.

"Y-yeah," I say, staring up at the sloped lawn.

The rest of school was tough. Not schoolwise, *Gemma*-wise. I kept my distance from her in our shared classes this afternoon, figuring that anything else I'd say would only make her more irritated.

I messed up with her today. We got off on the wrong foot. But even though Gemma doesn't know that she needs my help tonight, I'm going to be there for her. Just as soon as I work up the nerve to open the car door . . .

"Sure you're all right?" Pop prods. "You look kind of pale, kiddo."

I *will* stand up to Amberleigh. I know exactly what I want to say to her, to put her in her place. I can't clam up now. I've gotta move.

"I'm fine," I tell Pop.

It's not another Oscar-winning performance, but it'll do.

Pop chucks my arm. "You got this. And Da and I are only a phone call away."

"Thanks," I say.

It's showtime. *The Pool Party, Part Two: Vivian's Revenge.*

It helps to think of myself as a movie character, not the real Vivian. It especially helps to remember that, thanks to the magic, I can do whatever I want tonight with zero consequences.

So, I got this. I step out of the car.

Pop peels away from the curb as I make my way up the driveway. This time around, I haven't bothered pretending that I might go swimming. I'm still wearing Aunt Ximena's leather fringe vest, and I only carry a small purse with my phone, lip gloss, and an extra pad.

I'm prepared. This is *my* second-chance magic. That makes me as invincible as Torin in the Battle of Marigold

Field, when he wore armor spun from impenetrable elven thread.

I just wish that my hands would get the message. They tremble as I nudge open the back gate and join the party. Neil, Alex, and their soccer team friends are in the pool, jousting with foam noodles. Tonight, it's Tate and Amberleigh who sit together in the hammock, whispering over a book that Tate's holding open. I'm on the lookout for Gemma, and soon enough I find her sitting with the choir girls by the snack table.

"Hey!" I say, strolling up to them, trying to act chill. *Invincible*.

Some of the girls say "hey" back. One of them introduces herself and says that she likes my vest.

Gemma gives me a half smile. "Tate said it's your birthday."

"Uh, yeah," I lie. "I'm thirteen."

"Cool." Gemma's smile widens a smidge—enough to reveal the dimple in her left cheek. "Happy birthday."

"Thanks," I say, telling my heart to stop beating so fast.

I place my purse on a chair, but I don't sit down yet. I try to think of something to say—some witty remark that will keep Gemma's eyes on me. But the moment passes, and she goes back to talking to the girl next to her. My stomach sinks.

It's not Gemma's fault that she can't remember my other Mondays. Still, I want to shout, *We've hung out, remember?*

You said you wanted to be my friend. We held hands!

All I do is shove a handful of Cool Ranch Doritos into my mouth.

"So you're a Leo, huh?"

The girl who introduced herself—Maggie, I think, or Meg—is talking to me.

Actually, I'm a Cancer, but I'm in too deep now, so I nod.

"Do you like to be the center of attention?" says Meg-maybe-Maggie. "I swear, most of the sopranos I know are Leos. Are you a soprano?"

"I don't know," I admit.

Maggie-maybe-Meg looks appalled. "How's that possible? You don't, like, sing at all?"

I munch another handful of chips so that I don't have to respond. I'm feeling uneasy—and kind of attacked?—when I hear booming words from across the patio.

"'Number two: Join the school paper. Because that's how Q. S. Murray got her start.'"

I turn around, feeling dizzy. My eyes won't focus at first. Then they zoom in on Amberleigh. I see the book that she and Tate have been whispering over. *Really* see it.

It's my hyacinth journal.

My thoughts spin like a carousel gone berserk. How do *they* have my journal? I rack my brain until I land on a memory of this afternoon, when the journal slipped from my backpack at lunch, and Tate picked it up. I'd gotten distracted after that. I hadn't noticed that Tate never gave it back. Now it's in Amberleigh's hands, and she's bellowing my list of eighth grade goals.

"'Number three: Make Gemma Cohen my friend. Because I *need* one.'"

By now, Amberleigh's reading has caught everyone's attention. Beside her, Tate giggles uncontrollably into a beach towel. In the pool, the boys have halted their noodle war and are listening in.

"What are you reading?" Neil shouts from the deep end.

Amberleigh glances up. Her eyes land on me, and instantly my vision goes murky. The colors around me blur and bleed.

"Oh!" Amberleigh holds up my journal like she's inspecting it. "Did I not mention the title? This would be . . . uh, let me check . . . *Vivian Lantz's Foolproof Plan for the Perfect Second Chance.*"

All eyes turn to me. Tate's practically howling, dabbing the beach towel against her eyes.

Tate. When we were at lunch, I assumed that she was just mad about Amberleigh's dig. I thought that she was getting back at *her* by being nice to *me.* Now I see that lunch wasn't just about making Amberleigh jealous; Tate was playing the long game. She stole my journal to dig up dirt on me. She stole it to get back on Amberleigh's good side.

There's a new mistake for today: I supremely underestimated Tate Matthews.

Meantime, Amberleigh hasn't stopped reading.

She clears her throat and announces, "I was getting to the most important point of the plan. It's crossed out, but . . . yeah, I can *just* make it out." She clears her throat and practically shouts, "'Make Alex Fernandez my boyfriend.'"

It's so quiet, I can hear the patter of rain on the sunshades.

In this moment, I make a brand-new, desperate wish: to be invisible. To simply disappear, never to materialize again.

But I don't get my wish. Instead, I get whispers from the girls at the snack table and hoots from the boys in the pool. I get Amberleigh saying, with scathing sweetness, "Wow, Vivian. That's so *cute*. You thought you could steal my boyfriend, easy as that?"

I'm speechless. Amberleigh knows that she's got me cornered. I can practically see the stinger come out as she gets up from the hammock and saunters toward me.

"Good luck with the school paper, at least," she says. "Maybe that'll pan out for you. But come on, girl. Trying to make us your friends by pretending it's your birthday?" She winces, like she's sorry for me. "That's pathetic."

My hands are clammy. My legs won't move. Amberleigh stands inches from me, arms crossed tight.

"It's *over*, Vivian," she announces. "Quinn Doughty saw

you at opening assembly. I know it was you who ruined my shoes. I just hope your dads can afford to pay eight hundred dollars in damages."

No. This can't be happening. This isn't *Vivian's Revenge.* It's my downfall.

I splutter, but no words come out. My feet are stuck to the concrete. Then, I can't help myself. I look at Gemma. She's not whispering or laughing. She's staring straight at me, and she looks *mad.*

"Is that why you were talking to me today?" she asks hoarsely. "Why you asked to hang out? You wanted to *make* me your new friend?"

"N-no!" I protest. "It wasn't like that. I—"

"Did you write that stuff on Amberleigh's shoes?" she interrupts.

I gape at her, speechless, thinking back on my memories from last night.

"Yeah," I say, feeling suddenly bold. "I did. Because she deserved it. She's *terrible.* She totally betrayed you at camp, and she's been treating you like crap ever since. You said so yourself, so why are you defending her? She wouldn't do the same thing for you." I throw out my hands. "For *anyone* here. She only thinks about herself!"

Gemma's face has turned ghostly pale. "Wh-what are you talking about? I never told you anything about camp." She looks past me, to Amberleigh. "I don't have a clue what she's saying."

It's true. I know that I'm sharing what Gemma told me in private yesterday, but I *have* to make her see why I chose to do what I did. Shouldn't she be glad that I pranked Amberleigh?

"Don't you get it?" I plead with Gemma. "She's not your friend."

Gemma holds up a hand, like she doesn't want to hear more.

"Know what, Vivian?" she says, getting up from the table. "It seems like the only one around here who doesn't know how to be a friend is *you*. Putting me on your *to-do* list? That is so messed up."

She turns her back to me and heads into Tate's house through the patio door. I feel like my heart's been ripped out and shredded till it's nothing but bloody, torn muscle.

"Ouch," says Amberleigh, watching Gemma go. She gives me a pitying smile. "Guess nobody likes a fake friend, huh? I bet that's why Cami Ruiz moved: to get away from you."

Amberleigh opens my journal, thumbing the gold-foiled pages. "Let's see. Is there an entry in here about *that*?"

My face is on fire. I want to wrench the journal out of Amberleigh's hands.

But I don't get the chance.

The next moment, she's chucking it through the air, and

I watch in horror as my hyacinth journal—prized possession and sacred keeper of the Master Plan—lands in the pool with a sickening plunk.

I gape at Amberleigh. "Why would you *do* that?"

She shrugs. "It was a trashy plan. But then, you're pretty trashy yourself."

She steps closer—so close that I feel the heat of her breath on my face. In a whisper, she says, "I don't know where you heard about summer camp, but the crap you're saying about me is a *lie*. And trashy liars? They deserve to be punished. So . . ."

It happens in an instant. Amberleigh lunges, pushing the heels of her hands into my collarbone, and I'm flying backward, losing my balance, falling into the pool.

I gasp as cold water hits my body. It's pure sensation: freezing water, muffled sound, smeared blue vision. Then I resurface, choking on pool water.

The boys in the pool are laughing. Alex clings to a foam noodle, snickering gleefully. A girl at the snack table asks, "Can she even swim?"

Yeah, I can swim. So I do. I grab my bobbing journal, and I slosh my way to the pool ladder, hauling myself up. Aunt Ximena's vest is heavy as lead, and water squelches in my sneakers with every step I take. And then—my stomach plummets as I remember: *my period*. What if there's blood running down my legs?

Nothing can be worse than this. It's déjà vu from last night, only this time, I'm the one who got shoved, not Gemma. I can't think straight. All I know is that I have to leave. I grab my purse from the snack table and make a run for it. But right as I reach the back gate, my right sneaker slips, and I wipe out. Pain slices through me as I skid across the concrete. There's a new roar of laughter from the patio.

"Oh my god, is she okay?" a girl calls out.

My brain screams at me, *Get out. Get away. Leave.*

I push myself to my feet, and this time nothing slows me down. I race out the gate and down the driveway, feet flinging me over the sidewalk tiles. I *run*, and I don't look back.

❦ ❦ ❦

I call Dads, sobbing, from Mariposa Lane. They both come to pick me up, but they don't ask too many questions—not after I practically screech that all I want to do is sleep. Pop sets out astringent and Neosporin on the bathroom counter, and Da sets a hamper outside the door for my wet clothes. Then, they leave me alone, like I asked.

At first, all I can think about is the journal. I open it on the bathroom counter, frantically flipping through the soaked pages. I press a hand towel against my page of goals, trying to sop up the water. That doesn't makes a difference, so I yank out the hair dryer, turn it to full blast, and wave hot air against the page. I try to dry out the whole journal—page after page after page—but no matter how long I work, I can't totally fix the damage.

I howl in frustration, yanking the hair dryer plug from the socket and tossing the journal to the floor. Defeated, I sink down onto the edge of the bathtub, where all the memories from tonight begin to wash over me.

Gemma was right: a friendship plan *is* messed up.

The truth is, I don't want to be Gemma's fake friend; I want to be her *real* friend. But I'd be lying if I said that's how this started. When Gemma ran into me outside school on that first Monday, I only saw her as part of my Master Plan—a way to get into Amberleigh's group and Alex's heart. My stomach turns at the thought. How could I be so shallow?

It was messed up for me to think of Gemma as a means to an end. It was messed up to hope that Alex and Amberleigh would break up. Thinking like that? It's self-centered. Mean. And how does that make me any different from Amberleigh Allen herself?

So much for sweet justice. Turns out the girl who got her just deserts today was *me*.

I thought I'd at least feel better letting off steam today,

but I'm only queasy—the way I feel when I gorge on too much queso and guac before the main course. Today doesn't count. No one's going to remember it in the morning when the clock resets. So why do I feel like crap?

I guess it's because *I'll* remember what I've done.

I didn't have to be a jerk to Mike Brot. Sure, he can be annoying, but that wasn't a good reason to make up my poop story. I didn't have to send Ms. Maffett on a wild-goose chase, either.

Then there's Arlo. I'm still so mad at him; and somehow, even after saying and doing the meanest things I could think of, I don't actually feel better. Not at the end of the day.

Nothing's changed.

My phone goes off, blasting the Relevane theme song. Cami's call. But I don't answer. I don't have the strength. Instead, I finally start to clean up my knees.

As I unwrap a Band-Aid, I get a terrible thought: What if this is the way it's always going to be? No matter how much magic, no matter how many second chances—what if my first-day curse really is unbreakable? Maybe Q. S. Murray wasted her magic on me. Maybe I'm a lost cause.

I used to think my first-day curse was a sign that I was a hero in the making. Now? I'm afraid that I'm not like Torin the Rogue or Sage Miriel. Maybe I'm like the wretched Prince Lorace, Princess Dexalva's brother, who was cursed from birth to suffer all his livelong days. Someone's got to play the sucky characters, right? What if that's my fate, while people like Amberleigh get to be the heroines?

Ugh. Prince Lorace. I feel for you, dude.

There's a sharp jab in my abdomen. It feels like a ticked off lobster is in there, scraping and snapping its claws. *Cramps.* They're worse tonight than they've been before. I rummage until I find a bottle of ibuprofen stashed in one of the bathroom drawers. I take a tablet, washing it down with tap water. Then, dejectedly, I pick up my journal from the floor and leave the room.

I hear voices down the hall. Dads are talking in the kitchen, same as they were last night, and curiosity gets the better of me. I sneak toward the open door, stopping right outside.

"I thought my approach was more direct," Da is saying. "But now . . . and the band . . . I did everything wrong."

"That isn't true, Sean," I hear Pop say. "Arlo can't doubt how much we love him. We've disagreed about his plans, but we haven't said we won't support them, either. We trained him to assert himself. To spread his wings. Well, he's a teen. That's part of the job description. We spread ours when we were his age, didn't we?"

There aren't any words after that—only the sound of Da

crying. I can imagine the scene inside the kitchen, with Pop scooted close to Da at the table, arms wrapped around his shoulders. Tonight, I avoid the squeaky floorboard and sneak back to my room. When I crawl into bed, still clutching my hyacinth journal, I'm not thinking about my cramps anymore.

Dads aren't angry about Arlo leaving—not from what I can tell. They're not yelling about how he's drifted away from the family. They're not saying that they hate him. They're just . . . sad.

A scratchy grip tightens around my throat. Tears leak from my eyes, streaming down my face. What if I don't hate Arlo, either? What if that's why I don't feel better after screaming my heart out at him? Because I don't hate him. I'm just sad, too.

As hard as things have been with Cami leaving for Florida, and as tough as school has been for these four days—I thought that Arlo would be here for me, at least. I thought *that* part of my life wouldn't change. But no. That, too.

A memory hits me.

Barficorn, Arlo said, when he dropped me off. *I love you, okay?*

I think about the way he said that, with the *off* look on his face.

Since last night, I've been blaming Arlo for leaving me with no warning. But what if he did try to warn me, in his own way? What if I was too distracted to notice?

I swallow, trying to get rid of that scratchy feeling in my throat. When I can't, I open my hyacinth journal to the Master Plan. The paper is still damp, warped around the edges from all the hair drying, and the ink has smeared, but my goals are readable. I take a pen from my bedside table, wondering if I'll even be able to write without tearing straight through the paper. But somehow, it works. I'm able to dig new words onto the page.

It's a fourth goal:

4. Make things right with Arlo
   ('Cause I've taken him for granted all
   this time.)

My theory about the magic has to be right. My magical time loop *has* to keep looping. This can't be the Monday that I get stuck with. I need another chance to do things differently.

I stare at the new words on the page, hoping—*begging*—for that second chance. Then I close the journal and hold it to my chest, and I keep holding on as weariness wraps around me, dragging me off to sleep.

16

"WHOA, WHOA, WHOA!"

I wake to the sound of rain on the roof and Arlo's voice shouting from downstairs.

I open my eyes to a galaxy of plastic planets above me.

Yes.

Excitement whooshes through my body. *Yes! It's Monday again!*

I throw off my bedcovers, and there are my knees, perfectly unscraped. No Band-Aids. No trace of last night. Which means no terrible pool party. No one at school will remember what went down yesterday night.

I heave a giant sigh of relief. Then, I head for the door.

I'm padding down the hallway as Arlo yells, *"Dads. Get down here, quick!"*

He grimaces when he sees me at the top of the stairs.

A lump clogs my throat at the sight of Arlo. His hair is soaked with rainwater and impatience burns in his eyes.

Hours from now, he'll be gone. But I don't want to scream about that anymore; I'm too worn out. I just want to focus on the goal I scribbled into my hyacinth journal last night: I want to see if I can make things right.

"That's a weird look on your face, Barficorn."

We're in the back room, helping Dads unpack boxes. I'm holding out a damp beaded flapper dress for Pop to inspect, and Arlo's airing out the pages of an old book called *Breakfast of Champions*.

It's boring work. I've done it *twice*. But this is different from those other times. Today, I know what this moment is worth. It might be the last time in a long time that all four of us Lantzes are together, in the same room.

"I'm thinking," I tell Arlo. "Guess that makes my face look weird."

Pop lifts a velvet dress out of a box and shakes his head. "It's going to take all morning to wash and line dry these."

"I could stay home from school to help," Arlo says.

"Nice try," replies Da.

"What?" Arlo balks. "It's for a good reason."

I frown. I remember Arlo saying this, but it doesn't make much sense to me now. Why would he offer to work at the shop when he knew that he was going to leave us? Wouldn't he want to get out of this place as soon as possible?

Maybe Arlo feels guilty. Maybe he thinks of this morning as his last chance to do something for the family.

A last hurrah, I think pensively.

"Well," Pop says, "I don't think Vivian would appreciate her chauffeur bailing on her."

"You wouldn't mind, would you, Barficorn?" Arlo turns to me, a sparkle in his eye. "Eighth grade's a joke, anyway."

"Speaking of which," says Pop, "you two should be heading out soon. Da and I can handle this mess from here on out."

I glance resentfully at the clock. Pop's right: I have to get to school. There's no way he or Da would approve of me bailing, so I'll play along. I get ready upstairs, and I don't forget about my period. How could I, at this point? I put on my usual first day getup—no fringe vest today—and slip the hyacinth journal into my backpack as a reminder of my new goal.

I clomp down the stairs just in time to catch poor Trixie whining. Heaving a sigh, I let her out front and watch her do her business. By the time I return to the back room, Arlo's wearing his flip-flops. It's only once we're in the car that I snap off the radio and tell him, "Let's skip."

Arlo blinks at me. "Beg your pardon?"

"You're right," I tell him, adjusting the toggles of my rain jacket hood. "Eighth grade *is* a joke. Let's get pancakes instead."

I can practically see the gears whirring in Arlo's brain, invisible steam blowing out his ears. I know now that Arlo had always planned to skip school, and I bet he's deciding if he should be an accomplice to *me* skipping, too.

"I don't know about that," he says eventually. "It's your first day. You might regret it."

"Trust me," I say darkly, "I won't. And you won't get in trouble with Dads. I'll tell them you dropped me off at school, and I just didn't go in."

Arlo doesn't seem convinced.

"Look," he says, "just because I'm not a fan of school doesn't mean—"

"No, I know," I interrupt. "I'm not planning on skipping *all* of eighth grade. Just today. I'm improvising. That's what life's about, right? Like music."

Seconds tick by. Arlo stares at the gearshift, contemplating.

"Pancakes, huh?" he asks.

"Pancakes," I confirm.

That settles it. Arlo shifts the Civic into gear, and we both know where we're headed without saying the name aloud. Arlo and I have had the same favorite breakfast spot since I was five: Magnolia Cafe. It's pretty much an Austin institution, and lucky for us, it's only five minutes away from home.

It's a rainy weekday morning, so the café's not too busy,

and Arlo nabs a spot in the tiny parking lot. Together, we walk up the ramp to the front door, passing the neon sign that says, *Sorry, We're Open.*

The host seats us right away, at one of my favorite booths, right under a hanging pterodactyl skeleton. Arlo and I both know what we want without peeking at the menu. He orders a coffee, I order a milk, and we both ask for short stacks of the cornmeal banana pecan pancakes. Then there's the pièce de résistance: an appetizer of Mag nachos—that's nachos smothered in cheese and sour cream, topped with jalapeños fresh enough to burn off your taste buds.

The nachos land on the table first, and I scoop a chip into the gooey goodness. Every bite is worth the money I stuffed into my backpack this morning.

Arlo chomps through chip after chip, and when our pancakes arrive, he drenches his with a flood of syrup.

"Cheers," he tells me, raising a forkful of pancake.

"Cheers," I say, tapping his fork with mine.

In this moment? Life feels normal. It's me and Arlo hanging out, like nothing's going to change. But the feeling won't last forever, I think morosely. That's why I have to focus on goal number four.

"How're things with the Neon Spurs?"

I ask it casually, looking for a change on Arlo's face: the *off* look—some telltale sign that'll give him away. He stays unaffected, though, shoveling more pancakes into his mouth.

"They're good," he says, around bites. "We finalized the new set list."

I drag the tongs of my fork through the syrup on my plate, creating four parallel tracks. On to my next approach: come right out and say it.

"So you're stoked about the tour, huh?"

That gets a reaction. Arlo slows his chewing, raising his eyes to mine.

"It doesn't matter how I found out," I tell him. "But I know you're planning on dropping out and touring."

"Um," Arlo says. "That's—"

I cut him off. "I just want to know why you want to leave home so much. Is it something I did? Or is it about Dads? I know you fight a lot, but they really love you. Da *does* support you, even if he doesn't like the band."

Arlo's shaking his head at me. "Hey. I'm not leaving because of you. Or Dads. I'm leaving for *me*."

I squint at him. "That's cheesy to say."

Arlo smirks. "Yeah, but it's true. When I found the band, it wasn't me messing around with the bass by myself anymore. Everything clicked. When we play together, it's like . . . I don't know, symbiosis or something."

"Like magic?" I ask.

"Something like that," he replies. "I get *way* more excited

236

about practice than I ever did about studying for my SATs. So I decided that life is short. Why waste it on checking boxes when you can spend it doing what you love?"

"But you love us, too," I say—so quiet the words barely get out. "I mean, right?"

Arlo gives me a look, like I'm being absurd. "Of course I do. But things are really heating up for the band. I'm the only member still in high school, and I'll be eighteen soon. We've been planning this tour all summer, and we've got some great venues lined up. Right now, the band is everything."

"Not *everything*," I counter, setting down my fork. I've lost my appetite.

Arlo sighs, tapping the edge of the syrup bottle. "You're right. Not everything."

"Why were you going to leave without telling us?" I've started to cry. I'm mad at myself about it, but there's no stopping it now.

"This isn't about you," Arlo insists. "Like I said."

"But it is!" I pound the table, choking back tears. "I'm your sister, so it *is* about me. You leaving means something to *me*."

Arlo's eyes widen. "Look, I was planning on texting Dads tonight."

"That's not good enough!" I spit.

A couple of people are looking at us. I didn't mean to

cause a scene. The whole point of getting pancakes was to make things *right* with Arlo.

"Hey," he says, more gently than before. "I'm going on this tour, but that's not because I don't care about you, and it's not because you did something to make me leave. I have to go where the music leads. Maybe one day you'll understand."

The trouble is, the way Arlo's explaining things? I sort of understand *now*. I don't get his obsession with band life, but I can think of it another way—like how much I love writing. If someone offered to pay me to write fantasy novels, right here, on the spot? You'd better believe I'd ditch eighth grade.

"I understand a little," I admit grudgingly.

Arlo reaches across the table, tapping my index finger. "Then you're more open-minded than I gave you credit for, Barficorn."

I don't reply. I'm still thinking about my writing. About the *Jaguar Gazette* and my other goals, and how so many of them have changed at this point that I'm not sure *what* I want out of my Master Plan. What does a perfect first day even *mean* anymore?

My eyes fill with fresh tears. And then? It's spilling out. I'm telling Arlo about Q. S. Murray's MeetNGreet and *happening to life* and my Master Plan. It's like, for these five days, I've been a bottled-up, shaken-up soda, and now the top's twisted off and I'm spewing everywhere. Arlo's face grows slacker with every word I say, and by the end, he's straight-up gaping at me.

"Jeez," he says.

I rub a hand beneath my snotty nose. There's only one teensy detail I've left out of my big speech: the time loop. I nervously study Arlo's face, worried about how he'd react to that news. I think again of Prince Lorace and how the guy was driven out of Celater, all for sharing one measly secret. Up until now, I've been so cautious that I haven't even told *Cami* about my second-chance magic. But now, I think it might be the right time. I want—no, *need*—Arlo to know this secret.

"I'm gonna tell you something," I warn him. "It's sounds super weird, and you're gonna think I'm making it up, but I'm not. I *swear.*"

Arlo sets down his knife. "Uh . . . huh."

"I'm in a time loop," I say matter-of-factly.

Arlo's expression doesn't change. He's waiting for more.

"Today isn't the first time I've lived this Monday," I tell him. "It's the fifth. I made a wish after my first day of school for a do-over. It was the worst day ever, and I couldn't stand the thought that I'd ruined eighth grade. So I made the wish, and the next day it was Monday all over again, and I've kept waking up on Monday ever since."

Arlo sits back in the booth, causing the wood to creak.

"So, *Groundhog Day*," he says.

"What?"

"It's this movie from the nineties. A classic. This guy keeps reliving Groundhog Day."

I scowl at Arlo. I've just told him my big secret, and he wants to talk about an old movie?

"In the film," Arlo says, "the guy is a real jerk. The whole point of his time loop is that he learns to be a decent human."

My scowl deepens. "I'm not a jerk."

Arlo arches a brow. "Who have you asked?"

I frown, remembering last night and Gemma's words to me: *The only one around here who doesn't know how to be a friend is* you.

"Fine," I admit. "I can be jerky. But so can you."

"Nice deflection, Barficorn."

I don't know what "deflection" means, but I'm tired of Arlo not taking this seriously.

"Do you believe me?" I demand. "Or do you just think this is funny?"

"Who says it can't be both?"

I'm too tired for this. My eyes well up with tears.

"Whoa." Arlo's grin slips off his face. "Hey. Sorry. I'm processing. This is a lot to lay on someone at breakfast. But you know, I've asked myself something like this before: 'If someone came to you and told you the unbelievable—like, they'd seen Bigfoot in the flesh, or they'd been abducted by aliens—would you believe them?'"

"And?" I ask impatiently.

"I figured it'd suck to be in that position, with no one to believe me." Arlo shrugs. "So why wouldn't I believe you?"

I shut my eyes. I didn't realize till right this second how much I needed this. I needed to tell someone about the magic. Needed them to *believe*. Now that I have, there's so much more to say.

I open my eyes and tell Arlo, "I've figured out the *why*. Q. S. Murray is . . . an *actual witch*."

Arlo lets out a laugh so loud that people look our way *again*.

"Just hear me out," I insist. "She told me in her MeetN-Greet that she wanted to help. She said she'd be sending me *magical vibes*. When I wished out loud to do Monday over, I think Q. S. Murray must have heard my wish with her magical powers. Then she used those powers to make my wish *come true*."

"Huh," Arlo says, scratching the scruff on his chin. "Sure. Why not."

"As to the *how*," I say, "um . . . that's more of a theory. I think that if I make a wish out loud, like I did before—if I tell Q. S. Murray that I don't need the magic anymore—she'll make time go back to normal."

Arlo looks confused. "Wait. You think you can stop the loop?"

I gulp, remembering the night of my third chance. I thought that I could stop the loop *then*, and I was wrong. But that was different. I'd forgotten how magic works in the Relevane books. I didn't ask Q. S. Murray to dam up the magical flow. I won't be making that mistake again.

"I—I think so," I say, voice wobbling. "Yeah. I'm pretty sure."

"Well, then, what's the problem?" Arlo asks, tossing his hands. "God, Viv. You were making it sound like some purgatorial fate you couldn't escape. If you think you can stop today from repeating, why don't you?"

I stay quiet, looking down at my half-eaten stack of pancakes.

Arlo clucks his tongue. "Hang on. This is about that plan of yours, isn't it? That whole *happening to life* thing. You're trying to live the perfect first day of school."

I snort so hard that it sounds like a goose honk. "At this point? I'd just like to live a day that's not totally *miserable*."

"Come on. Has it been that bad?"

I glare at Arlo. The tales I could tell. One: got my period in the *worst* way, in front of the whole school. Two: got banana puddinged in public. Three: heartlessly betrayed my new crush. Four: found out that my *old* crush is a total jerk.

Five: discovered that my brother has been secretly plotting to leave me for a band tour. To name a *few*.

"Fine, fine." Arlo tosses his hands again.

Our server stops by, setting the check on the table, and when they're gone, Arlo speaks again.

"You know what I think of Q. S. Murray's advice?"

"What?"

Arlo smirks. "It's a load of crap."

Indignation flares in me, like a Relevanian funeral pyre. I start to protest, but Arlo says, "Hear me out. It's cool that she writes those books. I'm sure they're great. And I know that you think she's, uh, *magical*. But put that aside for a sec and consider that maybe Q. S. Murray is *just a person*. Honestly? I think it's dangerous to idolize someone like that." Arlo thumbs his chest. "Take Kurt Cobain. Love his music, but I wouldn't go to him for life advice."

"Q. S. Murray isn't a rock singer," I argue. "Anyway, her advice worked for *her*. How do you think she became a successful author?"

"You said it yourself: her advice worked for *her*. I'm sure she meant well, leaving you that message, but who's to say what worked for her will work for you? Take your newspaper idea. Do you *want* to write for a paper?"

I fold my arms. First Ms. Rose and now my own brother. Will folks stop hassling me about the *Jaguar Gazette*?

"What's your point?" I ask.

"My point is that it's pretty messed up, telling someone else how to live. Plenty of people can't just *happen to life*. What if you grow up without money? Or people are judging or hurting you because of stuff you can't change—like the color of your skin, or your gender, or who you love? Dads couldn't legally get married till I was in fourth grade. What would Q. S. Murray tell them? 'Happen to marriage harder?'"

I glare at Arlo. "That's not the same thing."

Arlo goes on, like he didn't hear me. "Yeah, you should chase your dreams, or whatever. But take me, for instance. I wouldn't be going on this tour—the *band* wouldn't—if Nigel's parents weren't loaded. They bought him an RV for high school graduation, and his uncle has music industry connections in LA. So, like, life *is* going to happen to you—the good and the bad. You can't beat yourself up when it's hard or unfair or not perfect. That doesn't mean you're doing it wrong; it only means it's *life*. And if you ask me, the point of all this?" Arlo waves his hands in the air—at the pterodactyl, the uneaten pancakes. "It's not about getting it right. It's more about getting it wrong."

Arlo gives me a look, like I'm supposed to be having some big revelation. All I do is stare blankly at him.

Sighing, he sinks back in the booth. "I'm just saying,

control is an illusion. We'd all do better if we gave it up. Focus on helping people instead."

I want to call Arlo cheesy again for saying something as goofy as "control is an illusion." Before I get the chance, though, his expression darkens.

"Viv," he says, "do Dads know about my tour?"

I shake my head. "Nope."

"Then how did you find out?"

"Time loop," I remind him.

"So, you're basically an all-knowing Time God," Arlo muses. "How many Mondays did you say you've lived?"

"Going on a thousand."

Arlo narrows his eyes. "That's . . . a joke. Right?"

I give him a look, like, *Duh.*

I still don't know if Arlo believes me, and I definitely haven't enjoyed his pointless lecture. But I do know one thing: this is the best talk we've had in a while. Even if the rest of today is a bust, I'm glad I'll get to keep this breakfast in my memory bank.

When I reach for the bill, Arlo grabs it from me, shaking his head.

"I've got money," I insist.

"Too bad," says Arlo. "I'm in a band."

I roll my eyes. "You don't make money from *that.*"

"Ouch, Barficorn."

Arlo sets down a wad of cash, leaving plenty of bills for a tip, and we head outside, into the pouring rain. My mind's sizzling with thoughts—about Q. S. Murray and second chances and Life, with a capital "L." Arlo nudges me once we're in the car.

"You cool?" he asks. "The weird look's back on your face."

"I don't know how I am," I confess.

"Huh." Arlo studies me a moment longer. Then he starts up the car.

He doesn't take us home. Instead, he drives farther up South Congress, parking in front of Home Slice Pizza—the Lantz family's go-to for takeout eggplant pizza and garlic knots.

I snort at Arlo. "Hungry again?"

"Nah," he says. "I just feel like strolling around. How about you?"

I'm dumbfounded. Arlo feels like *strolling*? In the *rain*? With *me*?

I consider my alternative: slinking in late to school for what will feel like my billionth pre-algebra class. And that seriously makes me want to cry.

So I tell Arlo, "Yeah. I wanna stroll."

17

SOUTH CONGRESS IS a big street in Austin. It stretches across Lady Bird Lake, leading right up to the state capitol. South of the lake, it's weird as all get-out, jam-packed with restaurants and kooky gift shops. My favorite part is the street art. There are the spray painted words *I love you so much* by Jo's Coffee and the Mr. Rogers portrait next to Home Slice. I grin as Arlo and I pass the *Willie for President* mural and Arlo starts whistling "On the Road Again."

We walk under the shelter of Arlo's big umbrella, not headed anywhere in particular. Arlo meant what he said: we're here to stroll. We pop into South Congress Books, where I open the oldest-looking hardcovers, breathing in the scent of yellowed pages. We check out the clearance sale at a gift shop that's selling local-made T-shirts featuring hand-drawn avocados. We pay a visit to the costume shop, Lucy in Disguise, where I try on a giant Care Bears head. Arlo and I get to laughing so hard about it, I nearly pee my pants.

It's only when I get to the bathroom that I'm reminded of my period. Funny how it felt like such a big deal the first day, and now? It's like I've lived through a *year* of periods. I'm getting used to it.

These past five days, I've seen and done so much, all while the date on my phone screen hasn't budged. And even though I know that the people around me don't remember the past days like I do, I feel a pang of guilt when Arlo treats me to a lemonade at Jo's.

"I've got something to tell you," I say, as we sit on the covered patio. The rain is still coming down hard, ricocheting off the concrete.

"You've already hit me with the time loop thing," Arlo says. "Slow down."

But I've got to say what I've worked myself up to confess.

"I was mean to you yesterday," I tell him. "I said terrible things to you on purpose, *and* I flipped you off."

Arlo takes a big slurp of his Topo Chico and then points the bottle's neck at me. "That's pretty weak. I thought you were gonna say you murdered me by suffocation."

I narrow my eyes at Arlo. "I'm being serious."

"So, what?" Arlo says. "You're apologizing to me for something I don't remember, which is *another* thing I won't remember tomorrow, if you keep on looping."

He starts looking pensive, like he's contemplating—I

don't know, quantum physics?

"Maybe it's pointless to apologize," I admit, "but I feel crappy about it. So, sorry."

"Well, I was the one who left on tour without giving you the heads-up."

"Yeah."

"You were really pissed about that, huh?"

I glare at Arlo. "You were so sneaky, I didn't even find out until my third Monday. And that's nothing to look *proud* about."

Because Arlo sure looks proud. He winks at me before letting out a carbonated belch. A nearby diner glances our way, looking scandalized.

"Huh," Arlo says. "I'm thinking how wild it would be if you really were in a time loop."

My glare intensifies. "You said you believed me."

"I do," Arlo says, "but I'm working out the logic. I've been thinking . . . how are you so sure you've got a grip on the mechanics?"

"What do you mean?"

"Well, you've got a *theory* on how to make the loop stop, but you haven't actually tried it."

I don't like how doubtful Arlo sounds. I swallow uneasily, the lemonade stinging my throat.

"D-do you think I'm wrong?" I ask, faltering.

"Look," says Arlo. "I'm not trying to give you an existential crisis, but the stories I've seen about time loops? It's not the person *in* them who's in control. It's some outside force that's, like, teaching said person a lesson."

"What lesson am I supposed to learn?"

Arlo ticks up a brow. "Don't flip off your brother?"

"Ha, *ha*," I say dryly. "Anyway, if that's it, I already learned my lesson. So, no problem."

"But what if you haven't?" Arlo challenges. "What if you're not even close to learning your lesson? What if you've got ten years of Mondays left?"

I stare at Arlo, the barstool beneath my butt feeling suddenly distant.

"You're just trying to freak me out," I say.

"I'm *not*. I'm just guessing there are only so many times you plan on sharing your secret with me in these supposed alternate universes. If that's the case, I figure I should try to help you out. Open your eyes to the possibilities."

"The dark, depressing ones," I mutter.

"Another thing," Arlo says. "Why are you so sure the loop is Q. S. Murray's doing? If she's a witch, or whatever, why hasn't she used her magic to become independently wealthy? Why put in all that effort to write a way-too-long fantasy series?"

I glower at Arlo. "Relevane is not too long. And maybe

she writes because she *likes* to write. Isn't that why you play music?"

"Eh. I don't know if it's the same."

I'm starting to feel annoyed. If some outside force is teaching anyone a lesson, why isn't it *Arlo*? Why doesn't he get a lecture about, I don't know, giving your family advance notice before you peace out forever?

I don't feel like fighting with Arlo, though. Not today. We finish our drinks in silence and head back to the street. We have to stand close together beneath his umbrella, and I can hear the hitch in Arlo's voice when he tells me, "I'm supposed to meet up with the band soon."

I peer up at him. "What if you were late?"

"I can't—" Arlo starts, but I cut him off.

"I'm not saying don't go. I'm not even saying you have to tell Dads your plan. Just . . . couldn't you leave a little later? We could have dinner together, one last time."

"Jeez, Vivian." Arlo laughs. "It's not like I'm dying."

"I know," I say, "but this feels like a big deal."

I'm trying to hold down the desperate feeling that's clawing up my chest.

This can't be it, my brain shouts. *This can't be the end of the Lantzes as I know us.*

"Dinner's your favorite," I tell him. "Grilled veggies and cheese, plus tangerine poppy seed salad."

Arlo is quiet as we walk down South Congress. My foot lands in a puddle, but I shake it off, keeping my eyes on him. I know the look on Arlo's face. He's actually considering my proposal. Behind my back, I cross every finger I can.

"Dinner," he says, at last. "But that's it."

I know it's not enough. Tomorrow, if the time loop resets, none of this will matter. Tomorrow, if it *doesn't* reset, Arlo will be gone.

But maybe that's why I need this dinner so badly. I feel worn down and—more than that—alone. I just need someone else to understand what I'm going through. I need my big brother to stick around a little longer.

☘ ☘ ☘

After Arlo makes a call to the band—a conversation that involves the word "flooding" and *plenty* of cussing—the two of us discuss our options. We consider staying out and maybe catching a movie downtown at the Violet Crown. Guilt is powerful stuff, though, and in the end we figure that Dads could use our help at the shop. We also figure they won't be *too* pissed if we come clean about playing hooky right away. I decide to tell them I skipped school because I was too nervous to go without Cami, and Arlo will tell them he skipped to take care of me, which . . . isn't a full-on lie.

Dads definitely aren't happy when we get home, but in the end, they don't try to convince us to go back to school. Instead, they swap solemn looks, and Pop says what I expected to hear: "We're not angry with you. We're disappointed."

"I'm a *little* angry," Da informs us, adjusting his collar. Then he puts both of us to work.

Pop and Da have a handle on the back-room situation, so I'm sent into the shop with cleaner and paper towels. I start by wiping down the curio cabinet near the stairs, and I shudder, like I always do, at Pop's porcelain doll collection.

I feel a sudden sprinkling sensation on my arm. Turning, I see Arlo two display cases down, whistling innocently with a spray bottle in hand.

"*Jerk*," I say, attempting to spritz him back. But my nozzle's on spray, not stream, and the cleaner mists into thin air before it can reach him.

Arlo hoots. "Nice try, Barficorn."

I'm tempted to call him a jerk again, but I don't. After all, the reason Arlo's cleaning displays with me is because he chose to come home. He put his big plans on hold for *me*.

Later, we set the table upstairs. Dads have mellowed out since this afternoon, but us playing hooky is still a *thing*, obviously. Over dinner, Pop asks about Cami and if I've talked to her today.

"Yes," I fib, but *is* it a lie? I've talked to her today, just not *this* day. "She's trying out for dance team, and she met this girl named Fatima."

"That's great," Pop says, watching me cautiously.

"I'm fine," I reassure him. "I just got nervous today."

"It's okay to miss someone," Pop tells me. "That's the most normal thing in the world. It only gets bad when we don't talk about *why* we're feeling that way."

I know that Pop's talking about Cami, and I get it; I'd sure be worried if my kid skipped their first day of eighth grade. But I'm thinking of Arlo. It's normal to miss him, too, I guess.

I look between Arlo and Da, wishing I had the guts to say something like, "Arlo, Da needs to hear that you love him." Or, "Da, Arlo needs to know he's got your support."

I'm no peacemaker, though. That's something you have to train at for six years in the Elystrian Court, and even then, wars still break out in Marladia. I can't force Arlo to talk, and he doesn't say much, but it's dinner with my family—the four of us, together. It's a big change to this Monday night, and I think it's one we all needed.

Arlo and I clear the table as Da and Pop head into the den and turn on the TV. And I know, even before Arlo says my name, that our time is up.

"I'll send you postcards, if you want," he tells me. "Like Aunt Xime does."

I smile, but my heart's not in it. All I say is, "Sure."

We stand at the top of the stairs. A Netflix show is blaring from down the hall, and Dads don't have a clue that Arlo is saying goodbye. Trixie must have an inkling, though. She's skittered out to join us, and she whines softly, leaning against my calf. Arlo and I kneel to scratch her in her two favorite spots: right over her tail and behind the ears.

"I'll text Dads later tonight," Arlo says, "but I want to do it in my own time. I know you think maybe that's not enough, but that's how I'm handling it."

I give Arlo a hard look. Then I tell him, "Okay."

This is Arlo's secret, after all—one I wouldn't even be in on if I *weren't* an all-knowing Time God.

"So. Is this your last Monday, or is it back to the loop?" Arlo stills his hand over Trixie's ears, and that's when I know, for sure, that he *does* believe me.

Something clicks into place then. Another realization. This was a weird day. No school. No *Jaguar Gazette*. No Gemma. Today was about my family, and . . . I *needed* that.

I was so sure of myself when I got my first second chance. Now all I'm sure of is that I don't know what the heck I'm doing. Something always ends up going wrong. If I start the loop again tomorrow, will I just end up needing a seventh chance, and then an *eighth*, and then a *ninth*? When will it end?

Something else I didn't expect about this time loop: it's *lonely*. I guess that's why today was a nice change. I've been keeping this magical secret to myself. Now, finally, I've told someone else, and he believes me.

Well, I don't want to lose that. I'm tired of being on my own.

If I'm seriously cursed to never have a perfect first day of school, then I might as well keep the Monday when I got to eat nachos for breakfast.

That's why I tell Arlo, "The loop stops here."

He breaks into a crooked grin. "Aw, Barficorn. You're keeping our special day together?"

"Don't let it go to your head," I warn.

I think about the goal in my journal: *Make things right with Arlo*. I don't know if this counts, but it's something.

We get to our feet, despite Trixie's plaintive snorts. Then Arlo does something super surprising: he pulls me into a hug.

"Love you, Viv," he whispers into my hair.

"Love you back," I say, and I mean it with my whole heart.

I watch from the landing as Arlo heads down the stairs. He throws me a final wave before slipping into the dimness of the shop. Then he's gone, on his way to . . . I don't know where. I never ended up asking him. Reno, maybe. San Diego.

I have to go where the music leads.

I close my eyes, wishing that if there's any magic left float-
ing around, it follows Arlo and keeps him safe as he sets off
on the road.

Back in my bedroom, I find a notification on my phone:
one missed call from Cami.

I could call her back. Could come right out and say, *Cami,
hold on to your butt, because I've got a Code Unicorn.*

But it's not as easy as that. I've kept Cami in the dark for
so long, hoping I'd have a perfect first day to tell her about in
the end. Now that I'm stopping this time loop, no better off
than before? That'll take some extra explaining. And I can't
do that tonight.

"Tomorrow," I say, crawling into bed.

The lobster claw cramps are back, but I don't get out of
bed—not even for ibuprofen.

It takes all the strength I've got to say out loud, "Q. S.
Murray? It's Vivian Lantz, and I want the magic loop to end.
I wish for it to be Tuesday when I wake up."

There. I've said it. No take backs.

No more attempts to break my first-day curse.

No more *exhaustion* over making another freaking mistake.

I'm just too tired to keep on looping. So, it's like I told
Arlo: the loop stops here.

18

"WHOA, WHOA, WHOA!"

I wake to the sound of rain on the roof and Arlo's voice shouting from downstairs.

I don't move an inch. Even though the fog of sleep is still clearing from my head, I'm awake enough to know this much: it didn't work.

I did everything right last night. I made my wish out loud, for Q. S. Murray to hear. I asked for today to be Tuesday.

It's not.

"Dads. Get down here, quick!" Arlo screams.

Footsteps thud outside my door, followed by Trixie's yelps. Arlo yells about the leak above his bed, and Da cusses like a pirate on the high seas.

I stare at the plastic planets above my bed in disbelief.

It's Monday again.

Arlo's words from yesterday whoosh into my memory: *How are you so sure you've got a grip on the mechanics?*

And it's like I'm being swept up by an ice-cold tidal wave.

Turns out, I don't have a grip. Turns out, I have no idea how the magic works after all.

I bunch the bedsheets in my hands. What if this is my fate—the *ultimate* curse? Am I doomed to live out the first day of eighth grade for eternity? I'm so freaked out, I could puke.

Yeah, that's the right idea: I'll fake sick. Dads will let me stay home, and I'll ride out this day in bed, eating Jell-O and rereading Relevane books. I'd way rather do that then slog through another terrible day at school.

Dragging my hands down my face, I consider my options: I really could fake sick. Or I could skip school with Arlo for another day. Heck, I could steal all the money from Dads' cashbox and skip town. I could hitchhike to Albuquerque or the freaking *moon*. I could do anything today, and none of it would matter. What does *anything* matter if don't know how to get out of this loop?

Cold dread wells up inside me. *Am* I cursed? Am I trapped forever? Am I supposed to be learning a lesson?

"Well, *what*?" I demand, slamming my hands on the comforter. "What lesson, huh?!"

Arlo told me that in that movie, *Groundhog Day*, the main guy had to learn not to be a jerk. Is that *my* problem? Am I supposed to act nicer? Do better? Try *again* to make today perfect?

The dread pools higher in my gut, thick as tar. I don't have it in me to aim for perfection anymore. If that's the lesson I'm supposed to learn, count me out.

The muted sound of voices drifts into my bedroom. Arlo is home. The back room is flooding again. And suddenly, I want to be there, with Arlo and Dads.

My brain is fried. My nerves are frazzled. My hopes are in the dumps. I can't spend another second wondering why I'm stuck in this loop. I need a distraction, so for once? I'm grateful for the rain.

Dads and Arlo are in the back room, scrambling to save boxes.

"Woof," I say, because even after all these days, it's still a disastrous sight.

I form an assembly line with Arlo, handing down boxes to where Pop sits, unloading each one, shaking out clothes, and tossing what can't be salvaged. As we work, I look around.

There's a crease in Da's brow as deep as the Celater Gorge, and he's muttering under his breath about gutters and flood insurance. Pop's wearing his favorite glasses—the sparkly rainbow ones—and the glow of a nearby lamp illuminates his eyes. Then there's Arlo, with his rain-dampened hair and wrinkled Aerosmith tee. I wonder what's going on in his brain as he lugs another box my way. Is he daydreaming about the Neon Spurs's first show on the road? Is he worried about what Dads will do when he leaves? Is he thinking at all about me?

Who knows? I'm a time looper, not a mind reader.

I get a tingly feeling standing there in the back room. Sure, it's a disaster, but . . . it brought us Lantzes together, didn't it? It gave us one last chance to join forces and take care of the home we share.

There's something in the air here, Aunt Ximena said about the shop. *It's magical.*

I wonder if that's what we've got on our hands here: magic that only *looks* like disaster.

I glance up at the secondhand clock to see that it's seven twenty. I'll need to leave for school soon.

Do I even feel like going?

I'm stuck on the question for so long that Pop follows my gaze.

He gasps. "My God. How'd it get so late?"

Frigid dread floods my guts again. I don't want this moment to slip away. Not yet.

So I try Arlo's line: "I could stay home from school to help."

Da gives me a look. "Nice try, Viv."

I know then that it's no use fighting. The magic of this

moment is slipping away, whether I like it or not. That's the way it's got to be. I sigh, resigning myself to my fate.

I leave the back room, but I don't head upstairs right away. Trixie comes first. I scoop her up from where she's huddled under a credenza, whimpering.

"It's okay, girl," I say, hooking on her leash. "When you gotta go, you gotta go."

When she's through with her business outside, I pat her dry and let her go scampering to a new hiding place, under a chaise longue. Then it's back to business as usual: a quick hairstyle, plus makeup, and a stop at the menstrual shelf. I put on my regular first day outfit—no change in the routine. It's just easier that way.

I'm slipping my phone into my backpack when I spot the hyacinth journal, sitting on the nightstand by my bed. The sight of it drags a weary rattle from my lungs. *The Master Plan.* I'm too tired to even think about goals number one through four. So I leave the journal where it is, gold blooms winking in the pale light.

Once I'm buckled into the passenger seat of Arlo's car, I inhale, taking in the familiar corn chip smell. At this point, I know the song on the radio so well that I can bob my head along to the drums. That's what I'm doing when I notice the station wagon veering into our lane.

"Hey," I tell Arlo. "Watch out."

Arlo notices just in time. He hits the breaks and his horn, but there's no crunch of metal. No wreck.

"Seriously, dude?" he shouts, as a never-ending line of taillights forms ahead of us.

Ah, yes. The traffic jam. I kick my heels up on the dash, accepting my fate. Sure, the wreck would've sucked, but traffic? I can deal with that.

Arlo turns down the radio, checking the clock.

"You might be late," he tells me.

"It's okay," I say. "Principal Liu always gives the same speech. I won't miss much."

Minutes pass, and we finally inch out of traffic, but when Arlo pulls the Civic in front of the school's empty entrance, I don't get out. I'm busy thinking.

Here's what I know I can expect from today: the backroom flood, the traffic jam, parabolas, tuna salad. What I *don't* know? How this freaking time loop works. This could be the sixth of *six hundred* Mondays, or it could be my last. There's no telling.

But in case this *is* my final chance to talk to Arlo in person, I'd like it to mean something.

"Hey," I say, nudging his elbow across the console. "I hope the tour goes well."

Arlo looks confused at first. Then? *Terrified.*

"W-what?" he stammers.

"Don't worry," I say. "I'm not telling Dads. Your secret's safe with me. Just maybe, when you text them? Say you love them. I know it's corny, but I think they need to hear it."

Arlo blinks slowly. "Oh . . . kay."

I heave open the door and get out, slinging my backpack over my shoulder.

"And for the record?" I say. "I love you, too."

I close the door, leaving Arlo frozen behind the wheel. Eventually, he shakes his head, like he's shaking off a chill, and lifts one hand in a kind of half wave. I wave back, watching as he drives off into the pouring rain.

Bye, Arlo, I think, shoving my hands into my rain jacket pockets. *Maybe for a day. Maybe for forever. What do I know anymore?*

Then there's nothing left to do. I turn, hurrying toward the school entrance, and—*wham.*

Pain cracks across my ribs and lodges in my gut. I'm losing my balance, reeling out from under the awning and into the rain. My back hits the ground, and air whooshes out of me. Rain smacks my face, causing my nose to itch. I sit up and let out a giant sneeze.

"Oh my gosh," says the girl standing over me. The girl who *ran into* me.

It's Gemma, of course.

"Here," she says, reaching out a hand.

I look up, my eyes locking on hers, and suddenly? I want to laugh. Here I am, late for school and sprawled out in a muddy heap—*again*. On my very first day of school, I thought this was a disaster to clean up and forget as fast as possible. I didn't know then what a cool person Gemma was. I didn't know what a massive crush I'd get on her. I didn't know that, *actually*, her running into me was the best thing that would happen to me all day.

And then it happens. It's like the heavens open up and flaming angels burst out, blowing trumpets in my face. My fall hasn't just knocked the wind out of me; it's jarred loose memories, too. I'm thinking of the back-room flood—magic that looked like disaster. I'm thinking of what Arlo said to me yesterday, over breakfast: *It's not about getting it right. It's more about getting it wrong.*

Holy crap.

All this time, I've been trying to use magic to break my first-day curse. I thought that, with the help of my Master Plan, I could use my second chances—however many it took—until I got everything *just right*.

Arlo said that maybe the magic was trying to teach me a lesson. But what if that lesson is the exact *opposite* of what I thought? What if my first day of school isn't supposed to be perfect? What if it's supposed to be messy and full of mistakes? What if it's about *getting it wrong*?

I've spent the past week trying so hard to rid myself of the first-day curse. But now I'm wondering—if it's okay to get things wrong, then maybe all of my bad first days haven't been cursed at all. Maybe they've just been . . . well, *life*.

So what if today there *were* no Master Plan? Sure, it wouldn't be perfect, but it would be real, at least. A real day of mistakes. That's what I want: a second chance at all my second chances. A chance to undo my attempts to make this the perfect day. I don't have to suffer on *purpose*; I'm definitely glad I'm prepared for my period. But as for the rest? What if I stopped trying to make today fit into my plan? What if the plan is *there is no plan*?

No more pressure. No more perfection. No worries about *happening* to life. I'm simply going to *live*.

"Uh, Vivian?"

My thoughts clear out of my head. Gemma's still looking down at me, and my butt is thoroughly soaked in mud. The eight o'clock bell sounds—*ding-dum-ding*.

Right. Time to start living.

I grab hold of Gemma's hand.

"Thanks," I say, as she hauls me to my feet.

Gemma looks me over in horror and asks, "Are you okay?"

I rub my sore tailbone but nod. "I'm fine."

Gemma looks uncertain. "I've got makeup wipes to help with your mascara, if you want."

It's only makeup wipes, but my heart nearly explodes. This moment with Gemma Cohen? It's worth me falling in mud a hundred times.

"We're late," I tell her, motioning toward the school. "Want to go in together?"

"Oh."

Gemma glances at the doors, and my breath catches. What if she says no this time?

I wait for her answer with bated breath.

Then, a small smile curls up Gemma's face, and her left dimple appears.

"Sure," she says. "That'd be nice."

I smile right back at Gemma, and then? We run. We sprint to the auditorium, and when we arrive, we take the seats that Mrs. Campos points us to. Gemma hands me a makeup wipe, and I rub it beneath my eyes, but I don't bother with being precise. I'd rather focus on the fact that I'm sitting here with Gemma. I'm not worried about Amberleigh anymore, or about making a good impression on Alex. There are no steps in my plan to cross off. Instead, a new idea hits me, and when the houselights come on, I whisper to Gemma, "You're in Ms. Lally's class, right?"

"Yeah," Gemma says, looking surprised.

"Wanna walk there together?" I ask.

Gemma's eyes widen. She glances into the crowd, and I

can guess who's on her mind: Amberleigh. I see her filing out of her row with Alex, and there's not much time left if we want to avoid them.

Gemma turns back to me, wearing a steely look.

"Yeah, actually," she says, "I'd like that a lot."

"Great." I pop out of my chair, practically zooming toward the doors at maximum speed.

"Whoa!" Gemma yelps, but she keeps up. She's laughing as she says, "You're *fast*."

"Something about pre-algebra class," I say breathlessly. "Really gets me fired up."

Gemma keeps laughing as we escape into the hallway. "Ooh, yeah. Same. Numbers are so sexy."

Which gets *me* giggling.

It's as we turn a corner that I see an iguana shirt passing by. I do a double take, and sure enough, the iguana is attached to none other than Mike Brot.

That's when another idea hits me. I grin, thinking it through, and decide to go for it.

"Hey, Mike!" I call out.

When he spots me, he waves and makes his way in my direction.

"I, uh, gotta talk to him," I tell Gemma.

"No worries," she says, shrugging. "I'll save you a seat in class?"

My stomach flips ten times in a row, but I manage to nod. Then Gemma's gone, and Mike is upon me, flashing his student council smile.

"Nice shirt," I tell him.

I mean it, too. It's taken me a few days to realize, but that iguana's pretty impressive—shades of teal and purple, with iridescent scales. More power to Mike.

See, I'm not sure I've ever given Mike Brot a fair shot, and I do feel bad about the time I made up the story about the pooping volleyball team. Now I'd like to make things right.

"Look," I tell Mike, lugging off my backpack. "I'm a terrible baker, and so are my dads, but I want to contribute to the bake sale."

I zip open the bag's back pocket, tugging out my wallet. There's a ten-dollar bill in there from the last time I helped Dads with inventory. I tug it out and offer it to Mike.

"Oh." Hesitantly, Mike takes the bill. "A-are you sure?"

"Totally," I say.

Mike looks like he doesn't know how to feel. I guess he settles on glad, because he smiles and says, "This means a lot."

"Happy to help." I turn to walk away.

"No." Mike puts out a hand to stop me. "Like, a *lot*. I'm in charge of getting people to sign up, and it's not easy. People ignore me or, like, run off. Honestly? I've been dreading asking for volunteers at lunch. But Ms. Vela is gonna be super stoked to know that we've already got a donation."

"It's . . . not that much," I say, starting to feel self-conscious.

Mike shakes his head. "It's the thought that counts. Speaking of which, um . . . hang on."

Mike opens his own backpack, rummaging through its contents. Moments later, he pulls out a soda can and hands it to me.

"Dr Pepper?" I say.

Mike shrugs. "Consider it a token of my appreciation."

Before I can even say thanks, he takes off in a sprint. I watch that iridescent iguana go, wondering how I could've been annoyed by Mike Brot before. I guess I was so obsessed with my Master Plan, Mike just seemed like an obstacle in its way. Now that I've taken the time to actually talk to him? He seems nice. *And* I got a soda. That's something new.

The hallway is emptying out, and I should be in room 1067. I pick up the pace, breezing past the restrooms. I don't have the time to clean the mud off my outfit, but that's okay. I make it to Ms. Lally's class, where Gemma's saved me a seat at the back of the room.

"Thanks," I whisper, setting down my things.

She's already opened her notebook, and I notice the purple-ink face of Princess Ruth.

I point and ask, "Do you draw?"

It feels a little wrong, asking a question I already know the answer to, but Gemma nods and says, "For fun." Then she eyes the front of the class. "You're not going to, like, rat me out to Ms. Lally?"

I smile conspiratorially. "No way."

Gemma makes a dramatic hand swipe across her brow, just as Ms. Lally calls the class to attention.

I still don't know much about parabolas, but I have a major appreciation for Princess Ruth. And today, by the end of pre-algebra, I've worked up the nerve to ask Gemma a big question.

"Do you want to have lunch together?" I say.

Gemma doesn't answer for so long, I start to worry I've said the wrong thing. This isn't a question I've asked before. Maybe it's a step too far.

But then she says, "That'd be cool."

And my heart soars.

"I don't want to eat in the cafeteria, though," Gemma adds, "if that's okay with you."

"Sure," I say, feeling lighter than air. "I don't like the caf, anyway."

"Oh?" Gemma quirks a brow.

I shrug. "Bad memories."

271

But the truth is, I'd eat anywhere if it meant spending time with Gemma.

❦ ❦ ❦

Today in language arts, I take the seat closest to Virgil's aquarium. I give him a friendly wave, and he glares back. That's fish for you.

Ms. Rose talks about American poets, and Jordan Gilday answers the metaphor question. Me? I'm lost in thought.

I'm remembering how Ms. Rose told me that writing should light a fire in me. What she said ticked me off at first, but if I dig down to the truth, I'm *not* lit up about the *Jaguar Gazette*. I never have been. Interviewing kids for the "Shining Spotlight" is fine, I guess, but I'd rather be writing stories about magical worlds.

Well, who says I can't?

I thought that because there wasn't an author club at Bluebonnet Middle, I'd have to pick newspaper writing instead. I tried to make that fit into my plan because that's what Q. S. Murray said I should do. But what did Arlo tell me over breakfast yesterday?

Who's to say what worked for her will work for you?

As Ms. Rose talks about Walt Whitman, my gaze drifts to the poster over Virgil's tank. I hadn't noticed it before.

I'd been so obsessed with making a good impression on Ms. Rose, rehearsing what I should say, I didn't see what was right in front of me: a bunch of names and author portraits, under the title *Famous Short Story Writers*.

There's Edgar Allan Poe and Gabriel García Márquez. There's Alice Munro and Shirley Jackson. There's Haruki Murakami and Flannery O'Connor and Anton Chekhov. They're authors from different times, writing in different styles and languages, but they have one thing in common: they loved to write *stories*.

And that gets me thinking . . . what if there are other kids at Bluebonnet who love writing as much as I do? Not writing news articles but writing fiction. Short stories. Novels. What if those kids exist, and I just don't know them because there isn't a club for us? *Yet*.

Sure, joining the *Jaguar Gazette* might make me a better writer. I could learn how to finish articles and be okay with people reading my work. But I could do all that in an author club, too. I could even start by writing *short stories*. Those might be easier to finish than, say, a six-book fantasy series. I could share those stories with other club members and get used to the feeling. I could have *fun*.

I think this is the fire that Ms. Rose was talking about. *This* is what I want to do.

All I had to do to get here was trash my old plan and open my eyes. The answer was hanging over Virgil's fish tank all along.

You sly devil, I think, smirking in Virgil's direction.

Then? I turn to a blank sheet of notebook paper and get to work.

🌷 🌷 🌷

After class, my heart is beating fast. I'm more nervous than ever before about talking to Ms. Rose. But I think that's a good sign—a sign of how much this idea means to me.

I ask Gemma if I can meet up with her in a few minutes, in front of the caf, and she says yes. She leaves the classroom, and soon it's just me and Ms. Rose.

"Hello," I say, approaching Ms. Rose's desk.

"Hello, Vivian!" She looks up from feeding Virgil his flakes.

Now it's time to change the script.

"So, I like writing," I say. "Mr. Garcia might've told you that."

Ms. Rose sets down the fish food, dusting off her hands. "He *did*. He said that you were a stellar student last year."

My ears burn, but I press ahead. I've got to get this out.

"I write stories," I tell Ms. Rose. "They're fan fiction, mostly, based on the Relevane series?"

Ms. Rose brightens. "Of course! The Q. S. Murray books."

I nod. I feel self-conscious, but more than that? I feel brave.

"Anyway," I go on, "I know there are online groups out there, but there's nothing here at school for authors, specifically. That's what got me thinking about *this*."

I hand over a folded sheet of notebook paper—the sheet I've been secretly drawing on in class. Ms. Rose unfolds it, looking over a makeshift flyer. In penciled bubble letters, it says,

Join the Bluebonnet Author Club!

And beneath that, in careful print,

Show up every Thursday after school to share your stories and discuss your favorite books.

Adviser: Ms. Rose

Student leader: Vivian Lantz

Ms. Rose takes a long time reading over the flyer.

I wait patiently at first, but then, when it gets to be too much, I clear my throat and say, "It doesn't have to be on Thursdays. Any day of the week is fine. And if you're too busy to advise, then—"

"No." Ms. Rose cuts me off. When her eyes meet mine, they're shimmering. "I think it's a fantastic idea. I'm sure there are other students who'd love to join. There is a procedure to starting up new clubs, and we might have to cut through some red tape. But if you trust me to, Vivian, I'd be happy to take up the cause."

"R-really?" I ask. I'm honestly kind of shocked.

"Really," Ms. Rose says.

I break into a grin. "Then *yes*."

Ms. Rose refolds my flier and asks, "Do you mind if I keep this?"

"It's yours," I say.

"Then I'll get to work. In the meantime, I can name a few young writer programs in Austin off the top of my head. Tell you what: I'll have a list written down for you tomorrow. You can show it to your dads and look up more about each program online—if that's something you want to do *outside* of school, as well."

I smile so wide, I must be showing every tooth.

"Thanks, Ms. Rose," I say.

She taps the flyer and tells me, "More on this soon."

On my way out of class, I'm careful to avoid that extension cord. I mean, making mistakes is one thing, but I won't go out of my way to cause a disaster.

"See ya, Virgil!" I call, as I leave class.

He watches me go with his all-knowing fish eyes.

19

GEMMA'S WAITING FOR me outside the cafeteria doors.

"Hey!" I call, running up to her.

She smiles, revealing the baby-pink bands on her braces.

"I brought my own lunch," she tells me, "and it's pretty big, if you want to share. But, like, I understand if you want to get your own."

Do I want to another round of tuna salad? My stomach gurgles sulkily at the thought. That's a no.

"Your lunch sounds great," I say, "if you really don't mind."

"Cool," Gemma replies. "Let's jet."

She leads me down one hallway and then another, and we reach a set of double doors. Gemma pushes them open, and we head into the east stairwell. At last, the great mystery has been solved. *This* is where Gemma has escaped to every Monday.

"Teachers never come this way during lunch," she explains, as we sit on the stairs.

Gemma takes out a lunch bag, unpacking a big container

of pasta salad with a plastic fork, a jumbo box of raisins, and a couple of string cheeses. She hands me a cheese and places the rest of the food on the step between us.

"I nabbed an extra fork from the caf while I was waiting," she says, tugging a fork from the front pouch of her backpack and handing it to me.

"*Nice*," I say, taking the contraband silverware. Before I dig into the pasta, though, *another* idea comes to me.

I open my backpack and dig out the can of soda that Mike Brot gave me.

"Want this?" I say, offering it to Gemma.

Gemma's eyes light up. "Oh my God, you *rock*. Dr Pepper's my favorite."

You told me, I could say, but don't, since that would be majorly creepy. All the same, it's nice to be living in the moment. I've lived so many Mondays now, but I've never ended up in a stairwell, eating rotini with Gemma and cheering her up with a soda. This is my favorite lunch by far.

"Have you eaten here before?" I ask, looking around. "Like, last year?"

"Yeah," Gemma tells me. "Once, after I went camping in Dripping Springs with Amberleigh's family. She and I got in a fight, and I needed space to think."

I chew my string cheese thoughtfully. "Is that what this is? Space to think?"

I feel suddenly guilty. I invited myself to crash Gemma's lunch plans. Maybe she wanted to be alone.

But Gemma shakes her head. "More like space. I've already done the thinking."

"What have you been thinking about?" I ask. "Um, if you want to share."

Gemma grimaces. "Well, there's this party tonight. Amberleigh, Tate, and I—we've been doing it since fifth grade. But this summer, they did something. . . . They were just . . . The thing is, I don't even know if I want to be friends with them anymore. But if I don't go to the party, Amberleigh will make a huge deal out of it."

"You mean, *she* won't want to be friends?"

"Pretty much."

"But . . . isn't that what you want?"

Gemma sighs. "I *think* so. But not going tonight feels permanent. It's like I'm making a giant statement, and I can't take it back. I don't know if it's better to go with the flow for now."

"Well, how's that worked out so far?"

Gemma sets down her fork. "Not so great. It's just that eight grade—"

"Sucks," I finish.

"Yeah," Gemma agrees. "It's not a good time to lose your only friends."

"Tell me about it." I think of Cami and the miles between us. Hesitantly, I add, "It could be a good time to *make* friends, though."

Gemma looks at me, and it takes all my courage to look back. I'm thinking of what she said three nights ago, about wanting to be friends with me and Cami. Then I start feeling bad. I wish that Gemma could know about the magic. It feels wrong to know so much about her when she's only spent one Monday with me.

In this moment, I make a promise to myself: if I get out of this loop, and Gemma and I become friends? I will tell her this secret. I don't think that she would laugh or treat me like I'm full of it. She'd believe me, like good friends do. And maybe, over time, we could be more than friends. Maybe Gemma would tell *me* a secret—that she's crushing on me as much as I'm crushing on her.

But that's a whole lot of *maybe*s, including a magical one. I refocus on the here and now.

Gemma mentions a new baking show she's been watching called *Pastry Legend*, and I promise to check it out. When I say how pumped I am for the next Relevane book, Gemma says she wants to read the first one, and I tell her I'll lend her my copy.

We swap numbers, and when we do, I see that it's almost one o'clock. Gemma and I scramble to pick up our trash and sneak out of the stairwell. It feels like we're spies on a secret mission, tiptoeing down the hallways; and once we've made it to the cafeteria trash bins, I tell Gemma, "That was fun."

"We could do it again tomorrow," she suggests.

"It's a date."

Whoops.

"I mean, a *friend* date," I correct. "Or, like, whatever."

"Yeah. Like, whatever." Gemma grins, revealing the dimple in her left cheek.

So naturally, I can't see straight for a full five seconds. Maybe that's why I don't notice Amberleigh headed our way.

"Gemma!" she shouts. "Where have you *been*?"

She strides up to us, holding a lunch tray, Alex by her side.

"Was your mom late again, or something?" she asks, practically in our faces. Tate and Neil are a few steps behind, hauling their own trays.

"Yeah," Gemma says tersely, crossing her arms. "There was traffic, too."

Amberleigh smooths a hand over her ponytail and gives me a long once-over, taking in my mud-caked clothes. "What happened to *you*, Vivian?"

I've gotta smile at a question like that. A *lot* has happened to me. Like, six Mondays' worth of stuff. Not that Amberleigh knows that. She doesn't remember tripping me at lunch or pushing me into Tate's pool or any of her other scorpion stings. But even if I *weren't* in a magical time loop that only I can remember, I don't think Amberleigh would care that she'd done those terrible things. I'm realizing something big: while I've been taking my second chances, I've given Amberleigh second chances, too. And every single time, she's ended up being plain *mean*.

Well, if a magical time loop can't change Amberleigh Allen, then I, Vivian Lantz, most certainly can't. Ruining her shoes won't make her better. Neither will dropping a trayful of pudding on her head. Even if I told her off in front of the whole cafeteria, it wouldn't make a difference.

While I've been stuck in this loop, I've learned a thing or two about time. I figured out a while back that it's not worth my time to be Amberleigh's friend. But now I'm seeing that it's not worth my time to be her *enemy*, either. I've got better things to do with my Monday.

That's why I choose not to answer Amberleigh. I simply turn and walk off. I *leave*, feeling more euphoric than the Queen of Elystria on coronation day.

"Uh, *excuse me!*" Amberleigh calls after me. "I'm talking to you, *weirdo.*"

This weirdo keeps on walking.

Then . . . *splat.*

Something hits my back. I can feel it through my ringer

tee. It's goopy and cold, and it smells sickly sweet. Around me, the cafeteria grows quiet. Kids whisper to each other. I hear the words "fight" and "banana pudding."

'Cause that's what Amberleigh has catapulted at me from her lunch tray: a heaping spoonful of banana pudding. It drips off my shirt, hitting the floor in pale yellow globs. I turn, facing her down across the room. She smiles smugly, setting the rest of her lunch on the conveyor belt.

"What?" she barks, when she notices Gemma glaring at her. "I was trying to get her attention."

Gemma isn't the only person staring at Amberleigh. Tate looks shocked; Alex, too. Neil is snickering. But some of the kids at the tables near us look mad.

"What the frick, Amberleigh?" calls a guy from our grade—Justin Schmidt.

"Yeah, not cool," mutters a seventh grader close by.

"You okay, Vivian?" asks a voice at my back.

I spin around. Mike Brot has jogged across the caf. He puffs out breaths, shaking his head, and says, "That was messed up. Here?"

He holds out a napkin, like he's asking permission. Dazedly, I nod, and he swipes some of the pudding from my back. My ears are ringing. I feel unsteady, the way I did my first fateful day in this caf. Then there's gentle pressure on my arm. Someone's talking to me. They're leading me out of the cafeteria, toward the restrooms. It's only once we're at the sinks that I register Gemma's reflection in the mirror.

"I'm so, *so* sorry that happened," she says, wetting a paper towel. "Amberleigh is on some next-level crap."

"It's okay," I say, still stunned.

Then, slowly, I start to smile.

My smile gets wider—so wide that Gemma asks, "Are you all right?"

"Banana pudding *again*," I say. "She's so unoriginal."

Gemma frowns, clearly confused, and says, "I just hope she gets in trouble."

I kind of hope so, too, but knowing Amberleigh's luck, she won't. If a teacher catches wind of what happened, they'll give her a warning at most. She won't get sent to the principal, won't get punished. Not Amberleigh.

That isn't the point, though. The point is that I stopped trying to beat Amberleigh at her game. I stopped playing the game, period.

Gemma waits for the water to turn warm before she pats down my shirt. I stay still as she blots at the stain, feeling little electric currents running down my spine.

After a minute, Gemma surveys her work and says, "Well. You've got a big water spot now, but . . . I guess it kind of goes with the mud?"

I look at her. She looks at me. Then we crack up, and I feel warm all over.

I'm not sure what the future holds for me and Gemma. I'm not even sure I'll be getting out of this time loop anytime soon. But I don't need more second chances to figure out that I want *a* chance with Gemma. A chance for her to get to know me, like I've gotten to know her.

"So, uh, do you want to talk to a teacher?" Gemma asks, tossing the used paper towels. "I bet they'd let you go home early, if you want."

That's probably true. But I'm still thinking of Arlo's words: *It's about getting it wrong.* That's why, in the end, I shake my head.

"Believe me," I tell Gemma, "I've had worse first days."

Pop picks me up after school, and the rest of the afternoon I help out around Be Kind, Rewind. I clean the curio cabinets again, and, just for fun, I rearrange the creepy porcelain doll collection so that a Victorian baby doll with soulless eyes is holding an antique letter opener like a lethal weapon.

Today, business is slow. Dads had to open late because of the leak, and even now the rain is keeping folks away. In the end, Pop locks the front door at six o'clock on the nose, and I head upstairs to help with dinner.

The kitchen fills with the scent of olive oil and grilled red onions as Da hangs up his cell phone and says, "He still won't answer."

This is the toughest part of today: knowing that Arlo is gone. Dads won't find out until they get his text, and I don't have the heart to tell them the truth before that. I'm half hoping that today will be different, and any minute I'll hear the Civic pull into the parking lot.

But Arlo's a no-show, and eventually, after Dads delay dinner by half an hour, we eat. Tonight, I tell Dads about the list of writing programs Ms. Rose said she'd give to me. I'm trying to make them feel better, to take their minds off Arlo's absence. In the end, though, I know that's not my job. This is my loop, not Pop's or Da's. They'll process Arlo's Southwest tour on their own, when the time comes.

I'm chewing the last tangerine slice from my salad when the Relevane theme song blares from my phone. *Cami.*

Oh *no.*

I forgot about her text this morning. For the first time ever, I didn't reply. She has to know that I didn't forget about her on her first day of school. In a panic, I jump from my chair.

"Gotta get this!" I yell at Dads.

Then I'm sprinting to my room, slamming the door, and tumbling onto my bed.

I answer the call with an out-of-breath "Hello?"

"Dolphin *Priiide*!"

There's so much life in Cami's voice, it's like I could reach into my phone and pull her out in the flesh.

If only.

I'd give anything for Cami to be here.

"Hey," I say, cutting her off. "Want to switch to video chat?"

"Um, sure! But I'm warning you, my hair is a mess. I'm still getting used to the humidity."

I scoff. "I've got thunderstorm hair. No big."

We hang up, and this time I call Cami by video. Her face appears on my screen, and I almost start crying.

"I missed talking to you," I say, trying not to choke up.

"Yeah, it's been since, what . . . last Wednesday?"

Something like that.

"Wait." Cami's eyes widen. "You got *bangs*!"

I blink, raising a hand to my hair. Oh yeah.

I've been keeping my Master Plan a secret from Cami for so long, I'd forgotten that she didn't even know about my hair. There is *so* much to fill her in on.

"Do you like them?" I ask her uncertainly.

"Totally! You look like . . ." Cami squints in thought. "A *rocker*! Yeah. Like, rocker chic."

I almost start crying *again*. Cami knows me so well. Of course she does; she's my best friend.

Cami tells me about her day—getting lost, meeting Fatima, and planning to try out for the dance team. She tells me new stuff, too, like how the school hallways are painted to look like the insides of submarines, and how there are outside lockers and more palm trees than she can count.

"I saw my first alligator," she says, looking chilled to the bone. "Mom and I were walking in a park, and it *popped out of the lake.* Mom said she peed herself a little."

That makes me laugh, but not as hard as I would if this were an ordinary day.

Cami must notice, because she asks, "What's up?"

This is the moment of truth. I could do what I've done before and straight-up lie, telling Cami that everything's fine and my first-day curse has been broken. But I'm finally ready to stop keeping secrets. I need my best friend tonight, more than ever. I'm ready to let it out.

"Today was a Code Unicorn," I announce.

Cami just about chokes on the Takis she's been munching. She coughs, raining bits of corn chip on the screen, and next thing, her phone's toppling, the screen a blur of bedspread and carpet.

"Ack!" she squawks, scooping up the phone and righting

it so I can see her wide-eyed stare. "Vivian Mare, why didn't you lead with that?"

I shrug pathetically.

"What kind of magic are we talking?" she practically screams. "Second sight? Thought transference? *Levitation?*"

"Cami, shhhh," I hiss. "What's your mom gonna think?"

Cami gives me a look. "Mama's seen me dress up as Sage Miriel six times in three years. If you're worried she'll think I'm a weirdo, that ship has sailed."

Cami always makes good points. I've really missed that about her.

This is how it happens: I tell Cami about my six Mondays and my four goals. I fess up about wanting to get in with Amberleigh's group and plotting for her and Alex to break up. I tell Cami about my period and the Louboutins. I tell her about Arlo leaving and the day he and I spent together. Then I tell her my theory: Q. S. Murray's MeetNGreet and her promise of magical vibes, plus last night's unanswered wish. I tell her how I'm beginning to doubt that I understand the magic at all.

There are things I still don't share. The private stuff. I don't mention what Gemma told me on Mariposa Drive or what I overheard Da and Pop say about Arlo in the kitchen. I keep to the big facts, the stories that are mine; and when I'm through,

I'm out of breath, and Cami is out of dramatic gasps. She stares at me through the phone screen, mouth agape.

"This is a big deal," she says.

"So . . . you believe me?"

Cami looks affronted. "Of *course*. It's a Code Unicorn."

Tears fill my eyes. I've never missed Cami more. And I've missed her a *lot*.

"There's something else," I say, wincing at the icky feeling in my gut. "I . . . haven't told you any of this until now."

Cami frowns, not understanding. Then light fills her eyes.

"You mean," she says slowly, "you didn't tell me about the magic on any of those other Mondays. You haven't told me until *tonight*."

I bury my head in my hands. "I didn't even tell you about my *first* bad day. It just felt . . . I don't know, too overwhelming." I raise my head, wiping away fresh tears. "I wish I had now. I wanted to before, but . . ."

I pause, trying to figure out what to say on the other side of that "but":

I was too confused?

I didn't want to bum you out?

I wanted to wait until I'd lived the perfect first day?

All of those things are true. Only, there's something else— another reason why I've been ignoring Cami's calls—and I'm just now realizing what that is. It's got to do with the goal that I wrote in my journal three nights ago. The one about needing a new friend.

"Cam," I say quietly, "I feel like we're growing apart."

Cami sits up straight on her bed. "What?"

I sigh. "It's not your fault, or mine. It's just, things aren't the same. Not even with FaceTime or texting. You're not *here*, and your life seems so different already. I've never seen an alligator, and I haven't met Fatima. We're both going through all this new stuff, but we're not doing it together."

Cami is silent for a long time.

"I guess I've been feeling that, too," she says softly. "It sucks, huh?"

"It seriously sucks," I agree. "And things will keep on changing. And you and Fatima will be best friends, and you'll learn all this stuff about dancing that I don't know, and we'll get *further* apart."

I half expect Cami to say "No way!" She doesn't, though. She looks as bummed out as I feel. We both know it's true: we *are* going to grow apart, whether we like it or not.

Cami meets my eyes. "You're still my friend, though, Viv. And we'll always have Relevane."

Tears trickle from my eyes, and I nod. Somehow, even though I'm crying, I feel a little better. I've said out loud the thing that I've been too scared to admit since Cami left for Orlando. And it's true that Cami and I might drift apart, but it's also true that we'll always be friends in spirit. It's true that Cami was my very best friend in sixth and seventh grade—through school and crushes and every important feeling about Torin and Sage Miriel. It's true that she's being a great friend *now*.

"I get why you didn't tell me before," Cami says. "This is . . . a lot."

I sink my head in my hands again. "I thought I had it figured out, but I totally don't. Why do you think my wish didn't work last night?"

When I look up, Cami is squinting into the camera. "Do you really think Q. S. Murray is behind this?"

I frown. "You don't?"

"Well, I don't know. It seems sort of dastardly, doesn't it? Sending you magic without telling you how to use it, letting it mess up your life, trapping you in time? That's pretty diabolical. Doesn't seem like her MO."

"Well, her advice *was* kind of crappy," I point out.

"Maybe. But there's a difference between crappiness and villainy."

"What other explanation is there?" I ask, desperate. "At least this one makes sense. Q. S. Murray writes about magic. She sent me a MeetNGreet. She knew about the curse. She said she'd send *magical vibes*."

"It lines up, I guess," says Cami, sounding unconvinced.

"Was there anything else you remember about that night? Something else you said or did? Anything remotely magic-y?"

I concentrate, but nothing comes to me. Nothing except—

"I *was* reading over my hyacinth journal," I say. "That's where I wrote the Master Plan."

Cami bugs her eyes. She raises a hand to her mouth.

"What?" I get nervous when she doesn't answer me. "Cami, what?"

"Oh no," she whispers. "I didn't even *think*."

"Cami! What?!"

Cami lowers her hand. "Uh. I told you about that journal, right?"

"Yeah. You said you found it here in the shop."

"Mm-hmm. Right. But. I didn't exactly . . . tell you the whole story."

I feel like jumping through my bedroom ceiling. "Sorry, *what*?"

Cami clears her throat once. Twice. "So, uh, remember the day you got back from that trip with your Aunt Xime? I showed up to surprise you, so we could hang out the rest of the day."

I think back to earlier this year, in May, when Arlo and I went to visit Aunt Ximena in Marfa. The day I got home, Cami was on the front stoop of Be Kind, Rewind, waiting for me.

"I remember," I say, wondering what this has to do with anything.

"Well, I got there early, so I sort of poked around the place. I'd been looking for the perfect birthday gift for you for *ages*, and your dads told me how they'd gotten in a new load of stuff that week—stuff you wouldn't have had the chance to see. That's when I found the journal. It was on a shelf with other new books and records your Pop had brought in. I couldn't believe it. It was one-of-a-kind and still blank inside, and there were *hyacinths*. It felt like it was meant to be. So I brought it to the register, and your Da was saying how gorgeous it was, and he told Pop that it was a great find, and *then* both of them got confused, because neither of them remembered buying the journal. They said they had no idea where it'd come from."

I frown. "That's . . . odd."

"Right? They checked their inventory spreadsheet, and it wasn't in there either. It was like the journal had showed up on its own. While they were talking about it, I flipped through the pages, and this note fell out. It was nothing special—just an old sticky note. But it said, *Use me wisely*."

I feel woozy. I grab Mistmorrow and hug him for dear life.

"Well, it was weird," Cami says, "but your dads figured it must've been an oversight, so they still sold me the journal. And, like, I wanted the gift to be a surprise, so that's when I concocted the big reveal, and by the time you got the journal in July, the note seemed like a silly detail to mention. But now I don't know, Viv. It sounds sort of . . . um, *ominous*, given everything's that happened. I'm sorry I didn't mention it before."

My fingers dig into Mistmorrow's mane. "N-no," I say faintly. "This isn't your fault. It was the perfect gift."

"Or so we *thought*."

I shake my head, dazed. *Use me wisely* is a strange warning to put inside a journal. And I don't get how my birthday present just *showed up* in the shop. I know Da, and he's meticulous about his inventory records.

Use me wisely.

Why does that sound familiar?

Then it hits me. Aunt Ximena's words from long ago play in my mind: *There's something in the air here. Or maybe it's in the floorboards or the eaves. It's magical, wherever it's at, so use that magic wisely.*

I've always thought that the shop was special, but *this* isn't what I had in mind. Is it possible? Could the magic have been coming from the journal this whole time?

I look across the room at my backpack.

"Hang on," I say through parched lips.

I crawl across the bed, grabbing my journal from the nightstand and plopping it down on the comforter. I stare.

The back of my neck goes cold, and my palms start to sweat as, in the moonlight, I see what I thought I'd only imagined on my birthday eve: the gold hyacinths are *moving*—petals softly opening, stems crawling up the border of the book. When I blink, the movement stops, but this time, I know better. It wasn't a trick of the light.

With trembling hands, I open the journal and read the words at the top of the first page:

VIVIAN LANTZ'S FOOLPROOF PLAN
FOR THE PERFECT ~~FIRST DAY~~
SECOND CHANCE

Second Chance. The original words—*First Day*—have been crossed out.

Goal number three has been crossed out, too, and replaced with a new one:

3. Make Gemma Cohen my friend
(Because I <u>need</u> one.)

And beneath that is a new, fourth goal:

4. Make things right with Arlo
(Because I've taken him for granted all this time.)

I'm in a daze. Everything about this Monday has reset each time I've woken up: my dirty clothes, my backpack, my period. Even the journal pages are flat and dry; there's no sign of their dunk in Tate's pool. But my *words*—somehow they've been preserved. The new goals I wrote down are still here. The crossed out words have *stayed* crossed out.

I stare at the scribbled words in the title again: *Second Chance*.

I changed that title to make a point to myself. But maybe the journal thought I was making a *wish*. Maybe the journal thought that "second chance" meant *a literal second chance*.

This is the source of the magic. It's not the wish I said aloud—the one I assumed that Q. S. Murray heard. It's the wish I wrote in the journal, without even knowing what I'd done.

Use me wisely.

Memories flood my brain: talking crap behind Gemma's back, writing on Amberleigh's fancy shoes, telling Mike Brot my bogus story, giving Arlo the middle finger.

I have most definitely not used this thing wisely.

I look at the phone camera, holding up my journal with utmost dread.

"Should I, like, *burn* it?" I whisper.

Cami looks solemn. "That never ends well in the movies.

Don't cursed objects always end up re-forming and making things worse?"

"*Cursed?*" I drop the journal like it's red-hot. "Who said anything about *cursed*?"

"Magical!" Cami yelps. "You're right. It's *magical*, not cursed."

I groan, collapsing into my pillows and flinging Mistmorrow across the bed.

"Hey, that journal is *not* evil," Cami insists. "I gave it to you in the spirit of sincerest friendship. How could there be anything bad about it?"

"I don't know," I wail. "That's just it: I don't *know* what's happening to me anymore."

"Well, don't panic," Cami says reassuringly. "It's not like you've been trapped there for centuries, just six days."

I snort. *Just* six days. "Easy for you to say."

"But you said yourself, some of those days sucked. So, it's lucky the loop didn't end on one of those, right?"

I sink deeper into the pillows, blinking tearfully at the glowing planets above. Cami's right: I've got to keep it together. I tell myself to breathe. The panic lessens, easing its pincer grip on my throat. I stretch across my bed, reclaiming Mistmorrow.

"Sorry, dude," I apologize, patting his head.

Cami looks concerned. "I didn't mean to freak you out."

My brain is still recovering from the shock. I've been convinced for so long that this was Q. S. Murray's doing. That explanation felt fitting. *Right.* But the magic wasn't coming from some*one* after all. It was coming from some*thing*.

I stare again at the hyacinth journal.

"So, don't burn it, huh?" I say to Cami.

It's mostly a joke.

"What are you thinking?" she asks.

I'm thinking a *lot*. I've got six first days of memories swirling around, and one rises above the rest, ringing as clearly in my ears as it did this morning on the school lawn: *It's not about getting it right.*

I tell Cami, "I've got an idea. A way to stop the loop."

She blinks in surprise. "Really? And . . . um, if it . . ."

"If it doesn't work?" I haul in a breath. "I'll deal with that tomorrow." I correct myself: *"Today."*

"Viv," Cami says. "You'll tell me tomorrow, right? Even if it's another loop. And if it's not, you *have* to let me know that you got out."

"I will," I promise.

Cami heaves a weary sigh. "Code Unicorn. Who would've thought?"

I shrug. "Well, we *hoped*."

After we hang up, I feel totally drained. My cramps have gotten bad, but I don't let them stop me. It's time to get down to business. I pick up the hyacinth journal, and I swear, a faint heat runs through my fingertips.

Magic. I'm sure of it.

The magic was right here at home, all along. I don't know what that says about me, a die-hard Relevane fan. For someone who's read about magic for most of her life, you'd think I would recognize the stuff when it's under my nose.

Better late than never, I guess.

I open the journal to VIVIAN LANTZ'S FOOLPROOF PLAN FOR THE PERFECT ~~FIRST DAY~~ SECOND CHANCE.

"Hello again," I say.

Then I make my move. I uncap the pen on my bedside table, and I bring it down, drawing a bold slash through the list. One slash, then two—a perfect "X" through all four goals of my Master Plan.

It's not that the list is bad. It's just that I don't *need* it anymore. Some things have changed. I don't want Alex for a boyfriend, and I've replaced my newspaper dream with a better one. As for the rest? I can keep my style. I can be a friend to Gemma without expecting anything in return.

And then there's Arlo. I know now that I can't force him to come home. I can't make him do anything he doesn't want to do, just like I could never *make* Alex Fernandez my boyfriend or Gemma my friend. Things between me and Arlo are as good as they can be right now. When it comes to the future? There's no planning for that.

I look over the crossed-out list, thinking back on all my second chances. One thing I know for sure: I don't need another one.

I shut the journal in one swift thud. Then I get out of bed, taking the journal to my desk. It's an old piece Da found in Houston, with engraved feet and a lockable drawer. I take the key from my jewelry box, open the drawer, and place the journal inside. I slam the drawer shut and lock it with a satisfying click.

I know it's only symbolic. My desk can't contain whatever magic is in those pages. All the same, I feel like I'm putting an end to what came before: Q. S. Murray's advice, my dreams of a perfect first day. I've shut them away for good.

When I get back to bed, I squeeze Mistmorrow with all my might. Nothing has changed. There's no skull-rattling earthquake, no crack of thunder, no flash of magical light.

But somehow? That's okay.

I know that magic works in unexpected ways.

20

I WAKE TO silence.

It's dim. Grayish daylight peeks through my bedroom curtains.

I rub my eyes and listen, but the house is quiet. There's no rain on the roof and no shouting from downstairs.

I reach for my phone, and my heartbeat kicks up: *whump, whump, whump.* I don't know if I can do it—this simple act of turning on the screen.

Okay. In three. I'll look at my phone in three.

One, two—

I tap the screen.

Tuesday, it says. *August 23.*

I shoot up in bed, screeching. I jump on top of my sheets, throwing a fist in the air.

Tomorrow. It's *tomorrow*!

I made it to the other side. The loop is broken. Time's

302

ticking again, the way it's supposed to. The magic is over, like I wished it to be.

It's a new day.

Then I have a terrible thought. What if this is a dream? I could still be asleep on Monday night, and my subconscious is playing tricks on me. I have to be sure, so I grab my arm, shut my eyes, and pinch. I wait, breath bundled in my lungs. I don't open my eyes for a long time.

Then I do.

Nothing's changed. I'm standing on my rumpled sheets. My clothes from Monday are dumped in the hamper beside my dresser, not hanging from the closet door. I'm wearing the pajama set I picked out last night. My backpack's sitting where I left it, by my desk chair. And the hyacinth journal? I have to be sure about that, too.

I jump off my bed, unlock the desk drawer, and there it is: my journal, right where I stashed it yesterday. *Yesterday.* There's finally a new one of those.

I pick up the journal, and Cami's words from last night smash into my brain: *Use me wisely.*

Huh. Yesterday, I took my second chance at second chances. It wasn't perfect. You might even call it another bad first day. But for once? I don't think of myself as cursed. For once? I'm happy about the way life happened to me. I think

I finally *did* use this thing wisely.

"Thank you," I say, tapping a hyacinth on the journal cover. "For *everything*."

But thankful as I am, I do not want this freaking *magical object* out in the open. I drop it back in the desk and nudge the drawer shut with my toe. I'll figure out what to do about that *later*.

When I turn, I'm facing down my stack of Relevane books. To think, the magic never came from Q. S. Murray at all. Her talk about magical vibes? It really *was* metaphorical. I'm still wrapping my head around that.

"Sorry, Quincy," I say, addressing the books. "Guess you're not as magical as I thought."

Actually, come to think of it, Q. S. Murray isn't a lot of the things I once thought. Maybe Q. S. Murray is a great author, but maybe I *also* don't have to listen to her advice. Maybe life's gonna happen to me today, and that's all right. At least today, whatever happens will be brand-new.

Then I think, *Cami*. I promised I'd let her know.

I scramble back to bed and grab my phone, where there's a text waiting for me.

Any luck? she's written.

This isn't a text kind of answer, so I call Cami's number. I'm bouncing up and down as the phone rings, but the call goes to voice mail, and I lower the phone with a frustrated grunt.

That's when I see it. All this time, I've been focused on the date, not the time. Now it's staring me down in big glowing numbers: *9:03 a.m.*

I look at Cami's text again. She sent it *three hours ago*.

I slept in. I didn't set my alarm last night, and now I'm late to school.

"*Dads!*" I yelp.

I toss open my door and race down the hall to their bedroom, only to find the door wide open, the bed perfectly made. Pop and Da aren't there. My blood runs cold.

Oh no. The time loop stopped, but what if another kind of magic kicked in? What if my dads have *disappeared*? Or I'm the only human left on the planet? Or—

"Viv?"

I whirl around.

Da's standing in the hallway, rubbing sleep from his eyes. Pop isn't far behind, staggering out of the living room. They look as bad as flattened roadkill, and that's when I remember: *Arlo*. They found out that he left on tour last night. I guess they stayed up late talking it through and fell asleep on the couch. *No one* in this house set their alarm.

Trixie appears behind Dads, snuffling and shaking out her ears.

It's Tuesday morning, and we Lantzes are a mess.

"What time is it?" Pop asks groggily.

"*Late*," I reply.

Back in my room, I throw open my closet, and the first thing to catch my eye is Aunt Ximena's fringed leather vest. I don't have to think twice. I quickly dress, then throw on the vest.

Here's something I've figured out: I really do like my new style. Not because I think it's what it takes to be Eighth Grade Vivian. Nope. It's because this style—the bangs, the rocker chic vibe—really is *me*. Only now, I'm not using it to impress anyone. I feel like wearing Aunt Ximena's vest 'cause it fits—my body, my mood, *myself*.

Once I'm dressed and ready, I swing into the kitchen, where Da's starting the coffee machine and Pop is grabbing the keys.

"I'm taking you to school," he tells me, as I stuff Pop-Tarts into my bag.

Carefully, I look at him. I know what he's expecting me to ask: *Where's Arlo?* For a moment, I don't know what to do. Should I play pretend?

I make my decision and say, "I know about Arlo. He, uh, texted me last night."

Da sets down his coffee mug way too loudly. He and Pop look at each other.

"How are you doing?" Pop asks.

He looks worried—even a little scared. I wonder if life

will ever go back to the way it was two nights ago, when the four of us sat at this kitchen table, eating as a family. Will we ever be the Lantzes we were before?

Maybe not.

"I'm not totally great," I tell my dads truthfully, "but I think I'll get there eventually."

They exchange another look, and I know this isn't the last of our talks about Arlo. But right now? We're behind schedule. Pop and I head out to the RAV4.

I'm not nervous on the drive. My knees don't bounce, and my brain doesn't race. There's no hyacinth journal in my backpack. I have zero master plans. I'm not even freaked out about being late, or the fact that I'm still on my period.

I smile, thinking back to my *first* first day. It was embarrassing to get blood on my skirt, but it's just blood, isn't it? It's a part of life, like traffic and homework and window leaks. I shouldn't have to be ashamed of that. From here on out? Bring on my period. Bring on cafeteria disasters. Nurse office visits. Awkward flubs. Pool party fiascoes. I'm ready to get it all wrong. Just preferably only one time around, please.

My phone lights up with a text, but it's not from Cami.

Hey! Missed you in first period. Everything cool?

Gemma.

My electrified fingers tap a response: *Slept in! On my way now. Lunch together? The caf or the stairwell, you decide!*

Before I can forget, I send a message to Cami, too:

IT WORKED. TELL YOU EVERYTHING AFTER SCHOOL.

I think about my conversation with Cami last night and what she told me over the phone: *You're still my friend.* I know that's true, no matter what happens this year. And I know another thing to be as true as the Vow of the Elystrian Council: we will *always* have Relevane.

As I'm hitting send, a new text arrives from Gemma:

Caf. Let's find our own table together.

I hold the phone to my chest, beaming. I've got so much more to look forward to now than I ever counted on: lunches with Gemma and an author club advised by Ms. Rose. Even postcards from Arlo. That's all in my future. There are so many days ahead that *aren't* Monday, August 22.

Pop's been quiet on the drive. As he pulls up to Bluebonnet's entrance, he throws the car into park and takes out a Post-it note from the console box.

"Writing you an excuse," he explains, scribbling on the paper. "If the front office has any questions, you tell them to call me."

"Sure," I say.

When he's through, Pop holds up the note to inspect it. He turns his attention to me.

"Viv," he says, sounding serious, "I hope you know that

Da and I want you to live your life however you want. We support you. You know that, right?"

He must be thinking of Arlo. It's not right that I eavesdropped on Dads before, but I can't unhear what they said. I want to tell them both what Arlo told me—how leaving wasn't about them. Maybe there'll be a time for that. Maybe it will help.

Time will help us, too, I think. It can be pretty magical like that.

"I know," I tell Pop. "I know all that."

He nods, handing me the neon-green note.

"Are you going to try to make him come home?" I ask.

"Your da and I discussed that," he tells me. "But we think this is Arlo's decision to make. We want him to thrive. Him and you both. Any dreams or things about yourself that you want to share—I hope you know you can do that, Vivian."

That's just it: I *do* know. I've known from the first wriggling feeling of the crush I have on Gemma that I could tell Dads about it, if I want. I know, because Pop told me that there's nothing weird about liking guys *and* girls.

Not that I'm going to tell Pop about my crush on Gemma *now*. Like, I didn't even tell him about my two-year crush on Alex. That'd be embarrassing.

Still. It's nice to know that I could.

"Love you, Pop," I say, leaning in to give him a hug.

He squeezes my ribs so tight that they just about snap.

I get out of the car, facing down the front doors of Bluebonnet Middle School like Sage Miriel approaching the Gate of Perpetua on her way to consult the Relevanian Oracle about her destiny.

I take my first step, and my sneaker slides on the slick concrete. I yelp, throwing out my arms and somehow catching my balance, managing not to wipe out face-first.

The car window rolls down behind me.

"You okay?" Pop shouts.

I turn around with a mortified smile and throw him a thumbs-up.

Pop waves and drives off, and I find myself snorting with laughter. Seems like the right way to start my second day of eighth grade.

I walk the rest of the way to the school entrance, a spring in my step.

First days might not be my thing, but second chances?

I guess I'm pretty good at those.

ACKNOWLEDGMENTS

Eternal gratitude to my agent, Beth Phelan, and to the entire team at Gallt & Zacker. Beth, it blows my mind that this is our *ninth* book together. Thank you for yet again being my advocate and answerer of anxious questions.

All my thanks to Stephanie Stein for facing down dizzying time loop challenges and providing the notes and keen observations that made this story the best version it could be. Were it not for you, there would be no Virgil the fish, and I don't even wanna contemplate that timeline! Massive thanks to Sophie Schmidt for your help and insight and for brightening my day with good news emails.

My heartfelt thanks to the many folks at HarperCollins who worked hard to launch this book into the world: Jessica Berg, Gwen Morton, Sean Cavanagh, Vanessa Nuttry, Delaney Heisterkamp, Patty Rosati, Mimi Rankin, and Josie Dallam. Thank you to copyeditor Martha Schwartz for ridding this novel of pesky typos and gaps in logic. Paula Zorite, your cover illustration still makes me swoon. Corina Lupp, thank you for the killer design.

Thank you, Katryn Bury, for a blurb that warmed every ventricle of my heart. As always, my thanks to the booksellers, librarians, and teachers who bravely bring much-needed books to readers, young and old. And thank you to the many fantasy authors who enriched my childhood and transported me to faraway realms—most notably Carol Kendall and J. R. R. Tolkien.

I've never had to repeat a day of my life (whew), but the publication process can feel like its own time loop. There's lots of repetition, existential angst, and dark nights of the soul when I question if I'm doing *anything* right. I couldn't have made it through that without the love and support of close family and friends. Thank you to each of you—you know who you are—for getting me through.

Annie, Matt, and Lorelei—I love you three to Jupiter and back. Vicki and Bob, thank you for always making me feel like family. Destiny, thank you for continuing to be the Red Panda to my Puffin. Megan, thank you for being a frieeend (insert astonishing vocal run here). Hilary, your friendship and artistry brighten my life. Mai, I love book clubbing with you across the miles. Ariana, cry-laughing with you over biscuits and gravy is always a weekend highlight. Kidron, my sweet Swiftie, thank you for keeping me, like, all hip with the 411 on Gen Z. Cleo, my dog-ter, thank you for inspiring the snorting gloriousness that is Trixie.

Alli, my love, my best friend, my sweet cheese—thank you for seeing me through another novel. You cheered with me about the good news and cheered me up on my bad days. You sustained me during rounds of drafting and revision, and you spent an entire rainy day listening to me hoarsely read this book. You are my favorite human in the universe. I'm so grateful to have spent these past five years with you.

Thank you, dear reader, for jumping into this magical time loop with Vivian Lantz. I hope that you, like Viv, embrace life with all the messy bits and imperfections included. Or don't take that advice! I'm just an author, after all. :)